Odd Girl Out

A Gold Medal Original by

A. BANNON

D1328059

Martino Publishing
Mansfield Centre, CT
2016

Martino Publishing
P.O. Box 373,
Mansfield Centre, CT 06250 USA

ISBN 978-1-68422-010-6

© 2016 Martino Publishing

Cover Design Tiziana Matarazzo

Printed in the United States of America On 100% Acid-Free Paper

Odd Girl Out

A Gold Medal Original by

A. BANNON

GOLD MEDAL BOOKS

FAWCETT PUBLICATIONS, INC.

ONE

THE BIG HOUSE was still, almost empty. Down the bright halls and in the shadowy rooms everything was quiet. Upstairs a few desk lights burned over pages of homework, but that was all.

There was one room in the sorority house, however, where no reading was going on. It was a big, warm room, meant for sprawling and studying and socializing in, like the others. Three girls shared it and two of them were in it now on this autumn Sunday night.

One was a newcomer. Her name was Laura and she had just finished moving all of her belongings into the room. It was a scene of overstuffed confusion, but at least she had somehow succeeded in squeezing all her things in and now there remained only the job of finding a place for them. Laura sat down to rest and worry about it. She tried to ignore the other girl.

Beth lay sprawled out on the studio couch with her head cushioned on a rambling pile of fat pillows at one end and her feet dangling over the other. She was drinking a Coke, resting the bottle on her stomach and letting it ride the rhythm of her breathing. She wore slim tan pants and a dark green sweatshirt with "Alpha Beta" stamped in white on the front. Her hair was dark, curly, and close-cropped.

Laura sat by choice in the stiff wooden desk chair, as if Beth were too comfortable and she could make amends by being uncomfortable herself. She was nervously aware of Beth's scrutiny, and the sorority pledge manual she was trying to read made no sense to her. The worst of it was that Laura wanted Beth to like her. Beth seemed like all good things to the younger girl's dazzled eyes: sophisti-

5

cated, a senior, a leader, president of the Student Union, and curiously pretty. She had a well-modeled, sensitive face with features not bonily chic like those of a mannequin, but subtle, vital, harmonious. She wasn't fashionably pretty but her beauty was healthy and real and her good nature showed in her face.

Laura flipped nervously through her pledge manual, not even pretending to read any more. Finally Beth saw that she wasn't reading and smiled at the ruse.

"One hundred and thirty-seven pages of crap," she said, nodding at the manual. "All guaranteed to confuse you. I don't know why they don't revise the damn thing. I've passed an exam on it and I still don't understand it."

Her attitude embarrassed Laura, who smiled uncertainly at her new roommate, thinking as she did so how many times she had smiled in the same way at Beth, not sure of how she was expected to react.

She had never known quite how to react to Beth from the first day she had seen her. It had been shortly after Laura's arrival at the university, when everything she saw and felt excited her to a high pitch of nervous awareness. Even the sweet smoke of bonfires in the early-autumn air smelled new and tantalizing.

Laura walked around the university town of Champlain, down streets chapeled with old elms; past the new campus with its clean, striking Georgian buildings and past the old with its mellow moss-covered halls; past that copy of the Pantheon that passed for the auditorium; past the statues; past the students walking down the white strip of the boardwalk, sitting on the steps of buildings, stretching in the grass, and talking . . . always talking.

It thrilled her, and it frightened her a little. Some day she would know all of this as well as her home town; know the campus lore and landmarks, the Greek alphabet, the football heroes, the habits of the campus cops. Some day she wouldn't have to ask the questions—she would be able to answer them. It made her feel a sort of grateful affection for the campus already, just to think of it this way.

She had been in school a week when she went up to the Student Union to join an activity committee. It seemed like a good way to meet people and get into the university's social life. Laura had an appointment for an interview at three o'clock. She sat in the bustling student activities center on the third floor waiting to be called, clearing her throat nervously and sneaking a look at herself in her compact mirror. She had a delicate face shaped like a thin white heart, with startling pale blue eyes and brows and lashes paler still. A face quaint and fine as a Tenniel sketch.

She waited for almost half an hour and the sustained anxiety began to tire her. She stared at her feet and up to the clock, and back to her feet again. It was when she glanced at the clock for the last time that she saw Beth for the first.

Beth was standing halfway across the room, tall and slender and with a magnetic face, talking to a couple of nodding boys. She was taller than one of them and the other acted as if she towered over him, too. Laura watched her with absorbed interest. She tapped the smaller boy on the shoulder with a pencil as she talked to him and then she laughed at them both and Laura heard her say, "Okay, Jack. Thanks." She turned to leave them, coming across the room toward Laura, and Laura looked suddenly down at her shoes again. She told herself angrily that this was silly, but she couldn't look up.

Suddenly she felt the light tap of a sheaf of papers on her head, and looked up in surprise. Beth smiled down at her. "Aren't you new around here?" she said, looking at Laura with wide violet eyes.

"Yes," Laura said. Her throat was dry and she tried to clear it again.

"Are you on a committee?"

She was strangely, compellingly pretty, and she was looking down at Laura with a frank, friendly curiosity that confused the younger girl.

"I'm here for an interview," Laura said in a scratchy voice.

Beth waited for her to say something more and Laura felt her cheeks coloring. A young man thrust his face out of a nearby door and said, "Laura Landon?" looking around him quizzically.

"Here." Laura stood up.

"Oh. Come on in. We're ready for you." He smiled.

Beth smiled, too. "Good luck," she said, and walked away.

Laura looked after her, until the boy said, "Come on in," again.

8 ODD GIRL OUT

"Oh," she said, whirling around, and then she smiled at him in embarrassment. "Sorry."

The interview turned out well. Laura joined the Campus Chest committee and turned her efforts toward parting students from their allowances for good causes. Every afternoon she went up to the Union Building and put in an hour or two in the Campus Chest office on the third floor, where most of the major committees had offices.

It had been nearly two weeks later that Beth stopped in the office to talk to the chairman. She sat on his desk and Laura, carefully looking at a paper in front of her, listened to every word they said. It was mostly business: committee work, projects, hopes for success. And then the chairman told her who was doing the best work for Campus Chest. He named three or four names. Beth nodded, only half listening.

"And Laura Landon's done a lot for us," he said.

"Um-hm," said Beth, taking little notice. She was gathering her papers, about to leave.

"Hey, Laura." He waved her over.

Laura got up and came uncertainly toward the desk. Beth straightened her papers against the top of the desk, hitting them sideways the long way and then the short way until all the edges were even.

"Beth, this is Laura Landon," the boy said.

Beth looked up and smiled. And then her smile broadened. "Oh, you're Laura Landon," she said. She held out her hand. "Hi, Laur."

Nobody had ever called her "Laur" before; she wasn't the type to inspire nicknames. But she liked it now. She took Beth's hand. "Hi," she said.

"You know each other?" the chairman said.

"We've never had a formal introduction," Beth said, "but we've had a few words together." Laura remained silent, a little desperate for conversation.

"Well, then," said the chairman gallantly, "Miss Cullison, may I present Miss Landon."

"Will Miss Landon have coffee with Miss Cullison this afternoon?" said Beth.

Laura smiled a little. "She'd be delighted," she said.

They did. And she was. An occasional fifteen- or thirty-minute coffee break was traditional at the Union Building. Beth and Laura went down to the basement coffee shop, and came up two hours later because it was time finally to go home for dinner. Laura couldn't remember exactly what they talked about. She recalled telling Beth where she was living and what she was studying. And she remembered a long monologue from Beth on the Student Union activities and what they accomplished. And then suddenly Beth had said, "Are you going to go through rushing, Laur?"

"Rushing?"

"Yes. To join a sorority. Informal rush opens next week."

"Well, I—I hadn't thought about it."

"Think about it, then. You should, Laura. I'm on Alpha Beta and, strictly off the record, I think we'd be very interested."

"Why would Alpha Beta want me?" Laura said to her coffee cup.

"Because I think it's a good idea. And Alpha Beta listens to Beth Cullison." She laughed a little at herself. "Does that sound hopelessly egotistical? It does, doesn't it? But it's true." She paused, waiting until Laura looked at her again. "Sign up for rushing, Laura," she said, "and I'll see to it you're pledged."

"I—I will. I certainly will, Beth," Laura said, hardly daring to believe what she'd heard.

Beth grinned. "My God, it's nearly five-thirty," she said. "Let's go."

After that it had been easy. Beth spoke the truth; Alpha Beta did listen to her. Laura had signed up for rush, with the secret understanding that she would pledge Alpha Beta. But even at that, it was a thrill when Beth called her two days after rushing was over and said, "Hi, honey. Pack your things. You're an Alpha Beta now. Officially."

Laura had cried over the phone, and Beth said, "You don't have to, you know."

"But I want to!"

Beth laughed. "Okay, Laur, come on over. You just joined one of the world's most exclusive clubs. And you have a new roommate. In fact you have two." ·

"Two?"

"Yes. Me. And Emily."

Emily had spent the day with them, helping Laura bring things in and put them away. Laura was so tired now she could hardly recall Emily's face; all she remembered was a warm, ready laugh and the vague impression that Emily was fashioned to please the fussiest males: the ones who want perfect looks and perfect compliance in a woman.

Beth had called a halt to their work early in the evening.

"We've done enough, Laura," she had said, dropping down on the studio couch. "We've even done too much."

"It was wonderful of you to help me, Beth."

"Oh, I know. I'm wonderful as all hell. I only did it because I had to." She grinned at Laura, who smiled self-consciously back. Beth liked to tease her for being too polite and it made Laura uncomfortable. She would have gone to almost any length to please Beth, and yet she could not abandon her good manners. They struck her as one of her best features, and it puzzled her that Beth should needle her about them. She knew Beth could carry off a courtesy beautifully at the right moment; Laura had seen her do it. But Beth was much less formal than her new roommate, and furthermore she liked to swear, which Laura thought extremely unmannerly. Beth made Laura squirm with discomfort. And in self-defense Laura tried to build a wall of politeness between them, to admire Beth from faraway.

There was a vague, strange feeling in the younger girl that to get too close to Beth was to worship her, and to worship was to get hurt. As yet, Beth made no sense to her, she fit no mold, and Laura wanted to keep herself at an emotional distance from her. She had never met or read or dreamed a Beth before and until she could understand her she would be afraid of her.

Laura had been thinking about this that afternoon while she filled the drawers of her new dresser with underwear and sweaters and scarves and socks, and had resolved right then that she must always be on her guard with Beth. She didn't know what she was trying to shield herself from; she only felt that she needed protection somehow.

Beth had suddenly put an arm around her shoulders, shaking the thoughts out of her head, and said with a laugh, "For God's sake, Laur, how many pairs of panties do you *have?* Look at 'em all, Emmy."

And Emily had looked up and laughed pleasantly. Laura couldn't tell if she were laughing at the underwear or at Beth or at the look on Laura's face, for Laura looked as surprised as she was. She stood there for a minute, feeling only the weight and pull of Beth's arm and not the necessity to answer.

In a faint voice Laura answered, "My mother buys all my underwear. She gets it at Field's."

"Well, she must've cleaned them out this time," said Beth, smiling at the luxurious drawerful. "I'll bet they put in an emergency order for undies when she leaves the store."

Emily laughed again and Laura shut the drawer with a smack and cleared her throat. She hated to talk about lingerie. She hated to undress in front of anyone. She even hated to wash her underwear because she had to hang it on the drying racks in the john or in the laundry room where everyone could see it. It was no comfort to her that everybody else did the same thing.

"Of course, I don't believe in underwear myself," said Beth airily. "Never wear any." She swept a stack of sweaters theatrically off the table and handed them to Laura, who gazed at her in dismay, reaching mechanically for the sweaters. Beth laughed. "I'm pretty wicked, Laur."

"Don't you really wear any—any underwear?" Her whole upbringing revolted at this. "You must wear some."

Beth shook her head, enjoying Laura's distress and surprised at how little it took to shock her. Laura looked at her with growing outrage until she burst out laughing and Emily intervened sympathetically.

"Beth, you're going to make your poor little roommate think she's fallen in with a couple of queers," she said with a giggle.

Beth grinned at Laura and the younger girl felt strangely as if the bottom had fallen out of her stomach.

"She has," said Beth with emphatic cheerfulness. "She ought to know the dreadful truth. We're characters, Laura. Desirable characters, of course, but still characters. Are you with us?"

Laura wished for a moment that she were all alone in a vacuum. She didn't know whether to take Beth seriously or not; she felt as if Beth were testing her, challenging her, and she didn't know how to meet the challenge. She transferred a sweater nervously from one hand to the other and tried to answer. Nobody was a more rigid conformist, farther from a character, than Laura Landon. But the bothersome need to please Beth prompted her to say weakly, "Yes."

She put the sweater in a drawer, turning away from Beth and Emily as she did so, and silently and secretly scraped the white undersides of her forearms. It was an old gesture. Whenever she was disappointed with herself she bruised herself physically. The sad red lines she raised on her skin were her expiation, a way of squaring with herself.

Beth, who could see she had gone far enough, confined herself for a while to friendly suggestions and answering questions. It was a great relief to Laura. She was almost herself again when Beth suggested a tour of the sorority house.

The two girls went first up to the dormitory on the third floor, where everybody but the housemother and the household help slept.

"Does anyone ever sleep in the rooms?" Laura asked as they mounted the stairs.

"Oh, once in a while. In the winter, when the dorm is really cold, some of the kids sleep in their rooms. The studio couches unfold into double beds. They can sleep two."

They had entered the big quiet dorm with its dozens of iron bunk beds smothered in comforters and down pillows and bright blankets. Laura shivered in the chill while Beth pointed out her unmade bed to her.

"We'll have to come back and make it up later," she said.

Beth had then led Laura down to the basement. She was enjoying this new role of guide and guardian, enjoying even more Laura's unquestioning acceptance of it. They found themselves playing a pleasant little game without ever having to refer to the rules: when they reached the door to the back stairs together, Laura stopped, as if automatically, and let Beth hold the door for her. Laura, who tried almost instinctively to be more polite than anybody else, readily gave up all the small faintly masculine courtesies to Beth, as if it were the most natural thing in the world, as if Beth expected it of her. There was no hint that such an agreeable little game could suddenly turn fast and wild and lawless.

In the basement Beth showed her the luggage room, shelved to the ceiling and crowded with all manner of plaid and plastic and leather cases. In the rear of the room was a closed door.

Beth turned around to go out and bumped softly into Laura, who had been waiting for an explanation of the closed door. Laura jumped back and Beth smiled slowly and said, "I won't eat you, Laur."

Laura felt a crazy wish to turn and run, but she held her ground, unable to answer.

Beth put her hands gently on Laura's shoulders. "Are you afraid of me, Laur?" she said. There was a long, terribly bright and searching silence.

"I—I wondered what the door in back was to," Laura faltered. Her sentence seemed to hang suspended, without a period.

Beth let her hands drop. "That's the chapter room," she said. "Verboten. Until you're initiated, of course."

"Oh," said Laura, and she walked out of the luggage room with Beth's strange smile wreaking havoc in the pit of her stomach.

On the way upstairs they met Mary Lou Baker, the president of Alpha Beta. She came down the stairs toward them, towing a bulging bundle of laundry which bumped dutifully down the stairs behind her. She smiled at them and said, "Hi there. How's the unpacking coming along, Laura?"

"Fine, thank you." Laura watched Mary Lou retreat into the basement, impressed with her importance.

"She likes you," said Beth as they headed back up to their room.

"She does?" Laura smiled, pleasantly surprised.

"Um-hm," Beth answered. "Usually she has nothing to say to newcomers for a few weeks. If she notices you right away it's a good sign. At least it is if you're interested in her approval." She said this rather disparagingly.

Walking down the hall behind her, Laura smiled.

And now here they were in the calm of a Sunday night, alone in their room, curious and shy at the same time. Beth finished her Coke and set the bottle down on a glass-topped coffee table in front of the studio couch. The clack of glass on glass startled Laura and the pledge manual slipped from her hands to the floor.

"Want to go make your bed up now?" Beth said. Her voice was soft, as if she were rather tired.

"Oh, yes. I guess I'd better."

"I'll help you." Beth sat up, swinging her long legs to

the floor. She sat still for a minute as if getting her bearings, looking at her feet. Then she lit a cigarette. "Come on, let's go do it," she said finally with sudden brightness.

"*I'll* do it, Beth," said Laura firmly. "You've done so much for me today, I just hate to have you do any more."

Beth blew smoke over the table top. "Laura, if you don't stop thanking me for everything you're going to wear me out," she said. "Or turn my head." She said this good-naturedly, to tease more than to scold. But then she saw that she had hurt Laura and she wanted instantly to reach out with comfort and reassurance. She was not impatient with Laura's hypersensitivity, only unused to it. She never knew when she might scrape against it and cause pain.

Laura's mouth tightened and she gripped the cover of her pledge manual in an effort to calm herself.

"Laura," said Beth in a gentle voice, and she got up and went over to her. Laura drew back in surprise as Beth dropped to her knees in front of the chair, putting a hand on Laura's knees and smiling up at her. Laura was too startled to pretend composure.

"Laur, have I hurt your feelings, honey? I have, haven't I? Answer me."

Laura said helplessly, "No, Beth, really—"

"I know I have," Beth interrupted her. "I'm sorry, Laur. You mustn't take me so seriously. I'm only teasing. I like to tease, but I don't like to hurt people. You just have to get used to me, that's all. Take me with a grain of salt." She looked earnestly at her with the shade of a smile on her lips and she thought how good it would be to skid her hands hard up Laura's thighs and . . . So she kept talking. It was better to ignore the peculiar feelings Laura awoke in her; she covered her confusion with words.

"Because I want us to be good friends," she went on. "And I'll try not to—to shock you any more. I guess I'm a little crazy—the results of a misspent youth, of course." And she grinned. "But I'm not dangerous, honest to God. Now—" she smacked Laura's knees amiably—"we're over the first crisis. Are we going to be friends, Laur?"

Laura wanted desperately to pull her knees together. "Yes," she said to Beth. "I hope so."

"Good!" said Beth and she bounced to her feet. "Come along, then. Let's make your bed."

It hadn't taken long to make up the austere box bed and Laura found herself back in the room and faced with the humiliating problem of undressing in front of somebody else. Her shyness settled in her cheeks and neck like a heat rash. As soon as she felt the burn, it spread to her shoulders and bosom. She blushed very easily and she despised herself for it. She wanted to scratch at her arms again, but because Beth would notice it she had to content herself with biting the tender flesh of her underlip until she was afraid it would bleed and cause her more grief.

She turned as far from Beth as she could and unbuttoned her blouse, somehow feeling that Beth's bright eyes were doting on every button. But Beth was subtle; she was humming a tune and busy with her pajamas. She saw Laura without seeming to and Laura began to envy her pleasant abandon. After a moment she said, "Laur, do you have a sweatshirt?"

"Yes." Laura eyed her quizzically.

"Better put it on. The dorm is a damn deep freeze."

Laura found the sweatshirt and pulled it over her head, and Beth led her up to the dorm. On the door was posted a wake-up chart with a pencil on a string hanging beside it. Beth signed Laura's name under "6:45."

"Think you can find your bed?" she asked.

"There it is," said Laura, pointing.

"Okay, in you go," said Beth.

Laura studied the upper bunk, which looked unattainable. "How?" she faltered.

Beth laughed quietly. "Well, look," she said. "Put your foot on the rung of the lower bunk—no, no, wait!—that's right," she said, guiding her. "Now, get your knee on the rung of the bed next door. Now, just roll in. Whoops!" she said, catching Laura as she nearly lost her balance. She gave her a push in the right direction. Laura rolled awkwardly onto her bunk, laughing with Beth.

Beth climbed up where she could see her and said, "You'll catch on, Laur. Doesn't take long." She helped Laura under the covers and tucked her in, and it was so lovely to let herself be cared for that Laura lay still, enjoying it like a child. When Beth was about to leave her, Laura reached for her naturally, like a little girl expecting a good-night kiss. Beth bent over her and said, "What is it, honey?"

With a hard shock of realization, Laura stopped herself.

She pulled her hands away from Beth and clutched the covers with them.

"Nothing." It was a small voice.

Beth pushed Laura's hair back and gazed at her and for a heart-stopping moment Laura thought she would lean down and kiss her forehead. But she only said, "Okay. Sleep tight, honey." And climbed down.

Laura raised herself cautiously on one elbow so she could watch her leave the dorm. Beth went out and shut the door and Laura was left to her strange cold bed in the great dark dormitory. She felt cut loose from reality.

It took her a long while to get to sleep. Her nerves were brittle as ice and they all seemed to be snapping from the day's pressure. She lay motionless on her back and studied the luminous checkers on the ceiling, laid there through the window by the light of the fire escape. She thought of Beth: Beth beside her watching her, whispering to her, reaching out to touch her.

The stillness grew and lengthened and Laura lay in it alone with her thoughts. Far away on the campus the clock on the Student Union steeple pulsed twelve times through the waiting night. Laura pulled her covers tight under her chin and tried to sleep. She was just drifting off when she heard someone stop by her bed and she opened her heavy eyes and saw Beth outlined by the night light.

"Still awake?" she whispered.

"I'm sorry. I'm dropping off now." Laura felt guilty; caught with her eyes open when they should have been shut; caught peeking at nothing; caught thinking of Beth.

"Just wanted to make sure you were all right."

"Oh yes, thank you."

"Shhh!" hissed someone from a neighboring bed.

"Sorry!" Beth hissed back, and then turned to Laura again. "Okay, go to sleep now," she said, and she gave Laura's arm a pat.

"I will," Laura whispered.

TWO

A T SIX FORTY-FIVE, Laura heard a soft voice whispering, "Time to get up, Laura." She sat up immediately in her bed as if pulled by a wire, and looked over to see an unusually pretty face staring up at her.

"Thank you," she said.

The face smiled and whispered, "Wow, are you easy to wake up!" and moved away.

Laura had a good morning. She spent a lot of it wondering about her strange desire for a good-night kiss from Beth, and hoping Beth hadn't understood her sudden aborted gesture. At lunchtime she sat with everybody in the big sunny dining room, talking while she ate. She glanced over at Beth, who sat two tables away from her and found Beth returning the look. Laura answered her smile and turned, in confusion, to prospecting for nuggets of hamburger in her chili.

After lunch they studied together for a while. Laura sat down with her book in a large green butterfly chair in the corner and struggled to get comfortable. She was still trying to conform to the incomprehensible chair when Emily ran in from the washroom, grabbed her coat and a notebook, and ran out again. Seconds later she was back.

"Hey Beth, if Bud calls tell him I'll see him at Maxie's at four."

Beth pulled her reading glasses down to the end of her nose and looked over them. "Right," she said.

"Thanks." And Emmy was gone.

Beth stared after her, shaking her head and smiling a little.

"What?" said Laura.

"I just don't get it. Or rather, I get it but I don't like it. He's too crazy for her. Emmy needs a steadying influence." She winked at Laura and turned back to her book.

Laura began to glance furtively at her, half expecting her to be looking back, and she was rather disappointed when Beth kept her nose in the book. After a while Laura gazed

17

openly at her, resentful of the book that claimed all Beth's
attention. And then she forgot the book and thought only
of Beth. . . .

The two girls walked to their afternoon class together.
It was a brisk day, snappy and sunny and invigorating.
Beth walked with long, smooth strides. She liked to walk
and she walked well, as if she were really enjoying her legs;
enjoying the rhythmic cooperation between legs and lungs,
crisp weather, space and speed. She had a lusty health that
almost intimidated Laura, who was breathless with trying
to keep up. And breathless, too, with pleasure at walking
beside Beth.

They arrived in class five minutes late, and the instruc-
tor had already started his lecture. He interrupted himself
to note, while gazing out the window with a wry smile,
"Glad you could make it, Miss Cullison."

Beth, slipping out of her coat, looked up at him with a
grin. They were friendly enemies, she and the teacher;
they liked to catch each other slipping up somewhere.

"I see," he added, "you're leading the innocent astray."

Laura blushed in confusion. It scared her to see someone flirt with authority as Beth did: she expected to see
the hallowed rules and traditions crash down on Beth and
crush her, and when they didn't she was as surprised as
she was relieved. To Laura, the things Beth said and did
were daring in the extreme. To Beth, who knew herself
and people better, it was just a half-hearted revolt; a small
scale protest that was more in fun than in earnest. She
didn't want to be an out-and-out character any more than
she wanted to be one of the herd, so Beth beat herself a
path between the two.

Laura was happy, when she saw the letter was from her
father, that Beth and Emily weren't in the room. Her divorced parents were a faraway sorrow she tried to pretend
out of existence. She opened the letter slowly.

"Glad to hear you like your new home," she read. "I
understand Alpha Beta is a pretty good sorority."

Yes, father. Pretty good. If you say so. She hated the
way her father phrased things.

"Anyway," the letter went on, "they had a good house
when I was in school. Your roommates sound like nice
girls, especially the Cullison girl. That's the kind of friend-

ship you should cultivate, Laura, with people who can really do you some good. This girl sounds like a real go-getter—president of the Student Union and etc. That's quite an honor for a girl, isn't it? She can probably do a lot for you—get you into the right activities and so forth. I'd treat her well, if I were you."

Laura sighed with exasperation over her father's ideas of friendship; if it weren't useful somehow it just wasn't friendship, only a waste of time.

"By the way," he continued, "Cliff Ayers's son Charlie is in school down there. I'd like you to give him a call—he'd like to hear from you, I'm sure."

Sure, thought Laura with futile resentment. He'd like to hear from Marilyn Monroe. But who's Laura Landon? He won't even remember the name.

"Cliff says Charlie looks just like him, which means there's probably a line of girls ahead of you."

Is that supposed to encourage me? Laura wondered bitterly. If Charlie Ayers wants to hear from me, which I doubt, he can call me himself.

"I understand that your mother has found a nice apartment. You will spend half the holidays wth her and half with me, of course. I must say, Laura, you took the divorce pretty well, though of course I expected you to."

Laura crushed the letter with angry hands and threw it into the wastebasket by the desk. Then she put her head down and wept, until she heard Beth and Emily coming down the hall. They found her dusting the already spotless coffee table and smiling at the job.

Beth looked at her oddly for a moment and then picked up a manila envelope and hurried out of the room. She would be at a committee meeting all evening long and left Laura and Emily to study alone in an embarrassed silence. Both of them wished rather uncomfortably that Beth would come back and mediate for them. After a while the dearth of words between them began to pall and they were both suddenly conscious that they would be rooming together for the rest of the year. It seemed an interminable length of time.

Emily could usually chatter easily with people. She was natural with them and they responded naturally to her. But every word and gesture of Laura's seemed to her to be rehearsed, calculated to please, and it threw Emmy completely. She got the feeling that she could smash a bottle over Laura's head and Laura would say, very calmly, "Thank you."

There was plenty of room for Laura on the couch beside Emily, but she wouldn't sit there, simply because Emily got there first. She sat down in the butterfly chair with a sigh. It defied her, as usual, and her narrow skirt made the problem worse. She shifted unhappily and Emily, trying to be helpful, suggested, "Why don't you put your p.j.'s on, Laura? Much more comfortable. Besides, nobody studies in their clothes."

Laura couldn't think of an excuse to keep her clothes on and she got up to change, wondering if Emily just wanted to watch her undress. She performed the operation with determined casualness. Her set teeth wouldn't show, but her manner would. Emily watched her on the sly, wondering why Laura was so embarrassed and self-conscious about herself.

"Hey, Laur, what a pretty bra!" she exclaimed spontaneously as Laura pulled it out from under her pajama shirt. "Let's see it," said Emily reaching out a hand.

Laura gave it a jerky toss.

"Gee, nylon," said Emmy. "They make 'em up just like this only padded, you know," she added. "They're terrific. Ever try 'em?"

"Falsies, you mean?" said Laura. The word struck her as mildly obscene.

"Yeah."

"No, I never did."

"You should," said Emmy realistically. "They're terrific, really. Nobody knows the difference. Unless you're dancing awful close," she amended.

"I guess my busts are kind of small," said Laura.

Emily smiled at her, wondering at the pathetic modesty that made it impossible for Laura to call the parts of her body by their right names.

Laura's small breasts bothered her. She would fold her arms over them as much to conceal their presence as to conceal their size. She wished that they were more glamorous, more obviously there. In their present shape they seemed only an afterthought.

She sat down with her book again when she was safely into her pajamas and Emily sat and toyed with things to say; she had made a start and she wanted to keep the communication line open. At nine o'clock she snapped her book shut and said, "How 'bout some coffee, Laur?"

"No thanks," said Laura, looking up from her book.

"Oh, come on. It won't keep you awake. We've got a big jar of Sanka." She pulled open Beth's bottom dresser drawer and took out the jar, and Laura noted with displeasure her familiarity with Beth's things. "Come on," she said again. "I hate to go down alone."

Laura gave in. She followed Emily down the back stairs to the kitchen.

"We have a coffee break almost every night," said Emily tentatively. She lighted a cigarette and cast about for something new to say. Her perplexity made her pretty face quite appealing.

"Say, Laur," she said cheerfully, "have you got a date this Saturday?" Emily was ready to be friends with Laura; she was willing to be friends with almost anybody. The best turn she could do Laura, as she saw it, was to fix her up with an acceptable male. Emmy knew dozens of them.

"No," said Laura doubtfully. "But in pledge meeting they said something about getting me a date." She thought with fleeting guiltiness of Charlie Ayers, and knew she would never call him; she hadn't the guts and she hadn't the desire.

"Oh. Well, they haven't done it yet, have they?"

"Well, no, but—"

"Listen, Laura, there's a terrific guy I'm thinking of—a fraternity brother of Bud's. I could fix you up with him. Jim's a junior, real tall." And she went on to describe an irresistible young man. They are always irresistible until you're face to face with them. Laura let Emmy talk her into it. She didn't know any men and it seemed a good idea to let Emmy take care of the problem.

"Bud and I will be along the first time out," said Emily, making plans. "It's much easier to have somebody else along for moral support." She laughed and Laura smiled with her. What she said was true enough. It might not be so bad.

"That sounds terrific," she said, borrowing Emmy's favorite adjective to amplify her gratitude. "If it wouldn't be too much trouble for you."

"Oh, Lord no," said Emily. She set one cup into another thoughtfully and went on, "Gee, I wish I could talk Beth into going out."

Laura was suddenly alert. She turned and looked at Emily. "Doesn't she go out?"

"Nope. Crazy girl."

"Not at all?" Laura thought it was a requisite for sorority girls.

"No." Emily stared quizzically at her sudden show of interest.

"I just thought—" Laura looked away in confusion. "I mean, she's so popular and everything. I just naturally thought—well—" If a girl didn't date was there anything wrong with her?

"Oh, she used to," said Emmy, taking the steaming water from the burner and pouring it over the little mountains of dry coffee in the cups she had set out. "She used to go out a lot the first couple of years she was down here. But nothing ever happened, you know? Every time she got interested— Sugar?"

Laura was so absorbed that it took her a minute to collect her wits and answer, "Yes, please."

Emmy dropped it in and handed Laura her cup. "There's no cream. There's Pream, though. Want some?"

Laura wanted to shake Beth's story out of her. "No, thanks," she said briefly. "This is fine." She was hungry for any crumb of information about Beth without stopping to wonder where her appetite came from. She was concerned only with satisfying it at this point.

Emily dipped into the Pream can with a spoon and sprinkled the white powder into her coffee. "You get used to it," she said. "I didn't used to like it, either."

"Well, what happened?" said Laura in a voice that was urgent yet soft, as if the volume might excuse the words. She didn't want to look interested.

"Oh . . . well," Emmy stirred her concoction. "Nothing happened, really. In fact, that was the whole trouble. Nothing *did* happen." She looked cautiously at Laura, as if trying to determine just how much she could be confided in. Laura's face was a picture of sympathetic concern. "She'd find somebody she liked," Emmy went on, "and they'd go together for a couple of months, and just when it seemed as if everything was going to be terrific, it was all over. I mean, Beth just called it off. She always did that," she said musingly, "just when we all thought she was really falling in love. All of a sudden she'd call it quits."

"Why?" said Laura.

Emily shrugged. "If you ask me, I think she just got scared. I think she's afraid to fall in love, or something. It's the only thing I can think of. Otherwise it just doesn't make sense."

"Were they nice boys?" Laura asked.

"Terrific boys! Some of them, anyway."

"Well, didn't she tell *them* why she dropped them? I mean, she must have told them something." Laura was groping for the key to Beth's character, for something to explain her with.

"Nope," said Emily. "Just told 'em good-by and that was it. Believe me, I know. I've had 'em call me by the dozens to cry on my shoulder. But she wouldn't say much to me, either. She just said she got tired of them or it wouldn't have worked out and it was best to end it now than later, or something."

"And now she doesn't go out any more?"

"Isn't that something?" Emily clucked in disapproval. "You'd think she was disillusioned at the tender age of twenty-one. She puts on like she doesn't care, but I know she does. But still, she did it to herself. After a while when the boys called up for dates she just turned 'em down automatically. As if she knew she wasn't going to have any fun, no matter who she went with. As if it just wasn't worth the trouble."

Emily had lost Laura's attention, but she didn't know it. Laura was thinking to herself, She's got a right not to care. Why should she care about boys? She doesn't have to. Emmy doesn't know everything.

"Of course," Emmy went on, "she's told me a thousand times she doesn't want any man who's afraid of her, and if they're all afraid of her, to hell with them. I'm quoting," she added, smiling. "She likes to swear."

"I noticed," said Laura a trifle primly.

"I don't know where she got that idea," Emmy said. "She says she won't play little games with them just for the sake of a few dates. Well, you know men. What's a romance without little games? I mean, let's face it, there isn't a man living who doesn't want to play games." She eyed Laura over her coffee cup and made her feel illogically guilty.

"Maybe she's afraid of men," said Laura. The words popped from her startled mouth like corks from a bottle. For a sickening minute she thought Emily was going to ask

her questions or stare at her curiously, but Emily only
laughed.

"Lord, she's not afraid of anything," she said. "It's more
the other way around. They're afraid of her. She just needs
a good man who doesn't scare easy to get her back on the
right track. Maybe we can find somebody for her," and
she smiled pleasantly at Laura.

Upstairs again, Laura settled into her malevolent butterfly chair and wondered why Emmy was so short-sighted.
It struck her as rather fine and noble that Beth didn't go
out with men. It never occurred to her that Beth really
might like men; without knowing why, without even
thinking very seriously about it, she knew she didn't want
her to like them.

Laura was a naive girl, but not a stupid one. She was
fuzzily aware of certain extraordinary emotions that were
generally frowned upon and so she frowned upon them too,
with no very good notion of what they were or how they
happened, and not the remotest thought that they could
happen to her. She knew that there were some men who
loved men and some women who loved women, and she
thought it was a shame that they couldn't be like other
people. She thought she would simply feel sorry for them
and avoid them. That would be easy, for the men were
great sissies and the women wore pants. Her own high
school crushes had been on girls, but they were all short
and uncertain and secret feelings and she would have been
profoundly shocked to hear them called homosexual.

It would never have entered her head to doubt that Beth
was solidly normal, because Laura thought that she herself
was perfectly normal and she wasn't attracted to men.
She thought simply that men were unnecessary to her.
That wasn't unusual; lots of women live without men.

What Laura would never know and Beth would never
tell her, was the real reason she had given up seeing men.
Beth had, over and above most people, a strongly affectionate nature, a strong curiosity, and a strong experimental
bent. She would give anything a first try, and morality
didn't bother her. Her own was mainly a comfortable
hedonism. What she wanted she went after. At the time
she met Laura, she wanted to be loved more than anything else.

Beth had always wanted to be loved. She wanted to feel, not to dream; to know, not to wonder. She started as a little girl, trying to win her aunt and uncle in her search for love. Loving them was like trying to love a foam-rubber pillow: they allowed themselves to be squeezed but they popped right back into shape when they were released.

Unknowingly, her aunt and uncle had started Beth on a long, anxious search for love. When she couldn't find it with them she turned to others, and when she grew up she turned to men. It was the natural thing to do; it was inevitable. For Beth grew up to be a very pretty girl, and when she began looking for a man to satisfy her she found more than one always willing to try.

But none of them made it. First there was George, when she was still in high school. She was just fifteen and George was a Princeton man in his twenties. Beth liked them "older;" and the older ones liked her. George fell very much in love with her. He was fun, he had been places, he could take her out and show her a good time . . . and he adored her. Her word was law.

Beth administered the law for two years. The time began to drag interminably toward the end of the second year. George smothered her with love, and she began to doubt and to despise herself for not returning his passion. Here was real love, what she had always craved to make her life complete and meaningful, and what did it give her? A headache. George bored her.

It was in this mood that she gave herself to George. She was seventeen. George, on his knees, had implored her not to go to college; to stay at home and marry him and make him the Happiest Man In The World. She said, "No, George, I can't."

And he said, "Why?"

"Because I don't love you." Her heart rose in her throat, in fear and pity—fear for herself and pity for George.

George wept. He wept very eloquently. "I'll kill myself," he murmured in a misery so genuine that she began to fear for him, too.

"Oh, no, you mustn't! You can't!" she said. "Here, George. Come here, George." She called him like a faithful spaniel, and he came, and let himself be petted. And very shortly he felt a sort of dismal passion rising in him with his self-pity; he began to sweat.

"Beth." He said her name fiercely. "Look at me. Look what you've done to me."

Beth gasped and then covered the lower part of her face with her hands so he couldn't hear her laugh.

"Oh, George," she whispered in a voice shaky with suppressed amusement. George took it very well; he thought her trembling voice was paying him tribute.

And suddenly Beth thought to herself very clearly, Oh, hell. Oh, the hell with it. She was quite calm and she said to George, "Come here." Somewhere in the back of her mind was the hope that this would solve her problem, answer her questions, set things right. She might not love George, but at least she would discover the end of love. Next time she met a desirable man, she would know everything there was to know. She would be prepared and it would all be beautiful as nothing with George had been beautiful.

Beth unbuttoned her skirt and let it slip to the floor.

Hesitantly, with a flushed face and a nervous cough, George approached her. And in less than a minute they were on the couch together and Beth was learning about love.

After that there followed a long procession of boys, mostly college men. The novelty wore off early for Beth, but not the hope and promise; she was an incurable optimist. It took her three years of indefatigable effort to convince herself that it wasn't the men who were at fault —at least not all of them. The laws of chance were against it. But it was one thing to realize that some of the men were good lovers and another thing entirely to admit that not even the best of them could rouse her. What was wrong? She was healthy and eager and willing; she wanted it, she had always wanted some kind of love. Was it George's fault for making her laugh at it? Or her aunt's and uncle's for making her weep? It took her a long time to see that it wasn't the fault of any one of them, but rather of all of them, and of herself. That was the bitterest pill. And after she confessed to herself that something prevented her from finding the love she so wanted she became rather cynical about it. The bitterness never showed, but it was there. She was just a little contemptuous of men because none of them had been able to satisfy her; it was much more comfortable than being contemptuous of herself for a fault she couldn't understand.

Laura, sitting alone in the room with Emily on a lonely Monday night, could not have known any of this. Even Emily, who had been Beth's closest friend throughout her college years, knew nothing of it.

At ten-fifteen Beth walked in and the atmosphere in the room lightened up noticeably. Laura gave her a glad smile.

"Hello, children," Beth said, smiling at them both.

"Long meeting?" said Emily, stretching.

"No, short meeting. Long coffee break." She dropped her notebook on the desk and slipped out of her coat. "Laur, for God's sake, aren't you uncomfortable?" she said suddenly, laughing. "Makes me want to wiggle just to look at you. Here, swing your leg over this thing." And when Laura hesitated she took her leg and lifted it herself over one wing of the butterfly.

"It comes up between your legs," she said. "Now put your head back."

Laura moved her head back gingerly as if she expected it to fall off her shoulders at any moment. Beth pushed it back against the high wing of the chair, laughing at her.

"Now, isn't that better?" she said, mussing Laura's hair.

"Yes, thanks. Much better." And Laura had to smile back at her. The real world, with its real bumps and backslides and perplexities, was never farther away.

THREE

ON SATURDAY NIGHT Laura went out with the two fraternity boys and Emily. They walked to Maxie's, one of the oldest campus joints, and drank beer and listened to the Dixie Six. Bud put on almost as much of a show as the musicians; Bud was Emmy's flame—Bud was "it." He would drop his head in his hands and groan at the bad notes and at the good ones exclaim, "Christ! Listen, Emmy!"

Bud was slender and tall, with thinning brown curls and round green eyes. He had remarkably sensual lips with straight white teeth behind them, and an impish smile. He was a well-known campus musician, one of the best; his reputation with a horn and with women far outweighed his reputation among his professors in music school.

He was a sort of perpetual student; the type that comes back year after year and never quite graduates. He loved music and he loved girls, and he seemed to exist quite satisfactorily on beer and slide oil and kisses. He was a campus character; one of the ones everybody knows, or hears about and wants to know.

Emily was the only girl who had ever come near to hooking him. It wasn't the physical attraction; Bud liked them all pretty; he wouldn't have taken her out the first time unless she had fulfilled that qualification. It wasn't her twinkling charm or her compliancy, either; it was all of these plus her willingness and ability to learn something about music—his kind of music. She was learning how to play the piano, spending long hours at it, so she could talk to Bud in his own language. All these attractions weren't enough to keep him from surveying the field and finding a little competition for her, but as it happened that was the best possible way to intrigue Emmy, who liked to "work for a man." He was fast becoming her major subject, and Laura and Beth had to sit through several monologues on his merits as man and musician.

28

Laura examined him curiously. The music didn't move her, but everybody else was so excited that she pretended to be. She didn't understand the mass fervor but she was afraid to say so, and she sat and watched the band like the others.

Fortunately it was not very hard to be friendly at beer parties, and the more beer you drank the easier it was. Not that Laura could drink very much. But Jim, Bud's friend, did famously. With every passing quart he got friendlier. Toward the end of the evening anything in skirts was irresistible, and the handiest skirt was Laura's. He made an effort to get better acquainted, draping an arm over her and squeezing her into the corner of the booth with the warm weight of his body. He put a hand on her thigh and began to press it, and Laura looked to Emily in sudden alarm. She hated to let a man touch her and she hated even worse to let him do it in public. But Emily was too preoccupied with Bud to notice that her roommate wanted help.

"Jim—" Laura said helplessly, and wondered wildly what to say next. Maybe all sorority girls did this. Maybe this was part of the price of membership.

When Laura hesitated in confusion, Jim thought she was searching for a way to encourage him, and he began, as he thought, to make it easy for her. He murmured, "What, baby?" in her ear, and "Tell me, come on," with a nauseating intimacy, and began to plant wet kisses on her neck and cheek, his hand closing harder on her thigh, until it started to hurt.

Laura trembled in revolt and he breathed, "Oh, baby!" and pulled her chin around and kissed her lips. The hot blush burned her face and she thanked God for the bath of pink neon that disguised it.

"I was all wrong about you, Laura," he whispered, and his lips brushed hers as they moved.

Laura wanted to claw at him, to burst from that terrible basement into the cold air and run and run and run until it was all miles behind her.

He kissed her again; a man's lips were claiming her own, and it was all so new, so alarming, that it took her breath from her.

"Jim—" she said.

He kissed her again, harder.

"Oh, Jim, please!" and she turned her head away sharply

against the wall of the booth. It was unbearable. No punish-
ment could be worse than this. She waited, shaking, for
him to reprimand her.

Instead he stroked her leg and leaned over her and said
softly, "I understand, baby. Believe me. We'll have time
later."

Laura thought she might be sick. It was no consolation
to her to suddenly discover that she might be attractive to
a man. She heard Emily's voice across the table with such
grateful relief that she almost reached out to clutch at her.

"Well, look here!" said Emmy. "Look who's hitting
it off!" She smiled a pleased smile. Emmy was a born
matchmaker.

Jim straightened up a little and grinned at her. "Why
sure," he said. "Just took us a little while to find each
other. Kinda dark down here." He was delighted to have
discovered an unexpected warm spell at the end of a
chilly evening.

They laughed, and Emily gave Laura an approving
smile that made Laura weak. It was apparently not only
right but expected that she should let Jim maul her. Beth!
she thought with sudden desperate force. Oh, Beth, if
only you were here! The thought came unbidden out of
the blue.

The two couples walked home together to the Alpha
Beta house, Jim with a tight grip around Laura. She could
feel his hip bone grind smooth and hard around its socket
where their bodies were pressed together. She hid her cold
helpless hands in her pockets and put her head down
against Jim's jacket. The grating of the wool on her tender
skin was a comfort to her; it was utterly disassociated from
human flesh and just irritating enough to assuage her
conscience.

She murmured "Yes" and "No" to Jim when she had
to and when she tried to keep him from kissing her, he took
it affably as part of the game. And all the while Laura
thought of Beth, so strong, so lovely, so gentle. She tried
to peer through the defiant dark for the lights of Alpha
Beta. But when they got there, she wasn't allowed to run
upstairs to Beth.

Jim hustled her out on the gloomy patio and emprisoned
her on the love seat. He thought she owed him a fair
measure of affection to recompense him for the evening's
entertainment. Laura's aversion to him mounted higher

with every kiss until it reached a screaming pitch inside her.

"Gee, Laura, I thought you were gonna be cold as hell," he said. "You're not, are you?" He chuckled at her.

Laura looked at him wide-eyed, held so hard that she felt she could count his ribs with her own. She hated him. She wanted to spit at him, hurt him, run. But she was afraid.

"Oh, yes," he said. "You and I are gonna get along just fine, Laura. Just fine." And he kissed her. "Just fine. Hey, open your mouth, honey. Hey, come on, Laura."

Laura turned away from him and whispered, "Jim, this is our first date. I mean—please, Jim."

"I know, baby. You're just a kid, you want to do everything right." He tickled her neck. "Well, believe me, Laura, this is right."

Laura's nails bit cruelly into the heels of her hands in a frenzy of revolt. Oh, God, stop! she thought.

"Hey, Laur, how 'bout next week?" He waited. "You busy next week?"

She waited too long; she didn't know how to make up excuses. She turned a helpless face to him.

"Good," he said. "Let's make it Friday."

"Oh, but I—"

"I'll give you a buzz."

The merciful closing chime sounded, and she sat up straight in a spasm of relief. Jim pulled at her arm. "Hey, Laura, they don't beat you if you kiss a boy, you know," he said, laughing and pulling at her.

"Jim, it's closing time," she said sharply.

"You're just nervous, baby," he said with a grin. He got to his feet slowly. "Okay, I don't want to make you a nervous wreck." He pulled his jacket on. Laura wanted to yank it on and force him out the door with all the histrionic haste of an old movie. He got one more long wet kiss from her and then she saw him out the door with an audible sigh of relief.

Laura walked up the stairs feeling weak and miserable. Jim was a handsome boy. Emmy said he was popular, and she had another date with him. She ought to be happy. But for the first time a tiny doubt slipped into her thoughts. What do I want? she asked herself. But she was afraid to answer.

Emily caught up with her on the stairs and said, "Gee Laur, Jim really likes you! I'm so glad. I thought for a

while you two weren't going to hit it off. When are you
going to see him again?"

"Friday." She wondered if Emily would notice her lack
of enthusiasm. . . .

Beth was still up. Laura felt a surge of affection for her.

"Hey, it's past your bedtime," said Emmy.

Beth looked up with a smile. "I wanted to hear about
the date," she said to Laura, and Laura had a sudden wild
desire to throw herself into Beth's arms and cry; to tell
her, with all the violence at her command, what she
thought of Jim. But she didn't dare. She looked at Beth
for a minute like a lost waif.

Beth smiled at her as if she understood. "How was it?"
she said.

"Oh—very nice," Laura said. Emily was watching her.

"Laura made quite a hit with Jim," she told Beth, strip-
ping off her clothes. Laura let her talk, wishing all the
while that she would go away. She wanted to be alone
with Beth; to talk, to be comforted.

Emmy kept them up for a while. Laura refused to go
to bed until Emmy did, and finally she won the game.
Emmy stood up and yawned.

"Guess I'll hit the sack, you guys," she said. "I'm beat
to the bricks, as my friend Bud would say. See you in the
morning."

"Night, Em," said Beth. She lighted a cigarette and
settled back to gaze at Laura and when Laura could think
of nothing to say, she walked over to the couch and sat
down beside her.

"What's the matter, honey?" she said.

"Oh, nothing!" The overemphasis rang false, and her
head ached and Beth was so close to her that she was dizzy.

Beth put an arm around her. "Tell me the truth, Laur,"
she said. And when Laura remained silent, she added
gently, "It's not a disaster if you didn't like the boy, you
know."

Laura looked down at her lap, still mute, afraid her tears
would start with her voice.

"What did he do, honey?"

"He—he— I don't want to talk about it. It wasn't anything awful. Emmy seemed to think it was all right. Only,
I—" her voice quavered—"I didn't like it." And suddenly
she put her head down on Beth's shoulder and wrapped

her arms around her and let the tears come out. The pressure began to lessen a little.

Beth held her and rocked her in her arms. "You didn't like it, baby?" she said softly.

"I hated it! I couldn't help it."

Beth smiled down Laura's back.

"Oh, Beth, I wish so much you had been with me instead of—of Emily." She had been about to say, "Instead of Jim." What a curious idea that was—to have a date with Beth!

Beth held her closer.

"I don't ever want to see that boy again!" she said into Beth's shoulder.

Beth broke the date for her.

FOUR

THE DAYS began to fly in Laura's life so fast that she lost them before she could reckon them. They got progressively brighter; she wanted to memorize each one but there was no time.

A letter came from her father; he was a better correspondent than her mother, but all his notes reminded her of the fresh wounds of their divorce. Laura was ashamed, even afraid to mention it to anyone. Her father wanted to know if she had called Charlie Ayers and Laura revolted vigorously at the thought. She tried to picture herself getting him on the phone and saying stolidly, "Hello, this is Laura Landon." Silence. He would get the point, of course. "Well—uh, gee, yeah, Laura, nice to hear from you. We'll have to get together some time. Tell your dad hello for me." Thanks, but no thanks.

Laura wrote her father that she couldn't get hold of Charlie. She gave the impression that she had given him up in favor of a clamorous press of beaux. Her father wanted her to be popular.

Life with Beth, she soon discovered, was busy and unexpected and at the same time relaxed as if nothing quite mattered enough to worry about. Beth was always occupied but somehow never in a rush. She had a phone installed in the room to accommodate her burden of calls.

"I just don't see how you do it," said Laura one night when the visitor count was high.

Beth stretched and came down from her stretch laughing. "It's easy," she said. "Lots of spare time. No social life. My God, if I had to mess with men I wouldn't have time for anything. I know when I'm well off." She laughed again suddenly, her eyes on Emily. "Look at Emmy," she said. "You don't believe a word I'm saying, do you?"

"Not that 'well off' stuff," said Emmy. "Neither do you."

"Sure I do. Now and then. My God, I have to. I'd go nuts if I didn't." She winked at Laura.

"Don't listen to her, Laura," said Emily in a motherly voice. "She's depraved."

34

Beth shrugged and got up with a grin. "You see?" she told Laura. "Nobody understands me, not even my best friend." She threw a pillow at Emily, who promptly threw it back. Beth dropped it elaborately on the floor.

"You're slowing up in your old age," Emily said.

"Oh, go play your piano!" Beth instantly regretted the remark. She knew why Emily spent most of her free time —and there was very little of it now, since she saw Bud every night—practicing on the old piano in the living room. There was an almost pathetic childish ingenuousness to her plan to capture Bud that made Beth feel sad and helpless. Aside from that, she missed seeing as much of Emily as she used to. Her peculiar schedule usually kept her out with Bud or down in the living room until bedtime. Emily was fun to talk to and gossip with.

Laura carefully put the pillow back where it belonged and then said good night. Pledge rules forced her to go to bed at eleven, and left the other two to talk as they pleased. The curfew irritated Laura. She was afraid that as soon as she left the room her roommates talked about her. She always felt that it was too early for bed, that she was wide awake, that there was more studying to do. It didn't occur to her for a long time that she was jealous of Emily.

Laura was right, in a way. Her roommates did speculate about her. They marveled at her two baths a day. They watched her scrub her face until it was almost raw and red and they noted how she always volunteered for the most dreary and uninteresting tasks in the whole house.

"Darn the girl," Emily said after Laura's polite goodnight, "I wish she'd relax. You know, sometimes when you burp nobody hears you. If you say 'excuse me' everybody looks up and knows you burped."

Beth threw her head back in a strong laugh.

"Well, that's the way she makes me feel," said Emily, grinning ruefully. She thought of Laura's eagerness to please, her conscientiousness, as a sort of magnified normalcy that made Emmy uncomfortable. "I like the girl, I really do," she said. "I can't complain about anything she does, but—I guess that's just it. I can't complain. I wish I could. It'd make her seem real, somehow."

"I don't think she understands herself very well yet," Beth said. "That's why she's so careful of everything she says and does. She wants to be sure it's right."

"Here we go again," said Emily cheerfully. "The old

psychology corner." That meant gossip about a particular female. "What's her family like?"

"I don't know. She won't talk about them at all. I'm afraid I scare hell out of her when I ask about them."

"Well, that's funny," Emmy said. "Wonder why?"

On a Wednesday in late November, just before dinner-time, Laura was called to the house phone. She picked up the receiver without thinking; it was probably someone from her activity committee at the Union, or maybe a man. She had continued going out; it was expected of her. But not with boys like Jim.

"Hello?" she said.

"Hello. Is this Laura Landon?" It was a good voice, strong and low and pleasant.

"Yes." Laura checked the files of her memory against the voice. It wasn't listed.

"This is Charlie Ayers. My father and your father are old friends."

Laura was silent, surprised.

"I just heard from Dad that you were down here. Thought I'd give you a ring."

"Oh. Oh yes, Charlie." She was flustered and awkward on the phone, especially with men.

Charlie sensed it and took over for her. "Well, look," he said, "maybe we could get together for a beer or something tonight."

She started to protest. It was a reflex action.

"Oh, come on, you can study any time," he said pleasantly. "I won't keep you long." Laura was struck again by his smooth voice. She paused a moment and he took it for acceptance. "I'll pick you up around eight," he said. "Okay?"

"Well, I—okay."

"See you at eight," he said.

She hung up wondering if the rest of him was as impressive as his voice.

Beth was interested. "Charlie Ayers," she said reflectively. "Isn't he an ADO?"

Laura nodded.

"Seems to me I've met him somewhere. Where'd you find him, Laur?"

"Oh, he—he just called. I met him on campus." She was amazed at her own fib, only half aware of her motives.

They were many and involved and they boiled down to impressing Beth with her own importance.

At a few minutes past eight her buzz ripped down the quiet halls. She jumped up nervously, pulled her coat on, and opened the door.

"Laura," said Beth, watching her with a smile. "You'll need your scarf. It's cold."

"Oh, yes. Thanks." She pulled it from the shelf and settled it around her shoulders, and started for the door again.

"Got your gloves?" Beth asked.

Embarrassed, Laura turned back to her dresser and pulled them out.

"How 'bout your purse, honey?" Beth chuckled at her.

"Oh!" said Laura impatiently, grabbing it and starting out again.

"Laura," said Beth in a slow teasing voice. "Aren't you going to kiss me good-by?"

Laura whirled and stared wide-eyed at her. Beth grinned. "Go on, honey," she said. "Have fun."

Laura backed out of the room and then turned and almost ran down the hall, her heart pounding, thrumming a thunderstorm inside her. Emily came out of the bathroom one door down and said, "Have a good time, Laur." Laura watched her retreat down the hall toward Beth with a sudden pang of jealousy so strong that she had to admit it to herself for the first time. Her buzz sounded again, and she had to go downstairs and meet Charlie.

She gazed anxiously around the front hall as she came down, and finally she saw a young man with dark hair glancing through a magazine, standing with his back to her. The lower she came the higher he seemed to stand from the floor. He wasn't aware of her until her heels clicked on the marble floor of the hall. Then he turned around, tossed the magazine down, and smiled at her.

"You must be Laura," he said, and walked across the room to take her hand. "I'm Charlie Ayers."

"Hi," she said, intimidated by his height and afraid her nervousness would betray itself. His face went very well with his voice.

Charlie took her arm and said, "Let's go to Pratt's."

He held the door for her and led her down the front walk to his car—an eight-year-old Ford with a dubious repaint job that left it generally green in tone. "It's not beautiful, but it runs," he said, laughing as he let her in. He was so sure, so calm and steady, that Laura began to relax a little. She tried to think of him, not of Beth.

Pratt's had a fair number of customers for a Wednesday night when Charlie and Laura walked in. They found a booth and Charlie helped her out of her coat.

He leaned over the table while she sat down. "Beer?" he said.

"Just a Coke, thanks."

He went to get it—no such thing as service in a student bistro—and left her to think. She made a powerful effort to avoid Beth and concentrate on Charlie. He was handsome and friendly and he didn't seem disappointed to find her ordinary-looking. She thought boys who looked like Charlie wanted only beautiful girls. She pictured him with a beautiful girl. She made a cigarette ad of them, a little TV commercial in which Charlie, in a tuxedo, leaned amorously over a white-clothed table to light the beautiful girl's cigarette, and she inhaled the intoxicating vapors till her strapless gown groaned with the burden of her breasts, and then blew the smoke out at the audience. And then she turned back to Charlie and smiled enchantingly into his wonderful face. They really made an eye-catching couple. When Laura recognized the girl in the picture it shocked her heart into action again. It was Beth.

Charlie set a Coke and a beer and glasses down on the table, and sat down facing her, interrupting her disturbing reverie. She couldn't think of anything to say.

"Well, I guess our fathers have been friends for a long time," he said.

"Yes, they certainly have."

Laura let him talk, but she didn't encourage him. She didn't like to talk about her father. It always made her feel sad and a little frightened, and after a while it tired her out.

"That's a fine house you're in," he said. "Let's see, I should know some of your sorority sisters. Baker?"

"Mary Lou. She's the president."

"Yeah, I remember her. Sort of pretty. Nice gal. Gloria Mark?"

Laura nodded.

"Gee, I knew a lovely dish over there a couple of years ago . . . Beth Cullison. Never see her around any more."

"Do you know Beth?" said Laura, uncertain and faintly alarmed.

"Oh, everybody knows Beth. I've met her a couple of times. I don't think she remembers me, though. This was a few years ago when she was dating a fraternity brother of mine. Pinned to him, in fact."

"Who?" she asked. She had to know.

"Oh, you wouldn't know him. Graduated last year."

"What was he like?"

Charlie smiled quizzically at her eagerness, without answering her. She began to feel the need to explain herself.

"Beth's my roommate," she said.

"Oh." He nodded, smiling. "Well, he was a nice guy. Quite an intelligent boy. They used to have long philosophical discussions. I guess Beth went for that in a big way."

Laura didn't like him, whoever he was. She didn't like to think that Beth had confided in him, kissed him, even. The thought produced a rash of gooseflesh.

Charlie ran his hand over the back of his head, the cigarette jutting out and away from his crisp brown hair, and he watched Laura as he did it. "As I say, I don't really know the girl. Just met her briefly. But I remember her . . ."

Laura didn't answer, and Charlie casually changed the subject. "When's your father coming down to pay you a visit?" he said.

"Oh, I don't know. I don't think he will. He's too busy," she answered, but she was thinking about Beth. What did the boy look like? Was he fun, had he been in love with her? Did she like him? Did she let him . . .

"Too busy?" said Charlie. "Must be traveling, hm?"

"No," she answered absently, "he and mother are—I mean—they—" She was suddenly staring at Charlie in confusion. It was too late.

"They what?" he said.

She looked around helplessly as if some way of escape might suddenly appear, and all of a sudden she felt very weak and lost. Her family was falling apart, and she was falling in love with Beth. The world was inside out, all wrong. She didn't understand it, she hardly even realized what was happening to her. She couldn't stop and she didn't know where she was going. Charlie's eyes burned her face.

Laura put her head in her hands and a tight silent sob shook her. He came around the table and sat beside her, putting an arm around her and trying to comfort her. "You know, we're really old friends, Laura. By proxy, anyway. I'm a great listener. Want to tell me about it?"

She couldn't control her tears. At last she said simply, "They've gotten a divorce. It's all over now. It shouldn't affect me like this. Please don't tell anybody," and she looked up at Charlie anxiously.

"Of course not," he said. "But just remember I've got a dandy shoulder for crying on, any time you're in the mood." And he gave her a warming smile. Laura returned it gratefully.

"Come on, let's go," he said.

At the Alpha Beta front door Charlie said, "I'm not going in with you, Laura." She looked up in surprise, and he chuckled. "You might feel obliged to kiss me good night. Gets pretty hot and heavy in the front hall at closing time —as I recall." He was not in the least tempted to kiss her.

It seemed to Laura a very special favor, one that respected her acute sensitivity, and she didn't know how to thank him. "Charlie—" she began. "It was very nice of you to take me out and listen to my troubles."

"Wasn't nice of me at all. I enjoyed it," he said with a smile. In the little silence that followed it struck him that there was only one way to prove that statement and that was to ask her out again. It occurred to Laura too, only to humiliate her. But Charlie saw her as a nice kid in an emotional jam, and because she seemed to need someone to lean on, because of their families, because she looked forlorn, he thought one more evening wouldn't hurt him. "When can I see you again?"

Laura was astonished. "Why, I don't know—" she said.

"Well, how about a week from Saturday?" he said, figuring only that he hadn't any other plans.

"Oh, that would be fine." She looked at him curiously.

"Swell. I'll call you," he said. And he went off down the front walk.

She went upstairs to the room, wondering why Charlie Ayers had asked her out for the night of the Varieties Show, one of the biggest campus events. Charlie didn't know he had until two days later when he checked the university calendar, and then he cursed himself. But he didn't break the date.

Laura came in the room to find Beth on the phone. She looked up from her conversation and smiled at Laura and after a moment she hung up. She spun around in her chair and said, "Well, is he as good as he looks?"

"Oh," Laura blushed. "He's awfully nice."

"Going to see him again?"

"Yes. For the night of the Varieties."

"Well!" Beth smiled at her. "He must be impressed." Laura didn't answer. "Finally remembered where I met that guy," she went on.

An awful suspense grabbed at Laura's stomach. "Who?" she said.

Beth frowned a little. "Your friend. Ayers. Charlie."

"Oh. Have you met him?"

Beth studied her and Laura could feel her amusement without understanding it. "Um-hm," Beth said. "Real handsome kid, isn't he?"

"Yes," Laura said briefly. She didn't like the way Beth and Charlie remembered each other at all.

"Well, I think I've got it now—I must have met him at a party somewhere."

"A fraternity party?" She was chagrined by her own jealousy.

"I guess so." Beth smiled. "Charlie been telling tales?"

"Of course not!"

Beth began to laugh softly. "Laura, you must be interested."

Laura's face turned red. "In what?"

"In Charlie, of course. What else?" Laura couldn't look at her smile. "I don't blame you," Beth went on, needling her subtly. "He's nice, as I remember. I thought it was a damn waste to give a brain to a guy with a face like that."

Laura wouldn't answer her. She wouldn't even look at her. Beth enjoyed the boycott.

"He's too handsome for me," she said. Laura rummaged defiantly in her closet, her back to Beth. "I like 'em ugly," Beth said.

"Oh, you're just joking," Laura said pettishly to a wall of wool skirts.

"No, I'm not. I like ugly faces. I like interesting faces better than pretty faces . . . You have an interesting face."

Laura turned around then and met Beth's provocative eyes for an instant and then looked at the floor. "I do?" she said.

The door opened noisily and Emily burst in, laughing. "Hi, roomies!" she said.

"Jesus, Emmy!" Beth got up with a grin and walked over to her. "Let me see your face." It was lipsticked from ear to ear and down her neck to the collar of her blouse. Beth laughed at her. "Laura, our roommate is bombed," she said.

Emily studied herself in the mirror. "And it's indelible," she wailed.

"Is she drunk?" Laura whispered to Beth.

"Sure," said Beth. "She's stoned." She took Emmy's chin in her hand and surveyed her face. Emmy submitted docilely to the examination, with her eyes shut. "Open your eyes, Em, I'm not going to kiss you," said Beth. "Bud went home, remember?"

And Emily got the giggles again. She took a piece of Kleenex and began to rub at the lipstick, which resisted her efforts and sat firm on her face. After a minute she gave up and stared at herself in dismay. Beth pulled open a dresser drawer and handed her a jar of cold cream.

"Not that you deserve it," she said. Emmy clung to her and laughed. "Come on," Beth said in a businesslike voice. She smeared cream over Emmy's face, rubbing it in carefully. "Every time she goes out with Bud, this is what happens," Beth told Laura. "She says it's good for his morale."

"Oh, Beth, I do not!" Emily said. "I said it was good for his music."

"God, I'll say it is. When you finish with him, Em, he can play in the key of Q."

Laura didn't like to see girls drunk. She sat on the studio couch and said hesitantly, "Well, it must be sort of exotic to date a musician."

"Exotic-exschmotic," said Emily. "He comes with the same basic equipment as any other man." Beth laughed, but Laura saw nothing to laugh at. "Only he's the deluxe model," Emmy added. She pulled her clothes off vigorously.

"Here, here!" exclaimed Beth. "You have to wear that again. God, Emmy, you act like you wear 'em once and throw 'em away!" And she rescued Emily's skirt and blouse from the floor. She pulled a towel from the rack on the closet door and draped it over Emily's shoulders, stuck her toothbrush in her hand, and propelled her firmly toward the door.

"Shape up or ship out, gal," she said. "You're just too damn sexy."

Emily pulled herself up regally in her underwear and said, "I'm beautiful, I'm beloved, and I have a secret."

"Well, hot damn!" said Beth, and she laughed.

Emily minced into the hall and turned back to announce, "And you're all jealous." And she left to wash up.

"How 'bout that!" said Beth in mock awe.

Laura looked uneasily around the room. She thought Emily had acted disgracefully and it embarrassed her to even think of it. Beth was silent for a moment and then stared at Laura thoughtfully. "Laur, honey," she said, "you free tomorrow night?" When Laura said yes, Beth gave her a friendly smack on the rear. "Be my date," she said. "For the movies."

From then on, they went to the movies regularly and Laura saw the old Garbo films, French imports and Swedish nature films, only to be with Beth. She often turned down parties to be able to go, a practice Beth would have stopped had she known of it. But Laura kept it carefully from her. She liked everything about the movie trips too well: sitting next to Beth in the dark theater, hearing her breathe and shift and laugh or whisper to her. The first time they'd gone to the movies together, Beth had reached over and helped her out of her coat. When Laura tried to do the same for her, Beth stopped her. "I've got it, thanks," she said. And after that they followed the same ritual, without ever referring to it.

Then the night came when *Cyrano de Bergerac* was playing at the local theater. Laura and Beth had hardly been seated before Laura, saturated with the sentiment, found the tears starting down her cheeks. She could never keep them back from an affecting story. Beth saw the quiet little tears and smiled at them. It was then she reached into Laura's lap and found her hand and took it in her own and pressed it. The shock stopped the tears as the warmth of Beth's hand began to spread all through Laura, strange, sweet and inebriating. It was ten minutes before Laura dared to look at Beth. She was gazing serenely at the screen.

They never mentioned it but after that their hands always found each other in the dark of the theater.

FIVE

It was Saturday, the day of the Varieties Show, the day Laura was to see Charlie for the second time. It was also the day that Beth's Uncle John chose to pay his niece a visit. He had made a habit every year of getting down to see Beth for at least one weekend. He liked the Varieties and he liked the football game and he liked to have dinner at the sorority house with Beth. The girls made a fuss over him, and he would sit beaming at the head table, flattering the house mother and flirting with her charges.

Laura was anxious to meet him, to see if he looked and acted anything like Beth. Emily told her he was a very impressive individual; he had been a colonel in the last war and he had a false leg.

Uncle John arrived just before dinnertime and Laura watched with mixed emotions as he folded Beth in a hug. He was a big man with a red, jovial face and he shook Laura's hand heartily and said, "Well, well, you're Beth's new roommate! How d'you do?"

"Fine, thank you," she murmured, overcome with shyness, but Uncle John didn't notice. He was following Beth into the living room and greeting the girls he remembered from the year before.

Laura turned to Emily and said accusingly, "He doesn't look anything like Beth," as if it were Emily's fault.

"Oh, heavens no," said Emily. "He's not her blood relation. His wife is. She and Beth's mother were sisters."

"Oh," said Laura, and had trouble concealing the disappointment she felt. "Does she look like Beth?"

"Nope. Beth looks like her father. He died a long time ago. She has a picture of him around somewhere. It's funny. You'd think she actually knew him if you ever heard her talk about him. She was two, I think, when he died."

After dinner they went into the living room and sat on the floor in the circle of girls talking to Beth's uncle. He

44

was enthroned on the couch with a pretty girl on either side of him, talking merrily in all directions at once. Beth sat in a chair across from him, watching him with a little smile. Every now and then he said, "Isn't that so, Elizabeth?" and she would nod in agreement.

Uncle John was a large man in many ways, fat, generous and well-heeled. He hadn't any idea of what sort of a girl his niece was underneath her pleasant exterior. All her life she had been a bright little girl and pretty, so he simply ignored her spells of melancholy and her love of books. He gave her plenty of spending money, kept her in nice clothes and nice schools, and saw her at dinner and on weekends. He didn't interfere with her private life and feelings; they simply didn't matter to him that much. She was charmingly grateful for his care so he was fond of her and had arranged for her to have an independent income on her twenty-first birthday.

Laura cringed when he began to tease Beth. "We're going to have to lock up her books until she gets herself a man," he said, and roared amiably at his niece.

Beth grinned at him. "He's scared to death I'll wind up an old maid," she told Laura, "and he'll never get me off his hands."

"Now, now, honey, you know that's not true," he chuckled.

Laura sat there almost hating Uncle John and his calm assumption that Beth wanted to get married. Couldn't he see how fine and pure she was? Her face a blank and her thoughts miles away, Laura didn't hear her buzz and it wasn't until one of the girls nudged her and whispered something that she remembered she was supposed to meet Charlie that evening.

He looked even more attractive than she remembered and he said, "Well, Miss Landon, you look very pretty this evening."

Laura tried to feel a spark of feminine interest in him, but she couldn't. She liked him, that was all. He took her arm and led her out to the car. In it was a young man sitting alone. Charlie pointed to him and said, "This is my roommate, Mitch Grogan, Laura. We have an apartment—"

"So called—" said Mitch.

"—over on Daniel. Couple of blocks from campus."

"Compensations of old age," said Mitch. "You don't

have to live in university-approved housing. As a matter
of fact, I don't suppose we could get anybody to approve
of our housing, Charlie."

"What's the matter with it?" said Laura.

The two boys laughed. "Everything," said Charlie. "You
name it, if it's bad we got it—bad pipes, bad wiring, bad
landlady, bad everything. But we can give a hell of a beer
party in the front room."

"And we keep our own hours," Mitch added.

"How old do you have to be to get an apartment?" said
Laura conversationally. They were driving toward the
auditorium where the Varieties Show was scheduled to get
underway.

"Real old," said Charlie. "God, twenty-two, at least.
Would you believe it, Laura, Mitch is damn near twenty-
five."

"Really?" said Laura, turning to look at Mitch in the
front seat beside her.

Charlie laughed at her seriousness. "He's going to die a
bachelor," he told her confidentially. "I just let him tag
along with me for kicks. Otherwise he forgets what women
look like."

Laura looked at Mitch again and he didn't seem in the
least disturbed over Charlie's prediction.

"See?" said Charlie with a grin. "God, they could put
him right in the middle of a harem and he'd ignore every
damn female until he got his homework done."

Trouble finding a parking space stopped all conversation
until they were inside the auditorium. From then on,
Laura made no effort to try to listen to Charlie and Mitch
over the wild shouts of laughter. She searched the huge
audience for Beth and Uncle John, but couldn't see
them. When the Varieties were over Laura tried to scan
every face she could see of the huge crowd streaming out
of the auditorium, but Beth was nowhere in sight. De-
pressed and silent, Laura walked with Charlie and Mitch
to Maxie's.

Maxie's was already jammed when they got there and
the Dixie Six was in action, as usual.

"My God, when did Bud Nielsen start playing with
them?" said Charlie.

"Where?" said Mitch. "Oh, yeah!"

Laura looked up, and there was Bud with his long gold
horn glinting through the smoke, standing in the fore of

the little bandstand that stood in the rear of the room.

"Do you know him?" she asked Charlie.

"Yeah, I know him. Fraternity brother. Good musician."

"My roommate dates him," said Laura.

"Beth dates this character?" Charlie looked at her in surprise.

"Oh, no! My other roommate—Emily."

"Oh," he chuckled. "I didn't think Cullison would go for this guy," and he nodded at Bud.

Cullison, Laura thought in irritation. Her name is Beth. Elizabeth.

"God, it's crowded. Do you see a place?" Charlie said, squinting through the smoky pink gloom.

Laura became suddenly aware of someone saying her name and she turned around a couple of times, straining through the half-light at the myriad faces.

"Laura!" It was Beth. Laura saw her laughing and struggling through the crowd and her first wild impulse was to blindfold Charlie. But it was too late for that. She looked up at him and he was staring at Beth with a smile on his face. Laura was too upset to see that Mitch was smiling too.

Beth was worth staring at. Her cheeks were flushed and her eyes were very bright, as if she had a romantic fever of some sort. Actually, she simply had too much beer in her, and it was making her laugh. The boys in the crowd were squeezing and pushing her and Laura was suddenly furious to see that she was enjoying it.

Beth reached a hand toward Laura and Charlie took it quickly and pulled her past the last few people that separated them. He pulled hard and she fell against him, laughing and off balance. He caught her around the waist to steady her and when she was quite steady he held her still as if he were afraid she might lose her balance again, or as if he hoped she would.

Mitch and Laura watched this artful maneuver together, Mitch with a mild twinge of envy and Laura with raging jealousy. She almost swore at Charlie in her anger. Furious tears gathered in her eyes and her whole body was rigid with emotion. She hated Charlie for holding Beth, she hated Beth for letting herself be held, she hated the two of them just for being near each other. She was afraid to see them together; they had spoken too well of each other.

"My God, I thought I'd never make contact," Beth was saying. "We're over there." She gestured vaguely behind her, still leaning on Charlie. "Emmy talked us into it. Uncle John is getting a lecture on jazz. Bud's playing. Did you see him?"

"We saw him," said Charlie.

Beth looked up into his face for the first time. "Hi," she said. "You must be Charlie." She leaned closer and studied him. "Yes, you are. I'd remember that face anywhere. I'm Beth Cullison."

"Yes, I know." He laughed, holding her a little tighter.

Laura could hardly contain herself. "And this is Mitch Grogan," she said in a sharp, impatient voice.

"Hi, Mitch." Beth leaned away from Charlie to take his hand. Then she said, "Come on back and sit with us. We've got loads of room." She looked up at Charlie again.

"Sure," he said, releasing her slowly. "Think you can make it?" He grinned.

Beth took a few steps away from him and then turned back and said with an air of injured dignity, "Certainly."

Mitch and Charlie laughed at her, and then Charlie took Laura's arm—he failed to notice how stiff and unwilling it was—and followed Beth back to the booth. Beth introduced the boys. Emily smiled beautifully at them.

"Well, now," boomed Uncle John over the racket, "you children can sit together over here and I'll sit next to Emmy. She's a trombone widow tonight." And he laughed at himself, getting up and moving over to Emily's side.

Beth slid into the seat he had left and Laura nearly followed her in an effort to keep Charlie away.

"Whoa, my dear," said Uncle John, catching her sleeve. "Let the gentleman in the middle." She was furiously embarrassed.

Charlie sat between Beth and Laura, and Mitch settled next to Uncle John where he could gaze undisturbed across the table at Beth. He wasn't the only interested party. Laura kept an anxious eye on her, and every time Charlie leaned over Beth to smile or say something Laura crawled with irritation. The loud music prevented her from hearing what they said to one another.

As for Beth, sitting next to Charlie and crowded tight against the wall, she was surprised by the size of him. His eyes were dark and his grin was wonderful and she began to feel inside her an almost forgotten excitement. It was too strong to fight and too sweet to ignore. She didn't do anything about it; she just let it happen, and when after a while she felt his hand on her knee she let it stay there and smiled imperturbably across the booth at Uncle John.

But she was not as calm as she looked. The pressure of the warm firm hand on her leg exhilarated her and confused her at the same time. It had always taken Beth a while to react to a man; there were some she had never reacted to at all, in spite of the fact that she had allowed them to touch more than a knee. But from the moment Charlie's arm had circled her waist she had felt an almost electric delight in him, in his touch and his presence. She almost resented it; she had tried so hard to give her affection to men she thought were worthy of it. But Charlie had done absolutely nothing to deserve it except touch her once or twice and talk to her a little. And that light touch, that low voice combined to thrill her strangely and bother her until she began to wonder if there was something wrong with her . . . or for the first time, something right.

Charlie's hand tightened on her leg and moved up a little while he talked to her. And then it moved up a little more, as if he were asking questions with it that had nothing to do with the words he spoke. Beth sat quietly letting him do as he pleased, too bewildered, too secretly pleased to stop him. She found that his touch made her shy; and the farther his hand traveled the harder it was for her to meet his eyes. But when she did she saw a promise in them.

Laura could see nothing but she suspected everything and she sat beside them, angry and tormented. Her sharp nails crept up her arms and threatened to come down them cuttingly. She was so tense toward the end of the evening that she almost gave a little shriek when Uncle John finally said, "Well, we'd better be on our horses, children." She wanted to get up and bolt.

They went their separate ways home and Laura was greatly relieved to get some distance between Beth and Charlie. She was silent in the car, still nettled, trying to think of a way to make Beth sorry for being nice to Charlie, to make her apologize for Laura didn't know what. Her jealousy rode herd on her, goaded her unmercifully.

Mitch asked her a couple of questions about Beth and

she hardly heard them or knew how she answered. Mitch was no threat, he didn't count; he hadn't sat too close to Beth and claimed all her attention and smiled at her and made her laugh.

There seemed to be only one solution, only one way to make Beth feel guilty, to make her stay away from Charlie, and that was for Laura to pretend that she really liked him. Laura made her mind up and set her chin in determination.

They reached the house and Charlie took her up the walk. Mitch leaned out of the car and called, "Hey, tell your roomie hello for me," and Laura ignored him. Charlie just laughed at him; Mitch admired all sorts of girls but he rarely had the guts to ask them out.

At the door Laura turned and faced Charlie, and began to talk before he said a word. "Charlie, we're having a Christmas party—a dance—two weeks from today. An afternoon dance. Would you—would you be able to come?"

Charlie was trapped. There were always excuses for evening parties but what the hell was there to do in the afternoon that was more important than a dance? And he had only seconds to think of something. He saw the little tremor in Laura's lips, her timidity and distress. There was a letter at home on his desk from his father that read, "Glad you met the Landon girl. Just heard about her family—too bad. Give her a good time if you can. Probably needs some cheering up." Still he hesitated. And then suddenly Laura came so near to tears that he said swiftly, "Why—I'd like to, Laura. Thanks."

His reticence stung and humiliated her, but at least he had said yes, and it was worth it to keep him and Beth apart. He smiled at her to make it up a little and gave her arm a friendly press. "I'll call you," he said. And Laura had to dash into the house without answering him before she lost the last of her composure.

SIX

Laura went heavily up the stairs and into the room. Beth was in her pajamas. She looked up at Laura with a smile as innocent as if she had spent the whole evening playing checkers with a maiden aunt. Laura stood staring at her, her face drawn and pale, and Beth's smile changed to a frown of concern.

"Hi, honey," she said. "You look pretty glum."

"I'm tired," said Laura briefly, and turned away to hang her coat up. She was too proud, too hurt to tell Beth what the trouble was—and she was too afraid.

Beth watched her for a moment in silence, and then she said, "What's the matter, Laur?"

"Nothing!" Laura snapped. She got ready for bed in resolute silence; Beth couldn't get a word out of her.

When Laura came back from the bathroom she found the studio couch opened out and made up like a bed. Beth was stretched out across it with her eyes closed and one arm lying across her forehead. Laura felt a sudden creeping shyness with her.

"Laura," Beth murmured sleepily.

Laura turned her gaze abruptly away. "Yes?" she said.

"It's awfully cold in the dorm."

Laura glanced back at her, her hand poised halfway to the towel rack. "It is?" she said.

"Um-hm . . . Want to sleep in here?"

Laura hung up the towel nervously. "But you're sleeping in here," she said softly.

"There's room for two."

"Oh, I—I think I'll be okay in the dorm." She felt suddenly a little panicky; she didn't know why.

Beth rolled over on her stomach and opened her eyes. She was smiling a little. "'Fraid of me, Laur?" she said.

"No," said Laura, trying to make it sound very casual.

Beth bounced up and down invitingly, laughing a little. "Come on, then. It's nice and warm in here."

Laura didn't know what to say. She opened her mouth and shut it again and then she turned around and looked

51

at Beth, as if that might give her something to answer
with. "Well—" she hesitated.

"I knew you would." Beth grinned at her.

Laura tried to remember that she was mad at Beth. "I
don't think I will," she said severely.

Beth turned over on her back again and laughed. "Open
the window a little, honey," she said.

Laura opened it slowly and the fresh cold air came in.
Then she went to the dresser and reached for the lamp
cord.

"Laura," Beth said in a drowsy voice.

Laura turned around, startled.

"Come here, Laur."

Laura stood still and gazed at her, wondering if she heard
right.

"Come here, honey," Beth said. "No, leave the light on.
Come sit here where I can see you."

Laura walked slowly to the bed with a strange alarm
growing inside her and sat gingerly on the edge. She was
trembling a little. Beth reached for her arm and said,
"Move over, Laur. Let me see you." Laura moved closer
unwillingly and trembled again.

"Are you cold, honey?"

"No." Her voice sounded too small for the rest of her.

"What's the matter, Laur? Did I hurt your feelings or
something?"

"No." Laura clamped her hands together and stared at
her knees.

"Tonight, I mean. I was acting kind of silly with Charlie,
wasn't I?" Laura refused to answer. "I was a little tight,
I guess. I didn't mean anything by it." She hardly knew
why she said this, why she felt the need to say it to Laura.
It was almost as if she were reassuring herself that it didn't
mean anything, when in reality she wasn't sure at all. "You
know that, don't you, Laur? Don't you?" She wished she
knew it herself.

"I—I hardly noticed it," Laura said, clinging to her
pride. Her arm felt like fire at the place where Beth's
hand rested.

"Yes, you did. You're upset, I can tell. Laura, baby, it
didn't mean a damn thing, believe me. Who's Charlie?
gentle; it almost persuaded Beth herself. She sat up and
My God, I hardly know him." Her voice was lovely and
put her arm around Laura. "Honey . . ." she said. "Am I

forgiven? Hey, Laur?" It was a teasing whisper. She lifted Laura's chin and Laura wanted to press her hands to her pulsing temples.

"Yes," she whispered, ashamed of her weakness.

Beth squeezed her and smiled. "Okay, you can turn out the light now," she said, and released her.

Laura got up and her knees were precariously weak. She hadn't time or strength to analyze the sudden violence within her. She pulled the lamp cord and let the darkness in. And then she stood perfectly still for a moment, knowing she was going to get into bed with Beth. She moved very cautiously across the room and found the bed; and then she crept in and pulled the covers up to her chin and lay on her back, afraid to move or make a sound, afraid even of her own breathing.

They lay in absolute silence for a minute. Suddenly Beth rolled over and tickled her hard in the ribs. Laura gave a little scream.

"Well, thank God," said Beth, laughing. "I was afraid you were dead. Don't you wiggle when you get in bed, Laur?"

"Yes—" She caught her breath. "No—" She didn't trust her voice, her thoughts, her body. She felt a great rush of warmth through all her limbs, electrifying, wild, radiating from the powerful thrust of her heart. "Oh, Beth . . . Beth . . ." she said, helplessly, drowned in it. Her voice shook and she realized that she was holding Beth's hands, that she had caught them to stop the tickling and held them still, held them hard against her ribs. Beth felt her quiver. "Laur, you are cold." She knew she wasn't. She wanted to make her talk. Charlie had left her in a state of strange elation that made her restless.

"No, no, I'm not cold—"

"Yes you are. Here, roll over. I'll keep you warm."

Laura turned on her side and Beth followed her, fitting her body to Laura's and pulling her close in her arms. "You'll warm up, honey," she said. "Just relax. Shall I close the window?"

"No," said Laura. Don't move, don't leave me, she pleaded silently. She wanted to stay like this in the velvet dark with Beth always beside her, touching her, her arms around Laura, her warm breath in her hair. Beth was torment so lovely, so amazing, so sweet, that Laura wanted to cry. She lay very still, afraid that if she moved Beth

would move too, and she would lose her. She felt her own
arm resting on Beth's, and Beth's clasped loosely about
her midriff, and all down her back the thrilling front of
Beth . . . their heads so near, her breath so light on Laura's
ear. The wonderful softness of her breasts, the strong
length of her thighs against Laura's. With the care of love
aborning, Laura pressed back toward her, trying to feel her
even closer as if that might make them inseparable.

Beth was immersed in a reverie of Charlie. "Hm?" she
said when Laura moved, rousing a little. "You all right,
Laur?"

"Yes," Laura whispered. Her whole body seemed to have
stopped functioning in an access of caution.

"Go to sleep, honey," Beth murmured, and pulled her
tighter to reinforce her words.

Laura lay wide awake in her arms for a long time, so
perfectly happy that nothing seemed real; full of a strangely
wedded exhilaration and drowsy bliss.

Beth fell asleep wrapped in her reverie. After a while
Laura raised up a little to let her move. She rolled over on
her back, groaning softly, and then lay still. In a moment
when she was quiet again, Laura turned to gaze at her, her
head lifted and resting on her hand. She studied the curve
of her lips and she wondered if Beth would know if she
kissed her, and she leaned toward her and then became
afraid again and stopped herself.

"Beth," she whispered in a voice not meant to be heard.
"Dear Beth . . . is this wrong? I'm so happy . . ." Maybe
she was wrong, but nothing, no one, was ever more right
than Beth. Laura looked at her face until she felt almost
dizzy with her; with the wild and foreign turmoil she
created in her heart.

"Oh, Beth, Beth," she whispered. "I think I—I think I
love you, Beth. I think I must love you." She pulled herself closer and brought her lips very near to Beth's. Her
heart felt twice its size in her breast and her breath wanted
to rush in and out in great gasps. She felt a sudden sweat
all over and she stared fascinated and shivering at Beth.

"We're so close, Beth . . . I could kiss you. I could kiss
you, Beth, we're that close . . ." She looked from Beth's
lips to her eyes, and still Beth slept peacefully, and Laura's
fever mounted until nothing mattered except Beth and
the intoxicating nearness of her. Laura made the first
concession to her passion. She leaned steadily closer to

Beth until their lips touched, and then she couldn't move away for a long time. She had reached, not a goal, but a first step. The kiss would never calm her—it taught her to crave.

She pulled away, shaking, and drew her hand across her mouth and she wanted violently to kiss Beth awake, to rouse her from slumber to sudden hot passion. Laura sat up in bed and struggled against her implacable desire with tears and tremors.

"Laur?" murmured Beth, and her hand found Laura's startled back.

"I'm all right," said Laura in a quick scared whisper. "I'm all right, Beth," and she lay down and faced away from Beth and drew the covers high.

She slept very little that night, and her whole being was consumed with wonder and hope and powerful misgivings. She had completely forgotten Charlie.

Beth slept, but restlessly. There was the mystery of Charlie to trouble her dreams, and there was the surprise of unexpectedly rousing Laura. She had begun to think that she would never reach Laura, never really be close to her; it seemed that all she ever did was tease, and all Laura did was answer her politely. But when she reached over in bed to tickle her she realized with a shock that she had struck a profoundly responsive chord in Laura. She felt Laura's cold hands grip hers and heard her breathe, "Oh, Beth . . . Beth . . ." and felt her cool, remote courtesy melt away. Beth was surprised and delighted. Unwilling to hurry her and just as unwilling to let her go, Beth simply held her in her arms and enjoyed the feel of her and marveled at the force of her heart. She knew it was more than fright that provoked Laura's heart so, and somehow Laura's reaction complemented the strange mood Charlie had brought upon her.

Beth took Laura in her arms that night, not because she had forgotten Charlie or because the effect he had on her was lessened; but simply because Laura was right there with her in the same place at the same time, because Laura was sweet and warm and accessible and Beth felt a tender fondness for her. And perhaps most of all because Charlie had aroused to painful new life her old craving for love.

It meant a lot to Beth to be loved. It would have meant

even more if she could have loved someone herself. But she had never been able to give her love successfully and so she was ready to take someone else's. She needed it; if she couldn't give it she would take it, that was all. And Beth was not afraid to take, to try new ways, to look in new places. She had not been afraid of George, nor of the boys that followed him. And she wasn't afraid when she felt Laura's unmistakably erotic response to her teasing; startled, intrigued, but not afraid. It did not frighten Beth that Laura was a member of her own sex; it made her only the more curious.

There was, in fact, only one thing that scared Beth a little that night, and that was her reaction to Charlie.

SEVEN

THE NOISE in the halls woke Beth the next morning. She moaned and stretched and turned to find Laura watching her, and she smiled sleepily at her.

"Morning, honey," she said, and yawned. "What time is it?"

"I don't know. Almost nine." Don't get up! Laura thought anxiously. It all went so fast.

"Ummm . . . got to get up." She raised her arm over her head and squinted at her watch.

"It's early," said Laura hopefully, still watching her.

"I know, but Uncle John rolls out at nine on Sundays. Always has." Her arm fell across her stomach. "He'll be by to pick me up in a few minutes for breakfast." She looked at Laura. "Sleep well, Laur?"

"Yes," said Laura, and she thought she had never seen anything quite so beautiful as Beth with her sleepy head on the pillow and her pale face set in the aureole of her dark hair.

Beth reached up languidly and pushed Laura's hair behind her ear, and that ear tingled to the ends of Laura's fingers. "My God, are you ticklish," Beth chuckled. "I thought you were going to snap at me last night."

Laura smiled sheepishly. "I didn't mean to. I was just— you caught me by surprise."

"I guess!" said Beth, and she lay still and looked at Laura for a long moment. She liked to be looked at the way Laura was looking at her. She was being admired and she enjoyed it. But still, Uncle John got up at nine.

She sat up and Laura's eyes never left her, as if they were trying to pull her back down on the pillow. Beth felt them and they were subtly exciting. She wanted suddenly to arouse Laura and she turned back and looked at her. Laura was propped up on her elbows. Beth put a hand on either side of her and leaned over her playfully. Laura's breath caught and her eyes widened in excruciating suspense.

57

"Did you finally get warm last night, Laur?"

"Yes. Finally." She smiled and Beth took her shoulders with a grin and pushed them into the pillow so that Laura lay flat beneath her.

"No 'thank you'?" she teased. "No 'yes, thank you'?"

"Oh!" said Laura, putting her hand over her mouth. "Oh, I'm sorry—" The weight of Beth on her made her feel a little crazy.

Beth laughed. "Don't be silly! It's a good sign. I've always thought you wouldn't stop being polite to me until you started to like me, Laura."

"Really?" Laura was astonished. Her beautiful manners came to nothing, then. "Oh, Beth, I—I do like you. I've liked you right along, right from the start. I—really." How could she possibly say it? Her earnest frown, her eyes, would have to speak for her.

"No, you haven't," Beth said, and she poked Laura in the ribs.

Laura gasped and twisted her body. "Oh, yes—yes, I have, Beth." She felt compelled to keep talking, to prove it. "Why, I liked you even before I met you."

"You did not," Beth teased.

"Yes, I did. Really, Beth."

"You didn't even know me. How could you like me?" She smiled.

"Well, I—well, I don't know." Her eyes fell then. It was the truth. She didn't. She knew only that from the moment she first saw Beth, nobody else interested her. And from the moment she spoke to her, no one else mattered.

"You must have some reason. Come on, Laur, tell me." Beth leaned over closer, smiling.

Laura had a brief fear of suffocating with her want, of betraying it through every hard breath, every drop of perspiration. "No, no . . . she protested weakly.

"No reason at all?" Her voice was almost a whisper.

"I just thought you looked like—such a nice person. That's all. You looked friendly. I thought you must be a nice person to know," she whispered lamely.

"Am I? Am I nice to know, honey?"

"Yes." She couldn't look at Beth now.

"I don't believe you."

"Oh, you must!" Her eyes flew back to Beth's. "You're

more than nice, Beth, you're—" And she stopped herself, swallowing compulsively, and looking away in something very near panic.

"I'm what? Tell me, Laur. Come on, honey, tell me," she coaxed. "What am I? Hm? Laura?"

"Beth—" Laura pushed her away in a sudden hot desperation. "I don't know!" She sat up panting and swung her legs over the edge of the bed.

Beth watched her with a smile. "Now you're mad at me, Laur. You're mad at me, aren't you?"

"No!"

"Yes, you are."

"Don't say I am when I'm not!"

Beth laughed gently at her and crawled over to her. She put her arms around her from behind with her legs coming around alongside Laura's and gave her a bear hug. Laura stiffened in the embrace, fighting her potent urge to return it and shivering again.

"Okay, Laura. You're not mad at me. You love me," Beth teased. She looked around Laura's head, trying to see her face.

Laura turned it furiously away, pushing at Beth's arms. "Don't make fun of me! Let me go!"

"I'm not making fun of you, honey."

"Let me go!"

"Say you're not mad."

"I've already said it."

"Say it again."

"I'm not mad," said Laura between clenched teeth.

"Okay, honey." Beth was laughing again. "Let's kiss and make up."

"Oh, Beth!" She was torn apart. "Beth, what a thing to say!"

"What's wrong with it? It's a nice thing to say."

"Let me go! Will you let go of me!" And she gave a hard push against Beth, who suddenly freed her and left her pushing against nothing. Laura got up seething with temper and an infuriating desire to turn back and throw herself into Beth's arms again and beg for kisses. But she dared not even look at her.

Beth sat on the edge of the bed and watched her pull her towel from the closet rack with jerky impatient movements. Laura couldn't bear being watched.

"I thought you had to get up and have breakfast with your uncle," she said testily. Her emotion unnerved her; she couldn't leash it and she hated to have it show. Beth sat still on the bed, smiling at Laura's irritation with gentle amusement.

She got up and came toward her. "Laura," she said in a soft conciliatory tone. Laura moved swiftly toward the door but Beth reached her before she escaped, catching her upper arms. She turned her around. "Hey, Laur?" she said. It was soothing and contrite. "Let me tease you, honey. Don't get so angry. I'm not trying to be mean . . . Do you believe me, Laur?"

"I don't know," said Laura as coldly as she could, and she trembled again.

Beth felt it with amazement. "Laur," she said. "Look at me, honey."

"No." And she stared in unhappy defiance at her towel.

"Laura, honey, listen. I liked you too, Laur. Before I met you, I liked you too."

Laura looked up slowly, disbelieving, yearning to believe, trying to hold her anger between them for defense. But it slipped away from her, out of her, and she was looking up at Beth like a little girl; like Laura six years old begging for a candy heart.

"You did?" she faltered, searching Beth's face.

"Yes. Yes I did." Beth was strangely excited again at the intensity in Laura's face and for a precious second Laura saw it. She found herself suddenly on the point of declaring her love, of clasping Beth in her arms. The tension spiraled up like a rocket and she gasped, "Beth!" and so startled Beth that she caught her breath like Laura and nearly crushed her arms with the sudden tight grip of her hands.

"Oh—oh, Laura," she said, shaking her head and trying to collect her senses. They were going too fast, they had to slow down. Her hands dropped and she turned to her dresser and picked up her comb, feeling the trembling in herself now. "We'd better get dressed," she said.

Laura stood paralyzed, watching every motion Beth made, the confession so tight in her throat that the pressure made her giddy. "Beth, I—I—"

Beth turned away from her into the closet. "Go wash up, honey," she said.

"Beth, please. Please, I—"

Beth straightened up suddenly and took Laura's face in her hands and bent over her and kissed her. And then she shut her eyes tight in pure surprise at herself and her hands held hard to Laura's shoulders for a moment. Finally she said, "Now go. Go on . . . For God's sake, Laur—scram!"

Uncle John stayed at the house for Sunday dinner. It was the traditional climax to his traditional weekend. He sat at the housemother's table and Beth sat beside him. Laura was at a table in the back of the room. With a little prudent rubbernecking she could just see Beth, but it was risky to keep looking. And still she had to look, almost to reassure herself that Beth was real.

They teased her about Charlie at the table. Emmy had pried the information from her that she was going to the Christmas dance with him, and when Emmy knew something the rest of the house knew about it soon after. Mary Lou Baker startled Laura at the table by saying, "Laura, it must be love!" Laura was straining to see Beth over the tops of rows of heads and her concentration gave her face a dreamy quality. She looked at Mary Lou with a startled expression until somebody said, "We hear you've got a date for the Christmas Dance!"

"Oh," Laura breathed in relief. From then on she was glad to play along with them. She needed a man just then as insurance against a dozen ills. Charlie stood for Laura-likes-men, men-like-Laura, everything-is-right-with-Laura-so-look-no-further.

When the girls across the table from her moved their heads apart, and the girls at the next table were nodding just so, she could see just enough to know that Beth wasn't looking at her. She was talking to someone, or laughing, or busy with her food, and Laura felt isolated and forsaken, envious of everyone at Beth's table. But between courses, when Uncle John was busy singing a song with the others, she glanced once more toward Beth's table and their eyes met and Beth gave her an almost imperceptible smile before she looked away.

Laura caught it and held tight to it, to the secret recognition in it, and she felt a sudden shock deep in her abdomen—so strong, so strange, so sweet that it invaded all of her before she understood it or could resist. She refused her dessert; she sat tortured in her place, yearning for the interminable meal to be over, for Uncle John to go home and leave Beth to her. She would have given anything to be rid of Emily.

She dared not look back at Beth. The curious feeling flared at the mere thought of her. The sight of her now would make the agitation unbearable. Laura began to fear her own words, her trembling hands, the telltale sweat on her face. It was with a long sigh of thanksgiving that she arose from the table and left the dining room, and went up to the room to wait for Beth.

She tried to calm herself, to tame the whirlwind in her stomach. She reached the room and opened the closet door to get her toothbrush and suddenly the funny feeling burst again inside her and she buried her face in the clothes and thought wildly, Beth, help me! Hold me, help me, Beth darling Beth I need you. Oh, I need—

The room door smacked against the closet door and Emmy said, "Who dat? Laur?"

A pang of caution sharply neutralized the feeling. Laura was on guard. She straightened mechanically and collected her toothpaste and said, "Yes."

Emily yawned. "We're going over to the Modern Design show in the art building," she said.

"You and Bud?" said Laura politely, as if it mattered. It cost her a terrible effort to appear calm.

"Yes, and Beth and Uncle John."

And suddenly it did matter.

"Should be a good show. Isn't Beth's uncle funny? Honestly, we nearly died laughing at him at dinner."

"Yes, he is funny. I thought he was going home early this afternoon."

"Well, he was, but we talked him into coming along to this show. Besides, he's the only date Beth ever has, and she needs to get out once in a while."

They heard Beth coming down the hall. She was talking to Mary Lou and she came into the room looking back over her shoulder and laughing at something. The strange feeling welled irresistibly in Laura at the sight of her back.

"We were just talking about you, roomie," said Emily, foraging through a muddled drawer for her gloves. Laura half envied her ability to be casual with Beth, and at the same time scorned her for not understanding Beth better.

Beth turned around and faced her roommates, and Laura couldn't stop looking at her. "Oh, you were?" she said. "Good things, of course." She smiled at them.

"We think you ought to go out more often," said Emily matter-of-factly, pulling out one glove triumphantly and tossing it on top of her dresser.

"You do, hm? With whom?" Beth gave Laura a quizzical smile.

Laura gave Emmy a brief venomous glance for having said, "We."

"Oh, anybody," said Emmy, burrowing in her drawer again for the other glove.

"Sure," said Beth. "Like, maybe, Santa Claus?"

Emily laughed. "Oh, Beth, you're hopeless. We'll have to make it our special project to marry you off this year, won't we, Laur?"

Laura glared at her, but Beth said, "And ruin a fine record? No thanks, Em. I'm stuck with Uncle John." She walked over to the closet and reached past Laura for her coat. "Hurry up, can't keep them waiting," she said to Emily.

"I'm coming. Can't find that other glove, darn it. I know it's here somewhere. I put it in here with the other one just two days ago. Can't just have walked away. Now where is it?"

While she talked Beth pulled her coat slowly off the hanger in the closet, all the while looking down at Laura, who stared hard at the floor until the wild feeling beat inside and lifted her eyes almost without her willing it. Beth took her hand suddenly and pressed it and Emily rambled on about her glove. Neither Beth nor Laura heard her for an instant. And then, when the instant grew a second too long, Beth drew her coat between them and turned and slipped into it.

"What are you going to do this afternoon, Laur?" she said.

"Found it!" said Emmy, and gave them a disgusted smile. "Underwear drawer."

"Nothing," said Laura. "Study, I guess."

"Why don't you come along with us?"

"Oh, no thanks, I couldn't. I—I have too much to do." She couldn't bear the thought of being so near to Beth all that time and unable to touch her.

Beth smiled at her. "I understand you're going to see Charlie again," she said. "You didn't tell me."

Laura turned hot with confusion. "Oh—oh, didn't I? Yes, for the dance."

"Hey, he's cute, Laur," said Emmy, grabbing her coat, and hurrying out the door.

Laura and Beth looked intently at each other, Laura with an uneasy smile on her face, and then Beth followed Emmy out.

Left by herself, the rest of the afternoon was a lonely one for Laura. Somewhere in the back of her mind was the sickening doubt that it was monumentally wrong to love another girl. And yet she did, and how much!

She thought of the kiss she stole in the night and her breath left her, first with delight and then with shame. And then she crept back to the thought and it was once again pure pleasure. She put her hand against her lips as if to preserve the kiss. Or prevent it? And then she thought of the way Beth had kissed her in the morning, so suddenly, so quickly, and she thought she couldn't have done anything so very wicked after all.

All afternoon, through her thoughts, the lines of print in her textbook, the wandering reveries in her head, slipped the word "homosexual." At first she seemed to glimpse it from very far away and it made her feel sick and frightened, but as the day waned it came closer. And finally she made herself look hard at it until she threw herself out on the couch and sobbed in an agony of self-accusation. She cried until exhaustion stopped her.

She sat up finally and looked at her mental picture of the Landons. They were normal. And then she looked down at herself, and nothing seemed wrong. She had breasts and full hips like other girls. She wore lipstick and curled her hair. Her brow, the crook in her arms, the fit of her legs—everything was feminine. She held her fists to her cheeks and stared out the window at the gathering night and begged God for an answer.

She thought that homosexual women were great strong creatures in slacks with brush cuts and deep voices; unhappy things, standouts in a crowd. She looked back at herself, hugging her bosom as if to comfort herself, and she thought, "I don't want to be a boy. I don't want to be like them. I'm a girl. I *am* a girl. That's what I want to be. But if I'm a girl why do I love a girl? What's wrong with me? There must be something wrong with me."

But then she thought irresistibly of Beth, and her clean wholesome beauty and her gentleness, and she thought that nothing Beth could do would be wrong. And Beth had kissed her. . . .

The interminable afternoon dragged on. Laura didn't go downstairs for supper but sat in the room ticking off the hours, thinking that Uncle John must surely by now have left and that Beth would be home soon. She was studying quietly on the couch at ten o'clock when her two roommates finally came in.

"Hey, you cleaned the room! That's terrific! Thanks, Laur," said Emmy.

Laura smiled. "That's okay," she said. She looked back to her book, but a hundred veiled side glances brought Beth to her eyes; Beth slipping out of her clothes, revealing her fine legs, slim-ankled and hard-calved. Laura wanted to know if she ever took dancing lessons. Her thighs were slender too, and firm, not wide and soft like so many girls'. For the first time Laura took a long heady look at Beth in the flesh and then Beth climbed laughing into her pajamas, teasing Emmy for running after "that no-good trombone."

Emily groaned and said she had millions of things to do and she would do them all tomorrow and thank God the evening was over and "Good night, you two, I can't fight it any longer." She went off to bed. It was a stroke of luck Laura hadn't counted on. She was worn out herself, but she didn't know it. She wouldn't have believed it.

Beth drew a book from the shelf and came and sat beside Laura on the couch.

"Don't know how long I'll last," she said. She felt Laura's warm glance on her and enjoyed pretending she didn't.

The torments of Laura's afternoon began to fade. Beth reached out and squeezed her knee, and Laura jumped.

"You are ticklish," she said with a smile, and then she turned to her book.

Laura looked at her book, waiting for a word, a gesture to invite her; but none came. Beth studied seriously and in a short time she was lost in another world. Laura, seeing her absorption, stared boldly at her, loving her nearness with its wealth of adorable details: the light hair on her arms, the fine skin, the violet eyes so unaware of the pale blue ones that searched them. Her hands were marvelous and long and firm, with trim hard nails on them;

her breathing so gentle, so peaceful, so welcoming. Laura wanted to put her head down on Beth's breast. And as she looked at it, moving rhythmically up and back, swelling with swift grace under the striped pajamas, she wanted more than to rest on it. Her hand tightened, disciplining itself against desire.

She shifted self-consciously on the couch and found her place in the book again and stared at it, unseeing, stamping with her will on the strange madness in her that begged for liberty. When Beth was near her, her careful senses loosened, yearned, burst suddenly from the bonds of caution. Her mail-fisted moral code unclenched, and right and wrong rushed out and ran whooping into limbo.

After half an hour, Beth threw her book down and yawned. "Can't keep my eyes open," she said.

Laura looked at her with nothing for her but a smile— such a beggar of a smile! Beth gave it a bag of gold.

"Laur, honey, will you scratch my back?" she said.

Laura's smile grew. "All right," she said.

"Wonderful. I love to have my back scratched." She rolled over on her stomach, giving Laura room to sit beside her, and she sighed with pleasure as Laura's hands began to trace the curves of her back. "Oh, that's marvelous," she murmured. "Mmmm . . ." She shivered a little, and Laura trembled with her. "Under my pajamas, Laur. Feels better . . ."

Warily Laura lifted her pajama shirt and her cool fingers groped for the ripe smooth warmth beneath them.

"Oh, yes . . ." Beth said.

Laura could see her smile, her eyes shut the better to feel.

"Oh, I love this. Emmy won't ever do it for me. Mmmm . . . you're wonderful."

Laura's hands shook and she lifted them for a moment. "Don't stop, Laur."

And her fingers descended to their enthralling task again, traveling like ten light feathers over the flawless hollows, the fields of grateful flesh, the sweet shoulders. Laura was lost to reason. She parted the hair that hid Beth's neck and drew her fingers lightly over the white nape. The hair was cool and delectably soft, and at the roots warm and thick. Laura leaned toward it, hardly realizing that she was moving. It smelled clean and faintly perfumed. She looked at Beth's profile, outlined against the burgeoning pillow, the eyes shut, the lips relaxed, the brow fair and faultless.

With a swift thrill of necessity she bent down and kissed the white neck for a long moment. A sudden acute fear pulled her up. She clasped her hand across her mouth and stared in terror at Beth, wondering how she could have let herself do it. Beth lay perfectly still with a faint smile on her lips.

"Beth?" said Laura. "Beth?" The whisper quailed. "Oh, Beth!" Laura clutched her shoulders. "Say something! Forgive me! Say something! Are you mad at me?"

Beth whispered softly, "No."

A wash of heat flooded Laura's face. She bent over Beth again, perfectly helpless to stop herself, and began to kiss her like a wild, hungry child, starved for each kiss, pausing only to murmur, "Beth, Beth, Beth . . ."

Beth rolled over on her back then and looked up at Laura, reaching for her, breathing hard through her parted lips and smiling a little, and her excitement burned the last rags of Laura's reserve. Her lips found Beth's and found them welcoming, and one after another after another shock of intense pleasure hit her.

Her frantic heart shot blood through her veins, the sweat burst urgently from her body and she felt answering movements from Beth's body. All of a breathless sudden it culminated in a sweeping release exploding and reverberating stormily through her.

She heard her faraway voice groan in ecstasy and she held Beth so tightly that it seemed they must somehow melt together. She couldn't stop, she couldn't let go, she couldn't think or speak. And when finally the furious desire abated a little it was only to gather strength for a fresh explosion.

At last Beth pulled herself up on one elbow and leaned over Laura. Her eyes were hot and her hair was wild, yet for all that she looked strangely ethereal.

"Oh, baby," she said in a husky voice. "We'll sleep in here. We'll sleep here tonight. I couldn't leave you tonight." She looked hard at her. "Oh, Laur . . ." she said and her voice trailed away and her lips came down on Laura's again and again and again. Laura answered her

Suddenly Beth pulled away from her and stood up with a with wordless passion.

quick movement as if that were the only way it could be accomplished.

"Beth!" said Laura like a hurt child, as if she were about to lose her.

"Got to fix the bed. Somebody might come in. My God, they can't find us like this. Open the couch, honey. I'll get the blankets." She leaned over to kiss her once more and then she went out of the room.

In a few minutes she was back with the bedclothes. Laura couldn't look at her without touching her. She went over and put her head down on Beth's shoulder, and Beth let her burdens drop around her to free her arms for Laura. After a while they got the bed made up and the light turned out and themselves tucked in. There was still a little noise in the halls.

"What if somebody comes in?" whispered Laura.

"Nobody will. Besides, if somebody does, it won't matter. They won't know. The dorm is cold as hell tonight. A lot of kids are sleeping in their rooms. Don't worry, don't worry," she whispered and drew her closer in her arms.

"Oh, Beth," said Laura, and her voice was light as a breath and as warm. "I love you. I love you so much."

Beth bent down and kissed her. "Hush," she said. "Sleep."

EIGHT

Laura thought nothing could ever awaken her. The days that followed were dreams. She wrapped herself in her secret; she wore it in her eyes, on her lips, in her stomach where it welled up hotly to ignite the star in her heart. Her moments with Beth were brief but beautiful, precarious and precious.

It took Beth some time to recover from her astonishment. In one swift strange night with Laura she had found that powerful delight that was supposed to be the crown and glory of romantic love. It had been effortless, inevitable, more wonderful than she had dared to hope. But it had been ironic, too, that it had come like this unbidden, so easily, with a girl. Beth thought of the many men she had looked to for it; the countless times she had searched, tried for it, even worked for it, with nothing for her pains but fatigue and eventually boredom. How had a simple girl like Laura been able to spring her emotions free of their trap? It was a little uncanny. Beth eyed her with a new respect, but she couldn't help wondering . . . if it had been Charlie she had slept with instead of Laura, would it have happened anyway? Would it have been as good, or better? Maybe Beth was just ready for it when Laura happened to come along. Or maybe she needed a woman to teach her how a woman can feel. Beth couldn't find the answer, and the more she looked for it the more perplexed she became.

Laura and Beth found all sorts of odd little gratifications. At house meetings Laura liked to sit behind Beth and scratch her back. It went unnoticed, since half the others were doing it too. At the Union they met each other for coffee in the afternoon and they walked home together for dinner. During the long quiet evenings they studied; beside each other on the couch when they could, across the room from each other when Emily got to the couch first.

Emily was now a thorn in the side, now the spice of danger. Her presence inhibited them and at the same time

69

made the least glance, the least casual touch almost unbearably sweet. If Emily sat down at the desk to write, their eyes met over her back and their lips smiled behind her. If she sat in the chair and left them the couch they found means to let their bodies touch somewhere, gently, with seeming carelessness. When she left the room they had a sublime moment to kiss and caress and tease.

Still, Emily wasn't the only threat. Beth was pursued regularly by phone calls and visitors to the room. Someone might walk in at any time. Her minutes with Laura had to be brief. And yet she made time or found it somehow. Then she would hold Laura in her arms, whisper to her, tell her how often she thought of her, kiss her, comfort her, make love to her. And Laura would pour her passion over Beth like honey—rich and sweet and natural, and yet somehow ensnaring. It was delightful, a balm and a succor to Beth, but it wasn't all-engrossing, all-satisfying, as it was for Laura.

Beth knew this, and she knew she had to be honest with Laura before she broke her heart. Once or twice she tried to explain her feelings, but her uncertainty stopped her. She was afraid of hurting Laura, even though she knew that a small hurt now was far better than a great hurt later. But just then any hurt at all seemed too much. It wasn't fair to hurt her so soon. Beth stuffed her logic into this ill-fitting mold, not just to spare Laura, but partly to preserve her own pleasure. It was selfish, and she knew that, but for a while her need was as great as Laura's—different, but just as strong.

It would have been nearly as hard for her to renounce the thing as for Laura, so she let things drift for a while and luck and happiness drifted along with them. They had each other and no one suspected anything.

Into the golden days sailed Charlie, like an unwelcome thunderhead. Laura had almost forgotten about him and the dance she had asked him to. She was ready to plead any strange malady to get out of it but Beth insisted that she go.

"You made that date almost two weeks ago, honey," she said. "You can't just suddenly break it. You can't just quit going out. It'd look pretty damn queer if you did. Besides, you need a little male company now and then."

Laura disagreed by simply not answering. But she didn't say no when Charlie called.

"Does your roommate have a date?" Charlie had asked.

Laura bit her underlip. "Oh, yes, she's got a date," she said brightly.

Charlie seemed to see through her ruse almost instinctively. "I don't mean the other one—Bud's girl—I mean Beth. She got a date?"

"Oh. Beth. No, I don't think so."

"Don't you know?" He laughed a little.

"No, she doesn't." Her voice was sharp, but Charlie ignored it.

"Well, my roommate wants a date," he said. "Mitch—you remember?" The whole thing struck him as something of a joke. Even Mitch wasn't serious about it. Two such disparate characters as he and Beth would never last, but they might brighten up the Christmas Dance a little. Besides it would be fun to have Beth around, and Charlie couldn't very well take her himself.

"Mitch?" said Laura.

"Yeah. Beth there?"

"Not till dinner."

"Okay, he'll call her after dinner. Talk to her, will you, Laura?"

"Okay, Charlie. I'll tell her."

She did, of course; she had to. But she didn't like it. The whole thing seemed ominous to her.

"He's a very nice boy, I guess," she said glumly. "I don't think you'd like him, though. He didn't say a word at Maxie's that night."

"Oh, I thought he was adorable," said Beth, and she reached out laughing and took Laura's hands. "Laur, you're jealous!" she said.

"No I'm not! Really, Beth, I'm—you mustn't— Oh, I guess I am. Just a little."

Beth mussed her hair and said, "I'd be crushed if you weren't. Just a little." She lighted a cigarette and said thoughtfully to the smoke, "Well, it might be fun to get back into circulation. Just for once."

"All right." Laura looked at her hands. "He's going to call you tonight after dinner." She got up stiffly and started for the door.

"Laur—where're you going?"

Laura didn't know. She just wanted to express her disapproval.

"Oh, Laura, honey," Beth said, laughing. She came up

and stopped her and put her arms around Laura's waist. "You mustn't be so jealous. You've been going out all fall. How do you suppose that makes me feel?"

Laura hung her head.

"God, Laur, we'll double date. How could I possibly two-time you?"

Laura apologized. "I won't be jealous," she said. "I swear I won't." And she underscored her intention with a kiss.

Charlie and Mitch arrived together for the dance and waited in the living room for Beth and Laura. Charlie was imposing in a tuxedo, and he looked faintly amused and detached from the proceedings. Like Emmy's Bud, he was something of a ladies' man, but unlike Bud, he didn't court crushes from every girl he knew.

The attitude became him, but he was hardly aware of it. It wasn't that he was immune to girls—far from it. It was simply that he was much more susceptible to women. Simpering college girls amused him. They were silly and scatterbrained, many of them, and once in a while he thought they were fun. But a beautiful woman, assured, alluring and feminine, was a wonder he could never wholly resist. He had begun to see the first signs of this mature loveliness in Beth, just as she had begun to find maturity in herself.

Charlie and Mitch stood off in a corner and surveyed the girls of Alpha Beta, and the girls milled about and returned the survey. Charlie was fun to look at because he was good to look at. His hair was wonderful stuff—a rich dark brown born of an early blond that left gold traces at his temples.

"A pretty nice-looking bunch," said Mitch. He was enjoying his favorite spectator sport.

"Yeah. I've been away from this house too long."

They grinned at each other.

"Who's that one over there? By the fireplace?"

Charlie followed his gaze. "Oh, in the red? Boy, you're coming back to life." He laughed and slapped Mitch on the back. "That's Mary Lou Baker, the house president. Nice gal."

"You know her?"

"Used to. Haven't seen her for a while. Let's go over."

Mitch hung back. He liked looking better than doing.

But Charlie was striding across the living room and rather than be left stranded Mitch tagged after him. Charlie in action made a beautiful study in *savoir faire*. Mitch admired it, with secret envy.

Mary Lou looked up and smiled at Charlie as he came up. "Well, Charlie Ayers!" she said. "How are you? Gee, I haven't seen you for ages."

"Mary Lou, I'd forgotten how pretty you are."

She laughed a little, pleased and embarrassed.

Mitch stood and looked at her in the same way he had stood and looked at Beth, with a sort of goodhearted and passive admiration that rarely asked for more than a look.

"I hear you've been seeing Laura Landon," Mary Lou said to Charlie.

"Um-hm." He smiled.

"Isn't she a sweet girl? She's one of our best pledges. We're really fond of her."

"Yes, she is a nice girl," he said politely.

"Here she comes," said Mary Lou.

Beth and Laura came in together in very different moods. Beth was luxuriously pretty. For once she had taken time for every detail of herself, to Laura's alarm.

"After all, I only go out once a year," she explained. "Might as well do it up right."

"Well, if Mitch doesn't think you look terrific, he's blind," said Emmy. "Isn't that so, Laura?"

"Yes."

Laura tried to keep Charlie occupied with her so that he wouldn't have time for Beth. She talked or trapped him into talking as steadily as she could. But the four of them sat together and the conversation jumped about frequently.

Laura couldn't help it if Charlie offered Beth a cigarette and lighted it for her, but Beth could help it if she took his hand to steady the light and watched him while she inhaled. Whenever she spoke or smiled or glanced at Charlie she aggravated Laura's irritation.

They went into the dining room to dance after a while, and Laura had Charlie to herself. Not that she wanted him, but for once she was happy to put up with him, just to keep him away from Beth. The dining room was romantically festive with green lights, and all the furniture had been cleared out to make a dance floor. At the rear of the room was a long elaborately decorated table loaded with punch and cookies. Now and then, at intermissions, Beth and Mitch met Laura and Charlie around the punch bowl. Inevitably, Charlie finally suggested that they trade partners. Laura hardly had time to think about it before Beth was swept masterfully onto the dance floor and she found herself moving off with Mitch.

Charlie was perfectly assured with women and he liked to be around them. It was almost second nature. They never gave him much trouble. He was easy and firm with Beth and she followed him docilely, faintly annoyed with him for attracting her and amused with his confidence.

"That's a very pretty dress," he said, looking down significantly.

"Thanks." She smiled at him.

"Good color for you."

"I think so, too."

He raised an eyebrow at her. "Do you always wear purple?"

"Um-hm," she said, pursing her lips sagely and nodding.

He laughed. "Always?"

"Of course. Even my pajamas are purple."

He grinned and gave her a squeeze that brought back to her the strange sensations in the booth at Maxie's.

"Don't you believe me, Charlie?"

"No," he said calmly. "A girl like you doesn't wear pajamas."

Beth had to smile at him but at the same time she wanted to shatter his beautiful composure. He seemed to know instinctively how to tease her and she couldn't catch him off guard. He thought he had her perfectly under control. She had to wait till the dance was nearly over for a chance to trip him up.

He bent down close to her and pulled her tighter in his arms and said softly, "Beth, my dear, you're beautiful."

It was just her cup of tea. "Thanks, Charlie, so are you," she said.

For the space of a few shocked seconds he was silent. Beth waited for a tantrum, but she guessed wrong. He put his head down against hers as the music ended and laughed at her. And at himself.

"It's my criminal charm," he said, and squeezed her again, and Beth looked up at him in surprise. And again she smiled at him against her will. . . .

The four of them went out to dinner together at the

Hotel Champlain. Laura became more and more quiet as her jealousy grew. Only Beth could see behind her deliberate courtesy to her hurt feelings.

The two girls went to the ladies' room and Beth tried to talk some sense into the younger girl.

"Are you all right, Laur?" she asked.

"Yes, of course." Laura looked down into the cascade of blue tulle flowing from her waist.

"Honey, tell me the truth. You look so unhappy."

Laura bit her lip, and then she said, "Beth, I told you I wouldn't be jealous, and I won't."

"Oh, Laura—" Beth couldn't help smiling. "You're such a foolish little girl. Do you know that?"

"Yes." It meant no.

"Who's Charlie Ayers anyway? Just a guy." Charlie was causing the trouble, of course. Not Mitch. "No more foolishness. Okay?" Beth talked to Laura as if she were a little child.

Laura nodded at her. The image of Charlie interfered with her every good intention, spoiled her every smile.

"Laura . . ." Beth's voice was very soft. "We'll be together tonight. We'll be together."

Laura looked full at her suddenly and momentarily forgot her rival till Beth gave her a little shake. "Come on, we've got to get back. They'll think we fell in."

And Laura followed her willingly then, as if a great weight had been lifted from her.

The evening went quickly after that, and everybody drank too much, except for Mitch, who was talking himself into a crush on Beth.

Beth had to stop Laura from a fifth Martini. "God, Charlie, what are you trying to do? Pickle her? She's not used to it," she said.

Charlie grinned and shrugged. "Give the lady what she wants," he said. His interest in Beth grew franker as his inhibitions grew fewer, but it didn't seem to matter. He couldn't stop himself. He began to get quiet and deliberate. When he got drunk he slowed down perceptibly, but there was nothing unmanageable or mean in him. He was quite pleasantly absorbed in pondering the enigma of Beth Cullison.

Now and then he would lean forward lightly on the table and study her as if she were a map. Beth gazed straight back at him in an effort to make him look away, but it was rather more like indicating the way to him; he wasn't in the least abashed. Beth was somehow half afraid that he would read in her eyes something of her concern for Laura; that he would see on her lips the illegal kisses, the extraordinary passion that the girl had inspired in her.

Charlie tried to ignore Beth out of regard for Mitch and Laura, but the other two simply didn't interest him. He asked Beth to dance with him again before the evening was over. The floor was small and packed. He guided her away from Mitch and Laura so they couldn't see, and he spent the dance pretty much in one place, holding her hard against him and talking to her. She had to look up at him to catch the words, and she tried to protest.

"Charlie, we have to get back," she said. And, "You're holding me too tight."

But he only shook his head and kept her there. He had never been so attracted to a girl. It just couldn't have happened any other way. He pulled her out of the crowd and into the shadow of the heavy drapes by the bandstand and gave her just time to say, "No—" before he kissed her.

When he released her she said, "Charlie, please, for God's sake—"

"I know," he said and gave her his handkerchief. "Don't talk about it. I know."

"No, you don't," she said, wiping off the smeared lipstick. "You couldn't. Let's get back." But she didn't want to.

It was a while before she could look at Laura again; the whole evening was different, irrevocably changed. It wasn't Laura she wanted that night, but it was Laura she would have.

NINE

Mitch was mad. It happened very rarely, but Charlie had muscled in on his date. He walked stiffly into their apartment. Charlie sighed and followed him in.

"Okay, Mitch, I'm sorry. So we both like the girl. We both want the girl. Okay, so we both call her."

"But that's just the point. You act as if you own every woman you look at, damn it. You—"

"I act like it but I don't."

"You make them think—"

"Oh, Mitch, for God's sake, that's a lot of crap. That's a lot of damn crap. You go around with your nose out of joint because you think I'm better equipped to seduce women than you are."

"Well, let's face it."

"Oh, let's face it, hell. Do you think a girl like Beth would fall for a face? For a lot of crap? Well, do you?"

"Any girl could be fooled."

"Well, would you like to know how well I fooled your precious date? I danced with her, remember? Do you know what I said to her?"

"No."

"I told her she was beautiful. Yeah, just like that. And what do you think she said to me?"

"I don't know," said Mitch with polite sarcasm.

"She said, 'Thanks, Charlie, so are you.' Now, what do you think she meant by that?"

Mitch glowered at him, and said nothing.

"She meant, 'You're an ass, Ayers. You're a damn ass and you're not fooling me.' Okay, I'm an ass. My God, I know what I am. It's just that women like that crap—most women. Now, do you think a girl like Beth thinks I'm Prince Charming, or something? Hell no, she thinks I'm an ass. Quit harping on the thing."

"Harping? Who's harping? You're doing all the talking."

"Oh, for God's sake," Charlie muttered. "All right, the hell with it. Do you want to know what your trouble is, Grogan? Do you want to know what your son-of-a-bitching trouble is? Well, I'll tell you. You don't want Beth Cullison; you just want a girl." Charlie sighed. "Let's just forget it. We'll talk about it later." Mitch sat motionless. "Women," Charlie growled. He went to the washbowl and brushed his teeth viciously and then he got into bed. "Come on, Mitch, you can't sit there all night."

Mitch stood up slowly and got out of his clothes and into his pajamas without a word. Charlie rolled over and shut his eyes and tried to figure out a way to see Beth, Mitch or no Mitch. He tossed around for a long while before he got to sleep.

Beth was a long time getting to sleep herself that night, too. Emily wouldn't go to bed until the birds were nearly ready to get up. Beth was too tired to want anything but sleep; too full of Charlie, too upset for Laura. But still, she was committed.

When Emily finally went off and Beth and Laura were alone, Laura could see that Beth was in a faraway and pensive mood. For a while she said nothing. Laura sat down on the couch and looked up at Beth as she might have gazed at a distant cloud, so lovely, too hard to know, so impossible to clasp and keep. The first drops of melancholy began to spatter in Laura when Beth turned out the light and came over to the bed and pulled Laura down in it beside her. She held her close and they lay still for a little while, warming each other, occupied with their thoughts.

"Beth," Laura whispered finally, "are you unhappy about something?"

"No, honey." Her voice was very soft. "Should I be?"

"I don't know. You sort of—acted as if you were."

"No, baby, I'm not unhappy." She frowned in the dark.

"Sometimes—sometimes I think I don't know you at all, Beth."

Beth said nothing. It was true.

"I know about the little things, but—I don't know anything about what makes you the way you are. I'm afraid I never will."

Beth squeezed her gently. "Maybe I'm not worth it. Maybe it doesn't matter."

"Yes, it does." She sounded urgent. "We won't always be together like this, Beth."

"Nothing lasts forever."

And Laura fell silent, as silent as her tears. Beth held her, unknowing; wondering sleepily at Charlie's invulnerable composure. She was startled out of near sleep when Laura said, some while later, "What do you really think of Charlie?"

"Mmmm . . . he's conceited."

"Is that all?"

"No. I don't know. He's a nice guy, I guess. I don't know . . ."

Laura felt her uncertainty as a worse threat than her positive admiration would have been. Under the spell of possible threats she snuggled closer to Beth, feeling, like a pain, the fragile sweetness of every moment with her. She thought briefly of Charlie, and she swore to herself, He won't have her! I'll fight for her!

"All right, baby?" Beth murmured.

"No!" Laura whispered. "No, Beth, I love you. Darling, I love you." Her sudden intensity brought Beth back to life. Laura had her way. She vented her passion with bouquets of kisses and her arms full of all the magnificent softness of Beth's body. Beth gasped in a thrill of surprise and then it was just Beth and Laura again, so immersed in each other that no wayward uninvited thoughts could threaten them.

It was the last time they were together before Christmas; the last time for several weeks.

Christmas. Laura went home to Lake Forest, Charlie went home to New York, and Beth went off to Florida to be with her Aunt Elsa and Uncle John.

There was little for Laura to do but visit one parent and then the other, and do school assignments. The holidays were a dreary parenthesis in her romance. She wanted to write to Beth every day but Beth forbade it.

"It would look too obvious," she said. "Just send a couple of notes, honey."

Her notes were rather more like chapters from a book, but at least there were only three of them. Beth's answers were short but affectionate in a noncommittal sort of way; Laura knew them by heart.

She spoke to her parents so many times of Beth that her

mother exclaimed, "Aren't you lucky to have such a nice girl for a roommate!" And she was thankful that her daughter was under the guidance of someone so "sensible" about boys. Laura had told her that Beth spent most of her energies on study and the Student Union.

Mr. Landon muttered, "She sounds like a damn puritan. A girl like that ends up an old maid nine times out of ten. I wouldn't take everything she says as the Gospel, Laura."

And Laura laughed to herself to think that her lovely, warm, passionate Beth could be so easily camouflaged without benefit of a single fib.

Beth, on the beach, sunned herself and studied and thought of Laura. She thought of other things, in her solitude, and all the other things, strangely enough, were Charlie. Her mind was vague, her thoughts indefinite; there was just a cloudy image of Charlie in her head. It could be dissipated like a cloud, but like a cloud it always re-formed and hung about to threaten a storm.

It came to her at odd moments, bothersome and wonderful and completely exasperating. Once, in a restaurant booth, Uncle John leaned past her to reach for the salt shaker, putting his hand on her knee as he did so. It couldn't have been a more innocuous gesture on his part and he was somewhat startled to hear his niece gasp audibly at his touch. The warmth and pressure of his hand in just that spot on her leg brought Charlie back to her with a shock; Charlie in the smoky booth in Maxie's basement, pressing against her, laughing, telling her nonsense, and feeling her leg with an experienced hand. She felt a sudden irritation at the thought of him, as she had so many times before; and as usual, she didn't quite understand it. Before the first week of vacation was up she was impatient to get back to school again.

Charlie, in New York, occupied himself with parties and people, but his head was full of Beth. In the past, whenever he found himself thinking too much about one particular girl, he'd deliberately ignore her and take out dozens of others, another one each night, and soon enough he'd be free of his infatuation. So it was with understandable confusion that he discovered that Beth could not be driven from his thoughts in this fashion. It annoyed him, but after four or five days he accepted the situation and quite simply gave up and thought only of Beth.

He knew her special kind of beauty appealed strongly to him, and she pleased him with her teasing, her talk, even her tantalizing independence. But he had found these qualities in other girls and never been so hopelessly fascinated with them. No, there was a unique delight in being with Beth, a curious essence in her that he couldn't put his finger on, couldn't explain. It was as if she were holding something of herself back, as if there were some secret unsounded depth in her that no one had ever touched. Charlie made up his mind then and there to touch her; to reach for her and find her as she really was, and hold and keep her.

The days dragged for all three of them. Laura crossed them off on a little pocket calendar she carried in her wallet on the other side of a picture of Beth. The picture was a reproduction of her yearbook portrait and although Laura knew every plane and shadow of it, she took it out frequently to study it.

TEN

Laura came back to school in a sweat of excitement. But when she burst into the room the one who turned to greet her was Emily.

"Where's Beth?" Laura demanded. She forgot to say hello to Emmy.

"Hi, Laur. Nice vacation?"

"Oh—yes, thanks. Where's Beth?"

"We just got a wire from her. She's not coming in till tomorrow. Bad flying weather, or something."

"Oh." It was a shocking disappointment.

Emily stared at her curiously. "She'll be back tomorrow, Laur," she said in a comforting voice that Laura was alarmed to have inspired.

"Oh. Oh, I know." Laura laughed nervously to cover her chagrin. "I—I just had something to tell her." She tried to make it sound casual. She had to have something innocent to be disappointed about.

"Oh, what!" said Emily, who loved secrets.

"Oh, nothing," said Laura. She turned away in confusion, suddenly afraid.

"Is it a secret?" said Emily. She was kneeling on the couch and smiling at Laura like a little girl with three guesses to spend. There was nothing malicious in her curiosity.

"Well, I—I don't know." Laura felt rather desperate.

"Can I guess?"

"Oh, Emmy!" she said in a sharp, angry voice. She stopped and caught her breath, and then turned to see how much damage she had done. Emily was looking at her, stung and astonished. Of all people, Laura was the last she would have expected a temper from.

"I'm sorry, Emmy," said Laura, and she was—sorry and scared. "I didn't mean to—say anything. I'm awfully sorry."

"Well . . . that's all right, Laura." Emily frowned curiously at her.

82

Laura undressed in a state of smoldering resentment, angry with Emily, furious with herself, and irritated with Beth for being a day late. Never mind what the flying conditions were; she should have been there.

Beth came the next morning. It was so good to look at her, to see the color of her and feel the substance, that Laura temporarily forgot her troubles and forgave her. Beth gave her a warm hug and said, "Miss me?" and laughed at Laura's bright eyes before she could answer. Laura was admiring her tan; she had turned a lovely gold-brown from the Florida sun and in her dark face her violet eyes looked almost luminous.

It took Emily only until that evening to wreak havoc. She didn't mean to; she never meant to. She thought there must be some sort of joke between Beth and Laura and she wanted to tease.

The three of them were settled quietly about the room when Emmy snapped her book shut and said, "Hey, Beth, what's this big secret between you and Laura?" She smiled at her.

Beth looked up suddenly with a long silent gasp of alarm. Emily didn't see Laura start in her chair. She was looking at Beth. Beth turned to Laura for an explanation but Laura was too frightened to say a word.

"What secret?" said Beth.

"Laura said you had a secret."

"She did?" Beth looked back at Laura with troubled eyes.

"Emily, I did not!" said Laura angrily, finding her tongue suddenly in this crisis. For the second time she had lost her temper at Emily. "I didn't say anything of the kind!" She had to shout at Emmy; she was afraid to look at Beth.

"Well, gee, Laur, don't get mad," said Emmy. "I'm not trying to start anything. What the heck is this, anyway?" She looked at Beth. "She said she had something to tell you, that's all. She was so let down when you weren't here last night that I asked her what was the matter and she wouldn't tell me. She just said she had something to tell you. Gee, I didn't mean to start anything. I thought it was a joke."

Beth pulled herself together fast. She had to in the face of Emily's sudden suspicion. "You didn't start anything,

Emmy," she said calmly. "You don't mind if I tell her, do you, Laur?"

Laura, who would have followed her naked into hell, shook her head in bewilderment.

"It was just a family thing, Em. Laura wanted to transfer out of journalism school. It all depended on what her father said. Sort of a difficult situation. Her parents didn't agree. I guess Mr. Landon finally decided against it. Right, Laur?"

"Yes." She stared in grateful surprise at Beth, with a sort of perverse pleasure in seeing her father rescue his daughter's Lesbian love affair. It was as good a thing as ever he did for her.

"One of those family things," Beth said. "Not so much a secret, Emmy, as just—sort of—awkward."

Emily was suddenly contrite. She never disbelieved Beth; she never had reason to. "Oh, Laur, I'm sorry!" she said. She looked anxiously at her, wanting to restore a sunny atmosphere.

Laura promptly absolved her, glad to have it over, to have got out of it so well. Emily took the thing at nearly face value, thanks to Beth. Laura was shaken hard and fast into the realization of the pressing need for tact and caution and highly refined hypocrisy.

Mitch called Beth, and ran headlong into the bruising fact that Beth didn't want to go out with him again. She gave him a charming runaround; he couldn't even get mad at her. But she said no, and it rankled in Mitch.

Charlie got out of the way and let him call first. It was the only way to keep peace. Besides, they were friends, they had an agreement, they even had a lease to bind them. But he intended to call and he said so, and there wasn't much Mitch could do about it, being Mitch. He didn't think he was in love with Beth any more, but he thought he might have been if he had had the chance.

Charlie came in and found him sitting by the phone. Mitch waved at it. "She's busy all week," he said with a sort of comic sarcasm. "Try for Friday night. She hesitated a little over that one."

"Mitch—" Charlie felt awkward.

"Go on, go on. We had an agreement."

He called. Beth was rarely called on a house phone.

Anyone with anything to say to her knew her private number.

"Hello?" she said.

"Hello, Beth, this is Charlie." He didn't believe in guessing games.

"Well, Charlie!" she exclaimed, strangely startled.

"I have a problem. I thought maybe you could help me out."

It was somehow possible to tell that he was smiling.

"Well, I don't know." She grinned back at him. "What is it?"

"Classics. An elective. Don't know how I got hooked. Anyway, I'm in trouble. I mean, I may very well flunk out."

Beth laughed at him. "Oh, that's a shame!" she said.

He ignored her. "Laura says you know something about the classics."

"Oh, she does?"

"Thought you might be willing to brief me. I wouldn't take much of your time. You're up at the Union every day, aren't you?"

"Yes—"

"I know you're busy—"

"Oh, I am—"

"But you must have a few free minutes."

"Well, sometimes, but—"

"Any time would do."

She realized that every answer she gave him was affirmative. "Charlie, I just don't know. I never know what to expect up there. My time isn't my own."

"Aren't you the president of the Student Union?"

"Yes, but—" Another affirmative.

"Well, hell, honey, make time. Just half an hour would do it. How about the Pine Lounge this afternoon? Say about three-thirty?"

"Charlie, I can't." She thought of Laura. "I just can't."

"Sure you can, Beth. Oh look, honey—I know you don't owe me anything, that's not the point. I just thought maybe you'd be willing to help me out. My God, I can't even tell you anything about Socrates! That's how bad it is."

Beth laughed.

"Please," he said, and she could tell again that he was smiling. "I'd really appreciate it, Beth."

She would tell Laura as soon as she got back to the room. There would be no cause for jealousy or suspicion. What's more practical and less romantic than a history lesson?

"Beth?"

She just liked to be with him. He was fun, he was different, he wasn't afraid of her. It wouldn't amount to anything.

"Hey, Beth—you there?"

"Yes. I—"

"Good," he said in a matter-of-fact voice. "Thanks a lot, honey. See you at three-thirty. Okay?"

No breath of ulterior motives. "Okay, Charlie."

Back in the room she told Laura, "It's for a Classics final. I guess he's having trouble with it."

"He likes you, Beth." Laura knew it right away.

"Not *that* way." She laughed. "Men like Charlie don't like girls like Beth. I'm supposed to be a real bookworm, you know. I guess I'm just a change of pace for him."

"Well, girls like Laura don't like girls like Beth, either. Until they fall in love with them."

"Oh, baby!" Beth laughed and pulled the troubled face up and kissed it. "I swear I'll tell you every word he says. And all you'll hear is a half-hour monologue on Greek philosophers."

With Laura watching her carefully, Beth only ran a comb through her hair before she left for the Pine Lounge. She had wanted to put on some cologne, change her sweater, freshen her lipstick—but she knew that would cause too great an eruption. She left the room with a great show of casualness and arrived at the Lounge a little early. She sat at a table with a notebook before her, daydreaming. She looked up and let her gaze wander out the window, where it rested motionless on nothing and criticized Charlie's face. She sat like that for almost ten minutes until suddenly a strong hand gripped her neck and she put her head back with a jerk, electrified. She laughed in spite of herself, hunching her shoulders and squirming to be free. Charlie held her firm, grinning down at her.

She said, "Charlie, don't!" still laughing, and then she realized that he wouldn't let her go until she stopped struggling. She froze.

He released her, tossing his books on the table in front of her.

"Sorry I'm late."

"Are you?" She was surprised.

"Um-hm." He took his coat off, pulled up a chair, and sat down.

"Charlie, you've been drinking beer," she said, pulling away from him as if his breath might intoxicate her, and grinning.

"Brethren," he said piously, "I repent."

Beth laughed at him. "Okay," she said. "What is it you want to know? As if you were in any condition to learn."

"I'm forced to agree," he said. "Let's adjourn. There's a jam session at Maxie's this afternoon."

"I thought you were flunking out of Classics."

"Oh, I am."

"Well, maybe you'd better do something about it."

"That's your job, honey." He pulled out a mimeographed list of names and places and questions and handed it to her. "Explain this damn thing to me, will you?" he said.

"All of it?"

"Well—the Peloponnesian War. I can't get the damn thing straight."

Beth gave him a skeptical smile and then she took the list from him. "Okay," she said. She bent over the paper and began to talk.

Charlie studied her hair and the line of her cheek, his head resting in his hand.

"You see, Sparta was up here," she said, and he didn't answer. "Do you see?" She looked up and saw him gazing at her.

"Mm," he said thoughtfully and let his hand come down. He leaned forward on his arms and looked down at the paper. "See what?"

"Charlie, are you listening to me?"

"You won't believe this, but I am. I don't know as I'm remembering any of it, though. Let's go over to Maxie's, honey."

"And let you flunk out of Classics?"

"And let me flunk out of Classics."

"I couldn't, Charlie, even if I wanted to. Sorry."

"Do you want to?"

She smiled a little, wondering why he had put it that way. "I can't," she said.

"That's not what I asked you, honey."

"I have work to do."

"So do I. So does everybody. Don't you ever play, Beth?"

"Charlie, I can't go."

"Half an hour?"

She laughed helplessly. "Ohhh," she groaned, flattered, and gave him a deploring look. "No!"

"Half an hour it is," he said. "Where's your coat?"

"Charlie—" she protested, but the situation struck her, and her laughter took the starch out of her protest. She did want to go. She obviously wanted to go. But she thought suddenly of Laura and her own good intentions, and turned cold.

"Where's your coat, honey?"

"Upstairs." Laura was tormenting her. "Charlie, I—"

"Come on, we'll go get it."

"I can't go, Charlie." She tried to make it sound serious and final.

Charlie stood up and pulled his jacket on and grabbed his notebook. He hustled Beth out of the lounge and down the linoleumed corridor to the elevator.

Beth leaned against the wall of the elevator while he pushed the button and it started up. "I wish you'd believe me, Charlie. I can't go."

He leaned on the wall beside her, one arm over her head, and looked down at her. "I wish you'd tell me why. You keep saying you can't go. Why can't you go?"

"All right, I'll give you a good reason. Mitch. What about Mitch?"

"What about him?"

"He called me this week, you know. Or didn't you know?"

"I know."

"And I turned him down."

"Um-hm." He didn't seem in the least perturbed.

"Charlie, he's your best friend! I agreed to see you only to help you out of a jam. Not to go out and drink beer with you."

"Am I supposed to apologize for asking you out for a beer?"

The elevator doors pulled open and they walked out slowly.

"How would Mitch feel?"

"He expects it."

"He expects it? Well, damn it, Charlie, what are you up to? What is this? You didn't want any help on that final." She sighed, but she was pleased. "Are you afraid to be honest?"

"You make it impossible, Beth. I suppose it's beside the point that I meant to be. I didn't organize the jam session." He followed her into her office and she turned and faced him while he talked. "Mitch was honest with you, and what happens? You force a man to use his ingenuity, Beth." It was the rare kind of compliment she couldn't resist. "Mitch says, 'Beth, I'd like to see you again, will you go out with me this weekend?' and gets a flat 'No.' So what am I supposed to do? Throw myself against the same brick wall?" He smiled at her and she had to laugh. "You can't say I'm not being honest now," he said.

"Still, Charlie," she said in a gentler voice, "it must be hard on Mitch." She was arguing for Laura, not for Mitch.

"Look, Beth, we had this out together. We both wanted to see you, we had a big argument over it, we finally decided to leave it up to you. It was the only way. Mitch called first. Then I called. He knows I called. My God, I'm not keeping any secrets."

Beth said firmly to herself, I can't go out. But she didn't say it to Charlie and when she looked up at him her resolution began to falter.

"Now, where's your coat?" he said, lifting a gray one from the rack. "This it?"

"No. Won't you please give up and go away?"

"This one?"

Oh, Laura—I can't help it, I want to go . . .

"Hey, Beth?" A girl put her head in the door. "Oops, sorry!" she said, catching sight of Charlie. "You leaving?"

"Well, I—what is it, Doris?"

"Nothing vital. Entertainment committee. You can see 'em tomorrow." She grinned at Charlie and left.

"Well, that's settled," said Charlie. "Which coat?"

"The tan one."

"That's more like it." He smiled and held it for her and she slipped into it with the feeling that she was slipping into a trap. She expected to pay for it somehow, but at the moment payment seemed far off.

They walked briskly over to Maxie's and Charlie talked

with her all the way, holding her arm, stopping her at curbs, leading her around puddles. Now she liked it and now it annoyed her but the curious excitement of being with Charlie overwhelmed her other feelings.

"Your friend Emily is over there," he said.

"She is?" Beth was vaguely upset. She would rather have had her escapade unobserved, but better Emmy than Laura.

"Yeah. Bud's playing. He's got her hypnotized."

"It's a way he has." And as a matter of fact it was true that he had held Emmy's affections longer than any other boy she knew.

"I'd like to know when that guy studies," Charlie went on. "Jesus, I only study the bare minimum myself. He studies about half as much as I do. Every time I go over to Maxie's he's down there playing. Damn near lives there, I guess."

Bud managed to stay in music school by conducting all his practice sessions down in Maxie's basement. Everybody loved it except his professors. He saw them only on the rare occasions when he went to class.

At the door to Maxie's Beth tried to hesitate once more, in deference to her conscience, but it was too late. Charlie pushed the door open with one hand and pushed Beth inside with the other.

"Get in there, girl, and behave yourself," he said.

She turned to glare at him and ended up laughing and doing as he told her. "One beer," she said weakly. "One."

The music floated up from downstairs. Maxie had moved the band permanently to the basement in the interest of maintaining the public peace. They went down the narrow flight of stairs to a huge dimly lit room full of long tables and smoke and music. The tables were full of people and the people were full of beer, as a general rule.

Bud was regaling the crowd with a trombone solo when Beth and Charlie found seats in a booth, and Emily was sitting on the floor of the bandstand at his feet, leaning against the piano.

"See?" said Charlie with a grin. He helped her out of her coat. "Be right back," he said, and went off to get beer.

Beth took out a cigarette and settled back to watch Bud perform. He stood with his head cocked toward the trumpet, building a duet for the clarinet to coast on. There was a cigarette jutting from his left hand and his shirt sleeves were rolled halfway up his long forearms. His legs were set wide apart and his right foot beat steadily on the stand beneath it. He belonged wholly at that moment to the melody and rhythm he was making, and Emily belonged wholly to him.

Beth studied them with the strange little prick of foreboding that Bud always inspired in her. It wasn't that she didn't like him; he was, as everybody said, a great guy. But he was no great guy to fall in love with. His eyes were always busy with other women and his head was full of music. He was crazy about Emmy, but he didn't love her. Beth didn't think he ever would. It wasn't Emmy's personal failure; he was just made that way. Some men are.

Charlie set a quart of beer under her nose and pushed her over into the booth. She looked up at him and smiled. He kept shoving until he had her pinned against the wall.

"Are you going to let me get away with this?" he said.

"Hell, no. I'm a lady," said Beth.

"Beth honey, you swear too much."

"I know," she said, "it's a defense mechanism."

He slid away from her and poured her beer. Beth felt the release of pressure from his body with regret. She watched him while he poured, wondering what it was that made her follow him, smile against her will at him, feel content just to look at him.

"Drink up," he said, and gave her her glass. "Cheers."

The music stopped and Charlie looked up and waved at Bud. Bud put his horn down on the piano for a moment and nudged Emmy. They both smiled and nodded and waved. Charlie beckoned to them to come over but the music started again and Bud picked up his trombone.

Charlie put his arm around Beth and she was astonished at the force of her pleasure. She turned to smile at him and it came to her as a shock that their faces were so close. Charlie pulled her closer and checked her sudden impulse to retreat with his own obstinate strength.

"Beth," he said, "do you know you bothered the hell out of me all through Christmas vacation?" She smiled away from him. "I thought about you all the time. And that's the God's truth, if I never told it before. I couldn't get you out of my head. Oh, I know what you're thinking." He looked at his beer and gave her a chance to watch him again. "You think I've said the same thing to a dozen dif-

ferent girls. Well, I guess I have, at that. I even thought
I meant it once or twice." He laughed a little at himself.
"Do I sound like a damn fool?"

"Yes," she said, but she smiled gently.

He leaned toward her. "I wish I knew you better, Beth.
I think there must be a lot to know about you." He
reached over and stroked her cheek with his index finger,
and she pulled away, still smiling.

"Why?"

"Because there's so little you tell. You won't talk about
yourself, honey. And yet you're talented, intelligent . . ."
He paused. "You're beautiful, Beth. I say this at consider-
able risk to my ego."

She laughed and looked at him.

"You are, you know." He reached into her soft hair and
caressed her neck with his hand. "Will I have to resort to
tricks to get you out next time? Or can I just say, 'Beth,
this is Charlie. I want to see you.'?"

"Try it," she said.

"I will. Do you remember meeting me, Beth? At a
party a couple of years ago? You were there with Don.
Remember?"

"Yes." She smiled, warm and aroused.

"Do you know what I thought of you?"

"No," she said and shook her head, wondering at her
wealth of monosyllables.

"I thought you were a beautiful girl who didn't know
she was beautiful. I thought you were antisocial, too. I
figured you for a born spinster. My God, I was blind! I
remember wondering if some guy would have the sense
to see how pretty you were and didn't give a damn that
you were such a square. Or maybe liked you square. I guess
Don did."

"We got along, for a while."

"God, isn't it funny how things work out? I had the
eyes to see you with and not the sense to do anything
about it. I guess I thought you were strange. I mean, it
didn't seem right that you should be so wrapped up in
books. Not you."

"Oh, I've always liked books." She couldn't get a re-
spectable sentence out.

"Better than anything else?"

"Not quite."

"I used to think so."

"They were an escape. They—filled an empty place. I guess you don't know about empty places, Charlie."

"I'm spoiled. I don't say that makes a better man of me. Will you tell me about the empty places, honey?"

It hit close to home.

"Can you talk to me, Beth?" he said gently. She looked down again, and he waited silently, watching her. "Hard, isn't it?" he said. "I remember when I was little I always used to say, 'Can I go outside?' and my mother would say, 'You can but you may not.' It's the other way around for you, I guess. You may, but you can't."

She looked up at him slowly and nodded. "I could, if it didn't matter," she said, and then, as if she had confessed too much, she turned away sharply and looked down into the cool gold in her beer glass.

"Afraid of me, Beth?"

She smiled a little at the heavily initialed table top, remembering the way she had asked Laura that same question, and then she looked up, straight ahead of her. "No," she said.

"Then look at me and say so."

She looked at him but it was very difficult to say it. It was difficult to say anything. She found herself just looking at him, wordless and wondering and excited. His arm tightened around her.

"No, Charlie," she whispered.

"I think you are."

"All right, I am." She swayed away from him but he followed her to the wall of the booth and held her fast. The force of the physical attraction between them overcame their sanity. They wanted each other with a violent desire; wanted to fit their bodies together to forge two physical promises. And still Beth fought him.

"Beth," he murmured.

She turned her head and his lips trailed over her cheek until his tongue found the corner of her lips. And then she turned back to him with the music and the noise and the excitement giving them privacy, and let her lips part a little and give themselves to him. All resistance washed out of her. She put her arms around him and held tight to him and when he stopped in surprise to gaze at her, she pulled his head down again and found his mouth, begged for it with her own, curiously thrilled with the light scratch of his beard, pressing her breasts against his broad flat chest as if she had suddenly found an excuse for their being.

"Beth!" he whispered in astonishment, putting his head down on her shoulder and holding her hard, feeling her tremble. Her response was so unexpected, so strong, that it caught him completely unaware.

"Jesus!" he said, and kissed her neck. "Let's get out of here." And sat up and started to pull her after him.

"Oh, no! No, Charlie, I—" She was frightened then, unwilling and unable to trust herself. They were safe in Maxie's basement; they couldn't do anything wrong. But Charlie had a car and he had an apartment, and Beth wanted him so much that she couldn't have put up a struggle. With another man it wouldn't have mattered; she had given up struggling long ago. It just didn't matter that much to her one way or the other. It was a sort of lost cause. But with Charlie it mattered enormously; with Charlie it *had* to be right. And the fear that it wouldn't be scared her almost as much as the growing feeling that it would.

"Charlie?" said a girl's voice. He looked around slowly with a frown. It was Mary Lou. "Hi!" she said. There was a boy behind her. "Freddie said there was a jam session down here. Well, Beth! What are you doing here?"

Beth mustered a smile. "Well—Charlie said there was a jam session down here."

"Uh—say, why don't you two sit down?" Charlie said to them. "We were just leaving. You can have the booth."

"Oh, there's room for four," said Mary Lou, sliding in on the opposite side. "Stay a little longer. This is the last set."

Charlie tried to object but she said, "Oh, look—isn't that Bud playing trombone? And look at Emmy." She turned to Beth with a disapproving frown. "Do you think she ought to sit up there like that? In public, I mean? It really doesn't look too good."

"I think it looks damn noble and romantic," said Charlie with a sort of irritated amusement. "Mary Lou, you worry too much."

"Look again!" said Freddie gleefully. "Maybe she's got something to worry about."

Mary Lou turned around in time to see Bud, flushed with beer and pleased with himself, give Emily a prolonged and melodramatic kiss. The audience offered some spirited approval.

"Oh!" said Mary Lou indignantly and the men laughed at her.

"That's nothing to worry about," said Charlie. "That's normal. Hell, be thankful she doesn't feel that way about girls."

Oh, Laura! Beth shut her eyes and put her head down to ease the pain in her clenched heart. And then she felt the pressure of Charlie's arm around her and she began to quiver again.

"She's got to stop that," said Mary Lou firmly, frowning at Emily. "It's just not fair. Not to any of us, especially her. Beth, can't you stop her?" she said earnestly. "I wish you'd talk some sense into her. I've heard all I want to hear about it. It's a campus joke. If she'd act like that right in Maxie's, I hate to think what she'd—"

The men leaned forward to hear what she said.

"Just talk to her, Beth," she finished loftily. "As a favor to me." Mary Lou had solid confidence in Beth. Beth was very sensible.

"I will," Beth said, and it was all she had strength to say.

Charlie got out of the booth and stood up, pulling Beth after him.

"We're leaving," he said firmly.

"Oh, why?" said Mary Lou. "Dinner isn't for another half-hour, Beth."

"It'll take me half an hour to get her back to the house," said Charlie with a grin, and they laughed at him.

"Okay," Mary Lou sighed. "See you later."

Beth felt a mounting sense of alarm outdistanced only by her rocketing desire. She tried feebly to protest again, but Charlie was too much for her; his utter refusal to let her intimidate him, his gentleness, his strength, his passion and her own overpowered her. She let him take charge of her.

Charlie put an arm around her and led her the three blocks to his apartment. She knew where they were going though she had never been there. They said very little to each other but when they stopped at street corners or turned and looked at each other their hearts started up again. Just inside the apartment door she stopped and turned back, the so-familiar doubts back in her heart.

"Mary Lou?" she said.

"I took you out to dinner. She won't ask questions."

"Mitch?"

"Field trip. Won't get back till tomorrow."

Laura? she thought, and the pain came back, but only for a moment. Charlie swept it away. He put his arms around her and embraced her so tightly that she couldn't breathe. And then he relaxed a little and pressed her to him, running his hands down her back. Her shoulders, her breasts, her hips felt the response of his smooth strength, his desire.

He picked her up and carried her to the bed. "Beth, you're lovely," he said. "So lovely."

A sudden awful fear clutched at her. What if it was wrong? What if it was as dull and empty and depressing as all the others? What if her instincts had misled her? "Wait, Charlie!" she said in a voice pitched high with alarm.

He heard the strain in her words and stopped to pull her close and comfort her. She clung to him on the verge of tears.

"Beth," he murmured. "Beth? Is this the first time?"

She held her breath in an agony of misgiving. What would he think of her if she told him the truth?

"Is it?" he prodded gently, thinking that was probably the cause of her fears. He was surprised to hear her whisper into his sweater, "No."

For a few moments they sat on the bed, neither moving nor speaking. Charlie was completely at a loss for words. Finally Beth lifted a pale face to him, and whispered, as if each word were costing her pain, "It was never any good. It was just a farce, a dirty little game. It was never right. At first I used to think it would be beautiful, if I just kept trying—if I didn't lose hope, if I found the right guy, if there was nothing wrong with me. If, if, if . . . But it never was." She stopped to conquer her trembling voice. "And finally, after a while, I just didn't care any more. I didn't care what they did to me. I guess I was lucky. Most of them were nice guys." A sob betrayed her, and Charlie held her a little tighter.

"And then I got sick of it," she said. "I got just old-fashioned sick of the whole business. I quit; I sort of swore off, I guess you could say. I figured it just wasn't for me. I didn't know why."

Charlie was silent and she began to get frightened again. "I—I don't know why I did it, Charlie. I'm ashamed—so ashamed. I—" She couldn't go on.

"You don't have to tell me all this, Beth," he said at last. He was shaken, surprised. And at the same time her confession made him feel fiercely protective.

"I had to tell you the truth," she said through her tears. "I couldn't lie to you."

"Why?" He looked down at her.

"Because this time I—I want it to be right. I want so terribly for it to be right and I was afraid it couldn't be if I —if I weren't honest with you."

He kissed the tears on her cheeks. "Is that why you're here now, Beth? To see if it's going to be right at long last?"

She hung her head. "I'm here because you told me to come with you," she said. "Because I couldn't help myself. Because for once I want it really and truly, for once I care about it. I care terribly." She looked up at him with tormented eyes. "Charlie," she begged. "Forgive me. Please forgive me."

"Forgive you?" he said softly. "What for? For being lost and mixed up and unhappy? For trying to set things right when you didn't know how? Hell, there's nothing to forgive you for. I'm only thankful they didn't turn you into a hopeless cynic."

She felt herself beginning to smile very faintly at him and in a sudden burst of gratitude she took his head in her hands and began to kiss him. The pain of her confession began to fade. Wherever he touched her she felt good. And when he had all that loveliness in his hands he pushed her down on the bed in a spasm of delight and kissed her all over, feeling her tremble with an almost unbearable pleasure.

Beth shut her eyes and said, "Oh, my God, Charlie, Charlie, Charlie . . ." And knew she had found what she had been looking for for so long.

And they fulfilled their promise in the dark and all the world spun away and left them alone in heaven.

ELEVEN

L AURA looked for Beth all afternoon. She looked for her at dinner. And when she went up to her room she felt lethargic and sad. Emily came up at seven and found her sitting in the butterfly chair, staring at a book.

Emily saw that Laura was worried, and she thought she knew why. Laura had a crush on Charlie and so Emmy hesitated to say anything. She just waited until Laura couldn't stand it any longer and said, "Laura, do you know where Beth is?"

"Well, I—she was out with Charlie this afternoon." Laura looked so unhappy that Emmy pulled the desk chair over to the butterfly and sat down.

"It didn't mean a thing, Laur, really. She'll tell you that herself when she gets in."

"Is she still with him? You mean she's been with him all this time?"

"Well, she—they dropped down to Maxie's to hear the music this afternoon." Emmy watched sympathetically as Laura's face fell. "Charlie was there earlier, Laur. Before he met Beth. He loves jazz, you know. I guess he just decided to bring Beth along. They really were good this afternoon." Laura's face was pale and hard. She said nothing. "Beth likes jazz too, you know," Emmy added, afraid of the silence.

"Yes, I know!"

"Laur, you mustn't take it so hard." Emmy reached out and put a hand on Laura's shoulder, but Laura shook it off and her nails pressed cruelly into her brow and scalp, trying to cut out the hurt they could never touch.

Emmy sat beside her in silence, miserable because she couldn't help. "Laur," she said. Her voice was all she could offer. Laura couldn't very well stop her ears. "Laur, please don't cry. She'll be home in a little while. She'll explain it to you, I know she will. Laur . . . there there, Laur, honey. Please don't—"

Laura stood up, suddenly furious, and turned on Emily.

98

"Don't call me honey! Don't call me that! I hate that word. Emmy, do you hear me?"

"Yes, I hear," said Emily in a whisper.

Laura sank back to the chair, frightened with her temper, her hurt, her jealousy. "Emmy," she said. "I'm sorry. You mustn't pay any attention to me."

"I didn't know you liked him that much, Laur."

"Oh, I don't. I mean, not really. Oh, I don't know what I mean; I can't explain. Please, Emmy . . ."

They sat in silence for a minute and then Emmy said, "Maybe you'd like to be alone for a little while."

Laura didn't answer. She was thankful, but too eager to be rid of Emily for graceful gratitude. When Emmy left she sat perfectly still with her lips tight and her eyes full, and had a talk with herself. She began to see that for all her tolerant teasing and tenderness, Beth simply didn't like her jealousy. And she knew Beth would expect a vindictive temper and tears and recriminations when she got home. Laura faced facts; her good sense was born of desperation. She couldn't swear off her jealousy, but she could tuck it under her love and hope it would smother. If it persisted, at least it wouldn't show. After all, maybe Charlie wouldn't last. Maybe it didn't mean anything.

The door opened suddenly and startled a gasp from Laura. She looked up quickly, but it was Mary Lou. The letdown knocked her temper off again.

"Where's Beth?"

"Not home yet," Laura said testily.

"Not home yet?" Mary Lou repeated in surprise.

"Try again at closing hours," said Laura. She stood up and turned her back on Mary Lou, gazing at the desk top as if she had important business with it.

Mary Lou stared at her back for a minute. The voice didn't sound like Laura's. "Will you tell her I dropped in? I'd like to talk to her when she gets back."

"Certainly."

"Thanks." Mary Lou waited just a second longer for Laura to say "You're welcome." Laura never passed up a chance to be polite. But this time she remained silent and finally Mary Lou turned and left, surprised.

Emily came back to study, and Laura waited with her heart beating high for the closing hour chime and Beth's return.

At closing hour Charlie and Beth said good night in his car. They couldn't let go of each other with any finality. Beth murmured several times, "I have to go in," and neither of them moved, except closer together.

Charlie kissed her, a long, deep kiss. In the pale radiance of the dashboard they gazed at each other.

"Oh, Beth, darling," he said. "I could look at you like this forever." It was unoriginally and beautifully true. "I never met a girl I wanted so much . . . so much . . ." He frowned at the mystery of it. "I can't let you go, Beth. I can't let you go."

"Charlie . . ." She traced the line of his brows with a finger and closed her eyes and felt his lips, and his warm breath flowed over her hand. He bent his head to kiss her hand and she pulled him closer and licked his ear, until he began to groan with the pleasure of it.

"Oh, Beth, where the hell did you come from? Why didn't I know you when I saw you? I've been looking for you for so long, darling."

"This is crazy, Charlie. It's just crazy," she whispered. "It happened so fast."

He stroked her hair. "Are you sorry, Beth?"

Her eyes fell. "I—don't know. I don't know, Charlie." She looked up to him and the sight of him scattered her doubts. "No, I'm not sorry." But when she looked away again she was. "Yes, I am. Oh damn, I don't know."

He pulled her tighter. "Beth—"

"Charlie, what time is it?" she asked suddenly. Laura was waiting. She went cold at the thought.

"Twenty-eight after."

"I have to go in." *Oh, Laura, forgive me!*

"Beth darling, listen to me—wait—"

"I have to go in."

"I want to see you tomorrow," he said. "What time, honey?"

"I don't know. Call me." She opened the car door, looking back at Charlie as she did so. He was frowning at her.

"Call you, hell. What's the matter with you? Tell me now."

She got out of the car and slammed the door, hurrying up on the walk in the direction of the house. Laura was suddenly looming in her thoughts and her conscience began to torture her. Charlie reached her side and took her arm and swung her about to a stop.

"Charlie, it's late—"

"I know it's late, Beth. What the hell's come over you all of a sudden? Wasn't it—wasn't everything all right?" His voice became soft, pleading.

"Yes—oh, yes, everything was—wonderful. Only—"

"Only what?"

"Nothing. I just don't want to be late. Please, Charlie." She tried to shake his arm off but he held her fast. Her concern for Laura chafed and grew with each second that he held her there, and at the same time she wanted to spend the whole night with him. She was helpless, rent between two loves, tormented.

At last he turned and started walking with her toward the house. "When will I see you, Beth?" He sounded a little grim.

"Just call me, Charlie, please. I don't know."

"What's the matter? What in God's name is the matter? Two minutes ago you were—you were happy. Now all of a sudden you panic because you're going to be a minute late. Am I supposed to swallow that?"

"You'll have to," she said. Her affection for Laura was crushing her with reproval.

Charlie spun her around again at the front door and embraced her.

"Beth, talk to me," he said urgently.

She shook her head and tried to pull free.

"Is it me?" he said.

"Oh, no! Oh, Charlie, darling—" She reached for him and he kissed her and let her go slowly. She shook her head at him wordlessly, wondering why she couldn't hide her troubles. They were so strong, so near the surface, that they threatened to spill over.

"I'll call you," he said finally, when the housemother called to Beth to come in. They stared at each other for just a second more, and then Beth left him.

She ran up the stairs, pausing for an instant on the landing to wipe off her smeared lipstick, and then she went down the hall to the room. Her roommates were studying quietly together. She glanced swiftly from one to the other.

"Well!" said Emmy with a big smile. "Welcome home."

Then she thought of Laura and fell suddenly silent.

Laura said nothing, and seeing her, so slender and wan in the big chair, Beth ached to be alone with her, to explain things. She began uneasily to undress.

"Have a nice time?" said Laura.

"Yes," she said cautiously.

"Where did you go?"

Beth was afraid to set off the volcano with every word. She went carefully. "Maxie's," she said. "And then it got too late to come home for dinner, so—we went out."

"Well, I'm glad you're home safe," said Emmy. She left Beth and Laura alone; she understood that Beth would want to talk to the younger girl, and she made a discreet disappearance.

Beth hung up her clothes, feeling as if she might explode with the tension. Charlie was so close, so warm in her head and the pit of her stomach, and yet there was Laura right beside her, real, and hurt. She couldn't let her go to bed before she had explained, or tried to explain, at least some of what happened. It hurt her sharply to know that she had to lie.

Laura sat hunched on the desk chair, her eyes fastened on the floor. Beth felt an unbearable pity for her and an almost exacerbating scorn for herself. She stood gazing at Laura for a minute, unable to talk, to find the right words. Finally she went over to her and knelt on the floor beside her. She took her hands and looked earnestly up at her.

"Laura," she said. "Laura, look at me." There was a film of anxiety over every word; a profound tenderness in her voice that touched Laura. She looked up and Beth reached for her to kiss her, but she resisted.

"Mary Lou wants to see you," Laura said unexpectedly.

"Oh, honey, not now. Not now."

"You'd better go, Beth. She might come looking for you."

"Laura, I don't want to leave you. I want to talk to you. I—"

"You'd better go."

Beth was surprised at her firmness. She squeezed Laura's hands and then lifted them up impulsively and kissed them. "I'll be right back."

She hurried to Mary Lou's room and found her still up. It would never have occurred to Mary Lou to question anything Beth did. Emmy's most casual behavior was subject to suspicion, but Beth's most suspicious behavior was just casual. To Mary Lou, anyway. She trusted her.

"Oh, hi!" she said. "I was just going down to your room. Guess what?"

Beth was in no mood for games. She tried to smile a little. "What?"

"Mitch Grogan called me."

It stirred a little interest. "Oh, that's great. Going to see him?"

"Yes, this weekend. Say, Beth? Is Laura all right?"

That rang the alarm bell. "Yes. Why?"

"She just seemed upset. About your date, I guess."

"Oh, no—"

"I guess she still likes Charlie."

"Oh!" She rubbed a distraught hand through her hair. It was an out; not the best, but the only one. "Yes, I— God, I feel terrible about it. I—"

"I understand," said Mary Lou. "Actually," she added confidentially, and confidence with her was a luxury, just as friends were a luxury, "I'm sort of glad it happened. You need somebody, Beth. I've thought that for a long time. It's a shame about Laura, but she'll find somebody."

Beth had to get back; her nervousness was likely to betray her. "I'm going to talk to her about it," she said. "I think it'll be all right." She turned and almost ran back to the room.

Laura was waiting for her on the couch. Beth went over to her, sat down and searched her face, and then took her in her arms and held her for a long time. Laura submitted docilely, letting Beth cradle and comfort her. As for Beth, every part of Laura that she could see and feel tore her heart; the quiet acceptance was harder for her than an out-and-out tantrum would have been. She touched Laura's face with her hand and felt her wet cheeks and said in a broken voice, "Oh, Laur, honey." It was all she could say for a minute.

"Beth, Beth, that's all right. Please—"

Beth got hold of herself. The immediate hurt in her arms loomed larger just then than the remembered pleasure of the evening. She hated herself for being false to this sweet trusting girl who loved her so completely. She was suddenly appalled with her own cruelty, her own bad faith. She should have told Laura long ago how she really felt and now it was too late. She must pay now; make it up to Laura, somehow heal the hurt.

"Laura," she said. "Laura, honey, get mad at me, or something. I can't stand it like this. I wouldn't hurt you for the world."

Laura made herself keep calm by an immense effort of will. "Beth, don't try to explain. I'd rather not hear ... I love you, Beth." She looked up at her and Beth bent down to kiss her, and Laura knew she had said the right things. No desperate anger would have brought Beth so close and made her so contrite.

The gentler Laura was, the more Beth's conscience hurt her, the more viciously her deception bit into it. "Oh, Laura, Laura, I don't know what to say. Forgive me, forgive me. I'd do anything to make it up to you."

"There's nothing to make up, Beth. Is there? I mean, you just went out with a boy, that's all. Well, I've been going out with boys too, all year. I'm as guilty as you are."

It was almost more than Beth could take. She had a brief horrible vision of Laura learning the whole truth and she stiffened against it, suddenly furious with Charlie for attracting her as he did. In an access of remorse she said, "Laura—Laura, I won't go out with him again, if you don't want me to." It was so easy to say, so magically comforting.

Laura was too powerfully tempted to refuse. She answered, looking up at Beth with a hopefully happy face that contradicted her cautious words, "Beth, I wouldn't ask you to do that. You know I wouldn't."

"You want me to. I can tell by your face." She took the slim face in her hands and it seemed so anxious and so trusting that she said, "All right. All right, Laur." She embraced her and looked into a dark corner of the wall and thought, Oh God, give me strength. I can't hurt her any more, I just can't. It took a woman, it took Laura, to teach me how to feel. I owe her my love. I owe it to her. She shut her eyes tight against Charlie and found him strong and clear in her mind.

And then Laura said, "Beth, darling!" and hugged her passionately and Beth thought, This is enough. This has got to be enough.

"Laura," she said softly. They fell back on the couch together and Beth let her have her way, tired though she was. A long while later she fell asleep, exhausted and unhappy, plagued by febrile dreams of first Charlie and then Laura and then Charlie again, wondering what Charlie would think when she refused to see him, wondering if she had the guts to stick by Laura. She hardly dared to think of Charlie, for she no sooner reviled him roundly in her head than her body gave him an unconditional pardon.

Laura lay still beside her, worried at her fitful turns but clinging obstinately to Beth's promise. She had a frightening premonition that Beth would resent her bondage, but at least she couldn't break it: she had forged her own chains. Besides, it was so thrilling to feel Beth bound to her, to feel Beth her captive, that Laura couldn't see the dangers clearly. She was too sensitive not to be fuzzily aware that there were dangers, but she couldn't really believe in them just then. Beth was hers.

TWELVE

Eммy could hardly wait to hear about Charlie. She had to run after Beth in a midmorning rush between classes and caught her speeding over the campus toward Lincoln Hall.

"Have coffee with me," she begged.

Beth was afraid; she knew too well what to expect from Emmy. "I have a class, Em."

"Well, cut it! Oh, come on."

Beth slowed down. "Well—" she said. She had to face it sooner or later. Emily would be wondering why she didn't see Charlie again. She'd have to make it sound plausible.

Beth let herself be led to the nearest coffee spot. Emmy could hardly wait to ask questions.

"How was it?" she said.

Beth stirred her coffee carefully, watching the brown and white unite in her cup and come tan. "He's a very nice boy," she said.

Emily waited. "Well, is that all?" she said finally.

"No." She pulled the spoon out and looked at it. It was a tricky business trying to fool Emily. Emily knew her too well. "We had a very nice time."

"What's all this 'nice'? That doesn't mean anything." She leaned back and folded her arms. "What happened, Beth?"

Beth wondered if she could possibly conceal it from her, and the weight of another lie pulled her spirits still lower. "He just doesn't have it, that's all. I know, I know, when you saw us at Maxie's I looked all excited . . . and I guess I was. But it wore off. He's—" She shrugged. "He's just another guy, Emmy."

"You're disappointed, maybe, but not with Charlie. Gee, Beth, I know you better than that. You're not in love with his face. At least that's not all you're in love with."

"Who's in love? With anything? Or anybody? I didn't say I was in love."

"You didn't need to."

106

"Oh, Emmy—" she exclaimed. *My God, does it show?* Emily took her confusion for confirmation.

"When are you going to see him again?"

Beth emptied the smoke from her lungs and said, "I don't know." If she had said "never" she would have provoked a storm from Emily.

"Is he going to call?" Emily felt her way carefully, surprised by Beth's evasiveness.

"Yes."

"When?"

"I don't know, Emmy. Today, I guess."

"You don't know? Didn't he say?"

"No."

"He's disappointed too, is that it?"

"I guess so. I don't know."

"If he's disappointed, why is he going to call?"

"Emmy, I—" She had to protect Laura. She looked down again, defeated. "I don't know."

Emmy frowned, reaching for Beth's confidence with her sympathy, her affection; wondering why Beth suddenly distrusted her. "What happened last night, Beth?" she said again. "Or don't you know that either?"

Beth wanted to scream at her. She made one last try to evade her. In a short dry voice she said, "We had dinner, we danced, we talked. We made love, we came home." She sighed, hurting because the relief of truth was denied her and because now it was Emily she had to lie to. But Laura must be spared; Laura, whose whole love she had taken for her some-time pleasure; Laura, whose trust she had wholly betrayed; Laura, to whom she owed the climax of love, and perhaps even her physical pleasure with Charlie.

"Beth," said Emily gently. "Why won't you talk to me? Is there something the matter?" Beth looked up at her slowly and Emmy took her hands and squeezed them. "Beth, you're my best friend," she said. "Don't you think I want to help, if I can? Gee, Beth, I tell you everything. I haven't a secret in the world from you. You know you can trust me." Beth couldn't answer. "Did he hurt you?" She shook her head.

"Did he threaten you or—or was he disgusting, or—"

"No, no, Emmy. He—" She stopped, helpless. After a moment she said, "No, he was very nice. He didn't do anything."

Emily released her hands and sat studying her in silence. Beth sipped her coffee and smoked and sweated in quiet misery. Finally Emily said pointedly, "It's Laura."

Beth looked up at her with such a startled face that Emmy said, "I thought so. I should have suspected this all along."

"Oh, Emmy—no!" said Beth. She was almost sick with apprehension.

"Don't tell me, Beth. I've got eyes. You won't go out with Charlie because of Laura."

"Emmy, I swear to God, it's not true, it's not—"

"Don't try to deny it, Beth. It's the only possible answer. Nothing else makes sense."

"Oh, Emmy, my God." She put her head in her hands, shaken to the core. "How did you know? How did you ever—"

"Simple," said Emmy. "You have the softest heart in the world. Too darn soft for your own good. You won't go out with Charlie because Laura's still got a crush on him." She smiled triumphantly. "I knew it. I'm right, aren't I?"

Beth couldn't answer. She wanted to laugh hysterically with relief, she wanted to get up and run.

Emmy sighed and spun her cup slowly around by its handle. "I know because Laura felt so terrible last night before you got home. She even cried a little. And finally she just plain got mad at me. She said she just couldn't explain it, but I knew it was you and Charlie."

Beth wondered if Emmy would see the tremor in her hands. "I talked to her last night," she said. "I think she's all right now."

"Now that you've told her you won't go out with Charlie, you mean."

"Oh, Emmy . . ."

"Beth, I know you wouldn't lie to me. You'd tell me if this wasn't true. Now listen to me. Laura's a sweet girl and I know you're fond of her, but this is ridiculous. You can't sacrifice a terrific guy—maybe your whole future—to one girl. You'll probably never see her again after next June. Beth, you're crazy about Charlie. Admit it . . ." Beth put her head down on her arms and prayed for her sanity. "Beth, you're hurting yourself forever, trying not to hurt Laura for a little while." For the wrong reasons, Emmy hit the right truth, but Beth was blind with her own distress.

"Oh, Emmy, you've got it all backwards, you—" She

broke off. "Let's not talk about it. Let's please not talk about it."

"But I don't understand."

"Please, Emmy." She restrained an impulse to grasp her shoulders and shake her into silence. She stood up abruptly, suddenly at the end of her endurance, and said, "I'm going up to the Union. I'll see you later, Emmy."

Emmy looked up, surprised and a little hurt. "I'll come with you, Beth," she offered.

"No, no. You—you stay here and finish your coffee."

Emily watched Beth stumble out of the lounge and made up her mind that she would interfere. Laura's crush would just have to give way to Beth's love. There were no two ways about it.

THIRTEEN

Mitch was curious. He pestered Charlie for the facts, and Charlie's evasions gave him the satisfaction of supposing the evening with Beth was a failure.

"How far did you get?" he asked.

Charlie sighed and looked up from his book. His temper was bad but he tried to hold it back. "I got nowhere, boy. I wasn't trying to get anywhere."

"Going to see her again?"

"Of course."

"When?"

"I don't know," he said with martyred patience. And then to illustrate his irritation he added, "God damn it! Now will you shut up?"

Mitch complied, grinning comfortably. To see Charlie make a mistake with a woman was to see Romeo take a pratfall under the balcony.

"What are you grinning at?" said Charlie.

Mitch chuckled. "I didn't know I was."

"You were."

"Oh, I'm just glad to know you're fallible."

Charlie plunged back into his book. He had been trying to reach Beth all day with no success. She wasn't at home or she couldn't be disturbed. They couldn't say where she was or when she'd be back. Sorry. Call again. And he did, again and again, with always the same results and the same obvious reason for them: she didn't want to talk to him.

It was incomprehensible. For a long while he imagined that he had done something wrong. But the harder he pursued the idea the less substance it had and finally he gave it up. Something else was bothering her. Maybe they had gone too fast. Maybe they both had wanted too much too soon. He hadn't pushed it, he hadn't insisted on anything. She'd wanted it as much as he did; it had happened naturally. He couldn't accuse himself of anything there. The whole evening had seemed so right, so fair and lovely, and he wanted her again so much that it was impossible

110

for him to admit that she didn't want him just as much. He didn't think she was a girl with a conventional conscience, but he was willing to admit that he might have been wrong there; she had certainly suffered enough over her past transgressions. What else could it be? He didn't think she was seeing anyone else; she came with him voluntarily and never made an objection to him. The more he thought of it the more puzzled he was.

Charlie didn't know he had an ally. Emily kept her peace as long as she could, but by the middle of exam week she couldn't hold out any longer. She knew Charlie had been trying to see Beth on campus, at the Union, everywhere; that he had been calling every day and getting nowhere; that he was upset and getting mad. She got half of this from Bud, who saw Charlie almost every day, and the rest from watching and listening to Beth, and pretty soon her Samaritan instincts got the better of her. She called Charlie. Mitch took a message for her.

When Charlie got home he found the note under the corner of the phone. "Call Emily at 7-4006. She says you'll understand. What's the mystery?"

Charlie chucked his books on the sofa and picked up the phone, pulling off his jacket while it rang.

"Good afternoon, Alpha Beta," said a bright young voice.

"Hello, is Emily there?"

"Just a moment please."

Charlie lighted a cigarette and waited, fidgeting.

Minutes later, Emmy said, "Hello?"

"Emmy?" he said eagerly.

"Oh, Charlie! I'm so glad you called. Listen, I'm going to be perfectly frank with you. I know you've been trying to reach Beth." She hesitated.

"Yeah?" he said, urging her with his voice.

"Well, she wants to see you, Charlie. I know it. She won't talk to you on account of Laura."

"Laura? What the hell does Laura have to do with it?"

"Beth's got it into her head that Laura's still got a crush on you."

Charlie was floored. "Emmy—my God—she never did! Our fathers were old buddies in college. I never would have met the girl if it hadn't been for that. She doesn't have a crush on me. She never did. What the hell!"

Emily was suddenly concerned. The words she phrased in such good faith seemed always to change character the moment they left her mouth. Not until she heard herself speak them did she understand them as other people did. She paused, trying to grasp the implications of the conversation. "Well," she said, uncertainly, "Beth doesn't know that, apparently. Anyway, Charlie, that's not the point. The point is she wants to see you. She's told me so. She's miserable, and if you could just *talk* to her—"

"How? My God, I've been trying—"

"I know, but she won't talk to you if she knows it's you. Call her on her private phone. We have one in the room. She doesn't know you have the number, so she'll answer it. Once she hears your voice, Charlie, it'll make all the difference, I know it."

"When can I call?"

"Call her tonight about seven. She'll be alone in the room then. Laura's got a final at Greg Hall and I'll just fade away."

"Emmy, you're a good girl."

"Oh, she'd do it for me. I just hate to see you two in a mess because of a silly misunderstanding. You just need a go-between." She laughed.

"What's her number?"

She told him.

"Thanks, Emmy," he said. "I really appreciate this."

They hung up, each wondering what sort of a game Laura was playing. Charlie figured it for some kind of petty jealousy, but Emily came closer. She began to review Laura's behavior systematically: the way she followed and imitated Beth; her disappointment when Beth wasn't at home; her temper when Beth wasn't there to greet her after Christmas vacation; her anger when Beth and Charlie went out.

Emily admitted that it might be some sort of obsessive friendship, but even that idea made her uncomfortable. She was unwilling to accept it but unable to dismiss it. But she said nothing to either of her roommates.

At seven, as arranged, Charlie called Beth on her room phone. He listened nervously to the ring. It rang four times before Beth picked up the receiver.

"Hello?"

"Beth—darling, this is Charlie. Don't hang up."

"Charlie?" She began to tremble.

"Don't ask me anything, Beth, just listen. I have to see you. Tonight. We have to talk. We owe each other that much. Can you be ready in fifteen minutes?" His voice was urgent and soft; it brought him too close to her.

"Charlie—" she whispered, sinking into the desk chair, and tears started down her cheeks.

"I'll be by for you in fifteen minutes," he said. "Beth?"

"Yes?"

"Fifteen minutes, darling." He hung up before she could say anything.

Beth put her head in her hands and gave one short dreadful sob, and then she ran to wash her face and get dressed. She was ready when her buzz sounded a few minutes later and made her heart jump. She sped downstairs as if speed would obliterate her thoughts.

Charlie was waiting at the foot of the stairs. She stopped when she saw him and moved toward him slowly, stopping in front of him in the hall. She hadn't even time to hate her weakness; she resolutely ignored the idea of Laura. She couldn't help herself. They stared at each other for a minute and then he put his arm around her tight and led her outside without a word and down the walk to his car.

He started the motor, and she watched him with her heart pulsing wildly and her hot hands knotted together. After a moment he turned and regarded her and, still without a word, took her in his arms. With a gasp she reached for him and they kissed for a very long time. And then again. He turned the motor off, and for almost an hour they sat there with no words, only their lips and their trembling bodies to speak for them. Finally she put her head down on his shoulder and cried soundlessly. Only her involuntary tremors betrayed her. When she was calm again he said gently, "Want to talk to me, darling?"

She shook her head. He tilted her face up and brushed away the leftover tears and smiled at her. "All right," he said. "I won't torture you with questions. You'll find a way to tell me. Only tell me this, honey. Did I do something wrong?"

"No." She smiled faintly at him and looking at him wanted him again and lifted her lips to be kissed. He took them almost violently and then, holding her, he said, "Is there someone else?"

She couldn't answer. She struggled with herself and couldn't answer.

"I'm sorry, I'm sorry," he said. "I said no questions, didn't I?" He released her, frowning and rubbing his brow. "Let's get a beer." He looked at her but she didn't answer. "I can only take so much of this, Beth. Beer, honey?"

"Okay," she said.

They went over to Pratts' and talked very little because there was only one thing to talk about and it couldn't be said. So they studied each other's faces in the candlelight and locked their hands together and got a little drunk, more on each other than on the beer. And Beth fought off the haunting image of Laura's face from time to time when it got too strong and began to accuse her.

Charlie had to say something finally. "Emmy called me," he said. "She gave me your number."

"Oh." She smiled at him.

"She said something that—made me think you might have a wrong impression, honey."

"Of what?"

He knocked a column of ash from his cigarette and said musingly, "Twenty-eight years ago, my father went to school here with a guy named Merrill Landon. They've been friends ever since. When I found out Landon's daughter was here in school last fall I called her up and we went out a couple of times." He paused to study her. "Do you see what I'm getting at?"

There was a line of worry between Beth's eyes. "What did Emmy tell you, Charlie?"

"She said she thought you wouldn't see me because of Laura—because you thought Laura had a crush on me. Darling, Laura never *did* have a crush on me. We're just friends. Or rather, the children of friends . . . Was that the trouble?"

Beth stared helplessly at him, her fingers pressed against her cheeks. He watched her for a moment, feeling that he was losing her again. "Beth, you can't let Laura come between us. She means nothing to me, except as a family friend. There's no reason—"

"It's not Laura's fault. Don't blame anything on Laura. She has nothing to do with it."

Charlie wanted to squeeze the truth out of her, but her worried face warned him it wouldn't work. She was as stubborn as Emmy had said she was. "All right, darling,

I won't push you any farther," he said. "On one condition. On *one condition*, Beth. Look at me." He pulled her toward him. "That you see me again." Her eyes dropped. "Beth!" His voice ordered her attention.

"All right," she whispered unhappily. She couldn't resist him when she was with him, just as she couldn't hurt Laura when they were together. "All right, Charlie."

"Tomorrow?"

"I don't know."

"Look, Beth," he said, suddenly getting disciplinary with her. "I know you've got trouble, honey, I know you're up against something. I'm not trying to force you or push you around or frighten you. Maybe you've got obligations somewhere else, maybe you can't help what you're doing. Okay. But damn it, Beth, you've got obligations to me, too, whether you want 'em or not. You can't play with people, honey. You can't do—" He groped a little. "You can't behave the way you did with me—say the things you did—and suddenly drop me like a hot potato. Nobody can take that, Beth. Not me, not anybody."

"I wasn't playing, Charlie. I was serious. Only—please, please, don't ask me what the trouble is. I can work it out. Just give me time." She raised her eyes again, imploring him.

He sighed and said a little crisply, "All right. I'll give you time, Beth, if that's what you want. But I won't sit around making phone calls that don't get answered and playing tricks on you just so I can see you. I'm *going* to see you. And you're going to make a date right here and now and stick to it. Do you hear me?"

She nodded.

"Do you have an exam tomorrow?"

"No."

"Okay, I'm out at four. I'll pick you up at five. We'll go out, have dinner, see a show or something." He paused. "Okay, love?"

She nodded.

He looked at the wall clock and said, "Okay, let's go. Almost closing hours."

Beth got up with a start. Laura would be home already. Her final couldn't have lasted longer than ten o'clock. It was ten-twenty.

At the house, Charlie stopped the car and turned to gaze at her for a minute, and then he got out without kissing her. Beth was chagrined, almost angry. He opened her door and let her out.

"Come on, honey," he said in a businesslike voice. "It's cold."

She got out, watching him hopefully. He took her arm, slammed the door, and started for the house.

"Charlie!" she said, pulling back, and the tone of her voice reproved him.

He stopped and looked at her, and she threw her arms around him and kissed him until he held her and answered her.

"Charlie darling," she said. It was as grateful as it was inadequate. At the door she clung to him, almost afraid to let him go, afraid to face Laura. But the housemother shooed him out with the others, and she had to watch him leave.

She went slowly up to her room and pushed the door open with a sort of dread, and walked in. Emily looked up from the desk.

"Oh, Beth!" she said. "How was it? Was it all right?"

Beth nodded. "Yes, Em. Thanks. Where's Laura?"

"In bed."

"In bed?" Beth could hardly believe it.

"Yes. She got home from the final and—" She shrugged. "She said she was tired."

"Didn't she ask where I was?"

"Well, she asked if you'd gone out and I said yes. She knew right away with who. I just told her you went out for a beer with him. I mean—I *had* to tell her. She would have found out anyway."

Beth turned and took her coat off. Emily watched her with a host of questions on her tongue.

"How's Charlie?" she said.

"Fine. We sort of—made it up. I'm going to see him tomorrow."

"Will you tell Laur?"

"Yes, I'll tell her." She shuddered at the thought.

"Will she understand?" Emmy was half expecting an admission—of what, she didn't know.

"Yes, she'll understand." The hell she will, she thought.

"Beth?" said Emmy, hesitating.

"Hm?"

"You aren't mad at me for calling him, are you?"

"No, Em, I'm not mad."

"You're acting sort of funny."

"I'm tired, Emmy."

Emmy went over to her. "Beth, are you in love? Really?"

"I don't know."

"Yes you do. Are you?"

Beth sighed and her strength seemed to leave her with her breath. "Yes," she said, and suddenly it felt good. "Yes, yes, Emmy . . ."

Emily hugged her. "Oh, Beth, I'm so glad!"

"Emmy, you make me feel—" She tumbled her hair with nervous fingers. "Everything's such a mess right now."

"But it'll all turn out, Beth. Things are never as bad as they seem. Most of the things you worry about never happen, you know . . . Have you told him?"

"No. I—I'm a little afraid to, I guess."

"Oh, well, you'll get over that. Beth, I'm so happy for you!"

Beth had to answer her smile and fight it at the same time. Emily's warmth brought the truth to the surface in her; she wanted awfully to confess. But the thought of Laura, so alone, so lovingly given, so badly used, stopped her again.

"Guess what," said Emmy wth her eyes bright and her yellow hair alive in the lamplight.

"What?"

"Oh, you won't even think it's the truth," she said, looking at her bare toes in the pile of the rag rug.

Beth smiled indulgently at her. It was a brief hiatus of relief from her own troubles. "Yes I will, Emmy. If you say so. What?"

"It's Bud. I really love him. I'd do anything for him."

Beth couldn't help laughing a little. "You've been in love with him all year, Em."

"Not like this. This is it, Beth." She gripped Beth's arms in dead earnest.

Mary Lou's request floated hazily back to Beth. She had completely forgotten to talk to Emmy in the press of her own difficulties.

"Emmy, you haven't done anything—"

"Oh, no, Beth!"

If it were real, as Emmy said, then it was wrong. Bud was too undependable, too uninhibited. "Emmy—don't get carried away. Use your head. Oh, Em—"

Emmy hung her head as if she might begin to cry. "Beth, you don't believe me," she whispered.

"Yes, I do, I do, Emmy. Only, be sensible, honey. I mean in public and everything. I mean—"

"Do you really?" She brightened. "Because I *do* love him."

"Yes, Emmy. I know." She was too tired to argue.

"And he loves me. He told me so."

"Oh, Emmy, I'm so glad." What else could she say? She fell into bed later too tired to think.

FOURTEEN

T HE NEXT DAY, Beth and Laura hedged with each other for a while before either of them would say anything. Finally Laura said in a tight voice, "You saw him last night, Beth. Why won't you just tell me? Why do I have to tell you?"

"Well—because I'm a little ashamed, I guess. Because I'm sorry, Laur. I didn't want to hurt you."

"You didn't have to. Why didn't you just tell me you were going to see him again?" She couldn't keep the bite out of her words.

"Because I didn't know it myself, honey."

"You didn't?" Laura gazed past her coolly and out the window.

"Oh, Laur, honey—" Beth tried to think of something better to say, but there was nothing. "No, I didn't."

"Beth, I didn't ask you not to see him again. You said you wouldn't see him again. You said it, not me. It was your idea. If I had asked you not to and you'd agreed— that would be different. But I didn't ask for anything. You went back on your word, Beth, after you gave it voluntarily." She was shaking with the force of her feeling, and she worked to keep her voice steady.

"Laura, honey, I— He called. He got my number. I didn't know. And when I talked to him, it—I owed him an explanation, Laur. I couldn't just drop him. Everyone thinks I dropped him because you still have a crush on him, don't you see? But he knows you don't, Laur."

"He knows?" Of course he knew. He took her out as a favor to her father. But did Beth know about her family, then? Had he told her of the divorce.

"Yes. He said your fathers were friends. He said you didn't have a crush on him at all. I had to see him—explain it—say something. I had to, don't you see?"

"I see," she said. "How did he figure all this out? If he knew I didn't have a crush on him, why did he think you wouldn't see him for my sake?"

"Well, I don't know. I—"

"Why didn't he figure out that there might have been another boy in your life? Or family troubles? Or something he did wrong? Why didn't he figure out any of those things, Beth? How come the first thing he thought of was me?"

"Laura, I—he didn't, exactly."

"Well, exactly what did happen, Beth?" She felt furious tears start up.

"He talked to Emmy, Laur. Emmy thought I wouldn't see him because of you. It was her idea."

"What right does Emmy have to go blabbing to him? What right does Emmy have to think anything about us?" She caught her breath, looking for words to cut with. "Why can't Emmy mind her own business and leave us alone?"

"Laur, please don't get excited, honey."

"Answer my question!"

Beth sighed and looked at her hands. "Emmy wanted to help. She knew I was unhappy. She knows me pretty well."

"Well, I guess I don't want to help and I don't know you at all and I made you unhappy. Is that it?"

"Laura—"

"Well, is it, Beth?" Suddenly an awful fear overswept her anger. "Oh, Beth—can't we be happy?" she pleaded. "We were so happy before. What happened? Why does Charlie matter?" The tears spilled over. "Do we have to quarrel and make each other miserable like this?"

"Oh, baby. No, no, we'll work it out. Somehow." She reached for her and Laura cried in her arms.

"Beth, we have such a beautiful thing together. We just can't let anything happen to it. We can't let anyone hurt it or come between us."

Beth wondered where the words were that would win her pardon. There didn't seem to be any.

"Beth," Laura whispered. "You won't see him again, will you?"

Beth was silent, not because she was torn again between the two, but because she hadn't the guts to say "Yes, I will see him."

"Beth?" Laura's voice was small and lost, like a child's in an empty room.

Beth pressed her close. "I don't know," she whispered. Laura took it in silence and in a moment Beth added, "I

might have to, Laur. I might have to—to ward off suspicion."

"Beth, please." It was almost inaudible.

"Laura, baby, I can't promise. I think I *have* to see
him."

"Why?" Her voice came out again, demanding.

"I've told you why. What will he think about you—and
me—if I don't?"

Laura sat up and pulled away from her. "I don't care
what he thinks. I don't care, I'm not ashamed. Are we
doing something dirty or wicked to be ashamed of? Are
we, Beth?"

"No." She shut her eyes and said slowly, "But other
people don't understand that, Laur. We have to keep it
secret—absolutely secret. People will say we're queer—"

"But we're *not!* I know what queer is. I've seen people—"

"Laura, we're just as queer as the ones who *look* queer,"
Beth said sharply, looking at her. "We're doing the same
damn thing. Now, let's not kid ourselves. Let's be honest
with each other, at least." Her own deception shut her up.

Laura sat and stared at her with a horrified face.
"Beth—" she quavered, shaking her head. "No . . . no . . ."

Beth grasped her hands. "I'm sorry. Oh, I'm sorry, that
was a terrible way to say it. I'm just so damn upset. I—"

"Are we really—" She couldn't say the word. "Are we,
Beth?"

"Yes."

Laura was mute for a minute, and then she said, "All
right. Then we are." She set her chin. "That still doesn't
make it dirty or wicked."

"No." Beth smiled ruefully at her and kissed her hands.
"It just makes it illegal."

Laura pulled her hands away and for a long while said
nothing. Finally she said, "Are you going to see him,
then?"

"Yes."

"How did he know your phone number?"

"Emmy."

Laura stood up suddenly and turned an outraged back
to Beth.

"Laura, Emmy's a friend. A very close friend of mine."

"Not of mine."

"Try to understand, Laura. She only wanted to help."

"Can't you make her understand you don't need help?"

"That would hurt her terribly. I can't hurt her, Laur."

"You can't hurt her, but you can hurt me?"

"Oh, Laura." Beth put her head in her hands. "I don't want to hurt either of you," she said from between her palms. "I don't want to hurt anybody."

"Well, choose between us, then. Because apparently one of us has to be hurt."

"Laura, will you stop?" Beth cried, looking at her. "My God, who's hurting who? What are you trying to make me do? What do you want me to say?"

Laura went to her and sank to her knees beside her. She put her head in Beth's lap, clutching at her, and said hoarsely, "I want you to love me, Beth, that's all. I want you to love me. Say that's selfish, say it's anything you want to call it, I can't help it. I love you more than life or death and I can't stand to think of losing you. I can't stand it, Beth, do you hear me? Oh, Beth, Beth, my darling, say you love me. Say that, and I don't care what happens. I don't care what else you say or what you do or even what we are. I don't care, if you'll only just tell me you love me . . . Beth? You do love me, don't you?"

"Yes, Laura."

"Say it."

"I love you, Laur."

Laura shut her eyes and didn't see the suffering in Beth's. There was nothing more they could say to each other then. And there was nothing more they could do. Emily would be back from lunch at any moment and both of them realized how dangerous it would be to continue as they were. They silently started tidying up the room.

Emily found her roommates in a state of apparent calm. Laura was collecting a pile of books and getting ready to leave.

"Where're you going, Laur?" said Emily conversationally.

"Over to the library." Laura wouldn't look at her. She was furious with Emily.

"I'll be down in Mary Lou's room, Emmy. We have that Comparative Lit. final tomorrow," Beth said, starting out of the room. "If anyone calls, I'll be down there." She looked cautiously at Laura, but Laura seemed unperturbed.

"Okay," said Emily. "Hey, when are you going out?" She knew instantly, from the look on Beth's face, that

Beth hadn't told Laura about her date. Emmy bit her tongue too late.

"I—don't know," Beth said, and she and Laura looked at each other. "He said he'd call. About five, I think."

Laura stod perfectly still with a book in her hands and stared at Beth. Emmy made the diplomatic move; the coming storm raised enough charge to frighten her out of the room.

"Guess I'll go see Bobbie," she said hastily, and backed out. She pulled the door shut behind her and walked down the hall in bewilderment. She didn't go to see Bobbie, she went to the living room and sat down in an alcoved corner and began, in spite of herself, to analyze the situation. She could put two and two together, but she could not believe in four until she saw it with her own eyes. It was the most difficult logic she ever faced: it was simple, irrefutable, and incredible—a lover's quarrel. Emmy gave an involuntary shudder.

Laura didn't say anything for a few moments after Emmy left. She sat down at the desk and stared out the window, speechless. Beth came up behind her, afraid to touch her, and stood behind her chair for a moment. Finally she said, "I meant to tell you, Laur. I just couldn't, after we got to talking. I can't bear to hurt you. Everything I say, everything I do, hurts you. It was cowardly, I know; I'll admit it. God knows I can't bear pain. And when I hurt you, I suffer too. I suffer terribly."

No sound, no gesture, came from Laura. Beth went around and sat on the desk and looked at her. "Laura, honey, you said—you said it didn't matter. You said nothing mattered as long as we had each other. You said you didn't care, as long as I loved you."

"Do you love me, Beth?"

"You know I do."

"No, I don't."

"I do, Laura."

"Then why didn't you tell me? Why do you lie to me, Beth?"

"Oh, darling—I'm afraid the truth hurts, sometimes. I didn't really lie to you, Laur, I just—tried to shield you."

"You should have told me, Beth. You never tell me anything. I have to guess, and if I ask the right questions, maybe I get the right answers. Otherwise I never learn anything. Not telling the truth is as wrong as telling lies, Beth. You knew all the time this morning you were going out with him this afternoon. It's yourself you're trying to shield."

Beth sighed. "I'm going out with him this evening, Laur. Because there's no way to explain to him why I won't go out."

"All right, Beth. Why didn't you just tell me that? I'd rather be hurt honestly than dishonestly."

"Oh, Laura, don't you understand—"

"I understand that I'm being treated like an irresponsible child," Laura exclaimed. "I'm being shielded from nothing, Beth. It's yourself you're trying to protect."

"Can't you believe I'd do something—anything—for you? Laura, if I've lied, and I have, it's been for your sake. Can't you understand that? My God, I've had to lie to Charlie for you and to Emmy, and—" And even to myself, she finished silently.

"And me."

"No, Laur."

Laura nodded at her. "Yes, Beth. Yes. Beth, I've been honest with you—absolutely honest—but you've got to be the same with me. I know I'm young. I know I'm inexperienced and childish sometimes. But you can't help me to grow up by treating me like a child; by shooing me out while you share your secrets with somebody else."

"Laura, I'm not sharing them with anyone else," she said, and her voice was tired.

"You haven't any right to deceive me, Beth," said Laura unhappily.

Beth's sorrows suddenly swelled and split inside and poisoned her. "God damn it, Laura!" she exploded. "Damn it, damn it, damn it! I've done nothing that I didn't do for your sake, nothing!" She stood up and strode to the other side of the room, and whirled to face Laura. "Will you never understand that? I've made mistakes, I know. I've hurt you, I know that, too. But do you have to harp on it? Do you have to cavil and pester and torment me, day after day—"

"Beth!"

"Like a damn silly little child—"

"Beth—"

"You make it impossible for me to handle this any other

way, Laura. I thought we could handle the thing like adults, but apparently we aren't quite capable of that."

"But Beth, didn't you understand what I meant—what I—"

"Yes, I understand. I understand that you're at least aware that I'm not the only one who's made mistakes. I suppose I'm to be grateful for it." The ache inside her was so awful that she went to extremes for the littlest relief; she hardly knew what she said, or cared. "What do you want me to do, Laura? Never speak to Emmy again? Never speak to Charlie? Lock myself in a damn garret with you somewhere and rot? Is that what you want?"

Laura looked at her, shaking her head, frightened.

"Well, there's a world around us, Laura," Beth went on as if Laura had said no, "and we're damn near grown up, however young we may act, and we've damn well got to go out and live in it. And crying over each other and clinging to each other and denying the rest of the world exists is sure as hell not the way to do it. That's a child's way, Laura. And if you haven't grown up enough by now to see it, then—then, damn it, I don't know. I can't help, I can only mess it up for you. If you're still a child, then go home. Go on back home to your mother and father where you'll be happy. Let *them* worry about you, let *them* take care of you. I can't; everything I do is wrong. Well, go back to your happy home and let your parents figure it out."

Laura put her head down on her arms, resting on the back of the desk chair, and never said a word. Beth wanted to see her temper, not her surrender. She wanted a fight and she persecuted Laura still further. She walked to Laura's chair and said, "The world is half men, Laura. The world is one-half men. Does that make sense? Well, does it?"

"Yes."

"And I like men, Laura. Now, that's honest. And I like Charlie. That's honest, too. Does it hurt enough for you? Honesty? Does it?"

"Yes."

"I like Charlie and I'm going to see Charlie, when I feel like it. Is that honest enough for you?"

"Yes."

Beth went to the closet and got her coat. "You can't

love a girl all your life, Laura. You can't be in love with a girl all your life. Sooner or later you have to grow up." She pulled the coat on and suddenly she couldn't look at Laura for knowing how horribly she had hurt her. It began to overwhelm Beth and she had to get out before it strangled her.

"Tell Mary Lou I had to go out, will you?" she said brusquely.

Laura lifted her head. "Where are you going?" she said. Her delicate face was discolored by the eruption of pain and on her underarms, where Beth couldn't see, her nails raised red welts, trying to call attention from the great pain with a lesser. "Where are you going, Beth?" she whispered.

"Out," said Beth.

"When will you be back?"

"Tonight. Closing." She paused at the door and looked at Laura. And she knew she'd never forget what she saw. Then she went out.

Downstairs in the hall she phoned Charlie. "This is Beth," she said. "Where's your final?"

"Math building."

"When will you be out?"

"About four, maybe sooner."

"I'll be at Maxie's."

"Honey, are you all right?"

"Yes. I'm all right."

"You sure?" He felt the tension and was doubtful.

"Yes. Charlie, I have to go."

"Okay, Maxie's." He hung up worried.

Beth went out and walked. She walked over to the campus, and across it to campus town, and down the block to Maxie's, half wild with pain and doubt and anger.

Girls didn't usually go into Maxie's alone, but Beth walked in without looking to right or left, stopped at the bar to get some beer—they didn't serve anything stronger —and found a dark booth in a back corner. There was only a small crowd and no one paid her much attention. She looked too grim for company.

She sat back there alone until almost four o'clock, with many trips to the bar for more beer. When Charlie found her she was slumped in the booth with her head back and her eyes closed. He slid in beside her and shook her gently.

"Beth . . . darling," he said.

She opened her eyes and looked at him as if she had never seen him before. And then she smiled.

"Let's get out of here," he said. He pulled her to her feet and helped her into her coat. She swayed a little, saying nothing and letting him steady her and lead her out into the cold air. He took her to his car and guided her in. "How long have you been there?" he said.

She put her head back on the seat. "Since two." She smiled a little at the ceiling of the car.

"Did you have any lunch?"

"Um-hm."

"What time?"

"Noon."

He started the car. "You need some black coffee, darling."

"No, Charlie." She turned her head on the seat and reached for the back of his neck. She stroked it with her long fingers and said, "No, Charlie. Come get drunk with me."

He looked at her with a curious smile. "What's the matter, Beth?"

"I won't tell you unless you get drunk with me."

"I don't want to get drunk."

"Yes you do, Charlie. Charlie, please, darling . . . yes, you do."

"What's got into you!"

She smiled. "Beer," she said. "I'm sick of beer. Can't we go somewhere and drink Martinis?"

Charlie laughed. "Oh, you're a funny girl." He caressed her hair with his hand.

"I know. You'll never find another like me, Charlie. Humor me, get drunk with me." She tickled his ears. "Please . . ."

He turned away, smiling a little out the windshield. "If I get you a Martini, will you tell me what the hell's the matter?"

"Um-hm."

"Promise?"

"Yes."

He paused a moment, and then he drove her downtown. There was a hotel two blocks from the railway station with a small bar in it and he took her there with some misgivings and a firm intention to drag her out after one drink.

She behaved very well. She didn't stumble or mumble and she wasn't loud. They sat quietly at a dark table and she teased him and they talked about nothing and pretty soon Beth wanted another drink.

"You said you'd tell me what the trouble was if I bought you one Martini," he said.

"Yes, I know. Well, I find I'll need two." She smiled charmingly at him.

"That's just what you don't need, darling. You're already loaded on beer. How much beer did you have?"

"Not very much."

"You were asleep when I came."

"I was not. I was thinking."

"Anyway, you promised you'd tell me after one Martini."

"Did I? I can't remember. It's a funny thing about me, Charlie. I never keep my promises. Never believe me when I promise you something."

"What's the trouble, Beth?"

"One more drink," she pleaded. He looked at her askance and she gave him a little-girl smile and said, "I'll be good. Honest." She felt a driving, desperate, relentless need to forget.

"I think you need some black coffee and some food."

"After this drink."

He shook his head. "I don't know," he said.

"Charlie . . ." Her voice was tender and soft. "Please."

With a sigh he signaled the waiter. "Two more," he said, and she smiled. He put his arm around her and said, "Now talk to me, Beth. Talk to me."

She cocked her head a little to one side and said with sleepy suggestiveness, "Charlie, let's go to bed. I want to go to bed with you, Charlie."

He smiled quizzically at her. "Later, honey."

"I want you to make love to me." She put her head back against him and looked up at him so that their lips were very near and Laura was very far away. "I want it. I want to be so close to you that I can't get any closer. I want you to hold me so tight that I can never get away . . . so it won't be my fault if I never go back. Can you hold me that tight, darling?"

Charlie felt his heart speed up and he tried to fight the feeling. "I'm worried about you, Beth. I'm worried," he said. He pushed an errant curl behind her ear and kissed her cheek and said, "Tell me why you want to get drunk."

She pulled away from him and lifted her glass and drank half the Martini. "I just want to get drunk. I like to get drunk. I haven't been drunk for years. Anything wrong with that? Besides, I can't think of anybody I'd rather get drunk with than you."

"That's the truth?"

"Um-hm."

"And nothing but the truth?"

"Yes."

"Beth?" His voice implied that he knew better.

She turned and looked him full in the face and said, "Charlie, I wouldn't lie to you," and shook her head to augment her honesty, and then she picked up her glass and finished her drink.

Charlie watched it go apprehensively. "Why not?" he said. "Why wouldn't you lie to me?"

"Why Charlie," she said, laughing a little. "Because you're the most beautiful man in the world. You know that, darling? You're beautiful."

"Yeah, I know." He grinned sardonically at his drink. "You told me once. But you can lie to anybody, Beth. Doesn't matter what they look like."

"Nobody ever told me that," she said. "Think of all the lies I could've told! I've been lying to the wrong people, Charlie. Maybe I should tell them the truth and see how they like it. Maybe they'd start telling lies themselves. It's awful to be the only one. It's lonesome."

He frowned seriously at her.

"One more drink," she said.

"No."

She picked up his glass and drank almost all the drink before he could stop her. "My God, you're a queer one," he said, laughing.

She put her head back and laughed with him. It seemed unbearably funny. "Oh!" she said, trying to catch her breath. "You called it, Charlie. You're so right. You have no idea—" and she laughed again. When she was calmer she leaned against him and turned her luscious eyes to his face and said, "Charlie, darling?"

"What?" he said, smiling at her.

"Can I excite you? Just looking at you, I mean?"

His mouth dropped a little and then his smile widened and he turned and fingered the stem of his glass. "Don't be foolish, honey."

"Charlie, look at me." He looked. "I'll bet I could."

"Not here, Beth. Not now."

"Oh, yes. Here and now."

"I think it's high time we leave," he said, making a move to get up, but she gripped his thigh and he stopped cold. "Beth, my God!" he said in a low voice. "Are you out of your head? Damn it, stop."

She didn't answer and she didn't obey. "Charlie," she said, smiling with her lips parted. "We can't go now. We can't go now, you'll make a spectacle of yourself."

"Beth—" He stared at her, astonished.

"Waiter!" she said, taking advantage of his confusion. The man saw her two raised fingers and nodded. And now when Beth started to pull her hand away, Charlie caught it and pulled it back. She felt his breath come fast and her own excitement began to mount. She leaned against him and said voluptuously, "We're going to have a nice slow drink. It'll calm your nerves."

"Beth, for God's sake," he said. "Oh, Jesus, Beth, you're crazy. You're absolutely crazy."

"I know. I'm crazy. That's my excuse. That's my excuse, Charlie. I need an excuse. I'm a girl in need of an excuse. You'd be surprised how I need—"

"I hear you," he said, smiling a little. "I need one myself right about now."

"What's it like, Charlie?"

"What's what like?" he said cautiously.

"What's it like to feel the way you do right now?"

"God, Beth," he said softly, and she felt a tremor run through him. "Stop talking, darling." He pushed her away.

The waiter brought their drinks.

"Beth, let's go," he whispered. "Let's go, honey."

"No," she said. "You haven't had your nice drink. Drink your Martini, darling, like a good boy."

"I don't want the damn drink. Damn the drinks. Let's go."

"No," she said and smiled at him. "You don't have to drink yours, but I'm going to drink mine." She drank half of it and leaned toward him. "How do you feel now, Charlie?"

"Beth, you damn little witch," he said.

"Tell me," she begged. "I want to know."

"I don't know," he said, "but I'm going to tear this God

damn table apart if we don't get out of here right now."

She patted his arm. "Drink your drink, dear. Maybe the table will go away."

"Beth," he pleaded. He trembled again and pulled her hard against him.

"Charlie, what will the neighbors think? I mean, we have to think of our reputations. I mean, my God, here we are in public, and everything." She felt giddily funny. Everything was funny. Charlie started to take her drink away from her, but she snatched it back and finished it, and some spilled on her blouse. "Charlie, darling, look what I've done. Wipe it off." She smiled at him like a malevolent siren. "Wipe it off, darling," she whispered.

He looked at the drops of liquor melting slowly into her cotton blouse and swallowed hard.

"You're sweating, Charlie," she said.

"Beth, we've got to go—"

"Oh, no!" she said. "Charlie, you can't."

"Can't, be damned. I have to."

"Your drink. You can't leave your drink."

He picked it up and drank it all down and set the glass hard against the table top. "All right, let's go." He got up holding his coat and pulled her after him. He put an arm around her to steady her, and guided her out of the bar.

They walked toward the car.

"Charlie, you're wonderful when you're drunk," she said. "You're wonderful when you're excited. I want to kiss you, darling."

He propelled her sternly toward the car and when they reached it he sighed with relief.

"Can we go back to the apartment?" she whispered when they pulled away from the curb.

"No. Mitch is there. We'll go out to the motel on Forty-five. Out near the air base."

"Anywhere," she said. She put her head down in his lap.

"Charlie, how long will it be? How far do we have to go, darling?"

"Beth, don't ask me questions. I've got all I can do to drive."

He reached down with one hand and tore her blouse open. Beth chuckled at him and heard the buttons chink on the floor. At stoplights he pulled her up and kissed her

violently, nearly crushing her. The tires screamed when
he rounded a corner and he drove a wild eighteen miles to
the motel.

He pulled Beth out of the car and into the room so fast
that he had her laughing again, dizzy and wild and hot,
like carousel music. He almost tore her clothes off her. He
didn't even turn the light on. She fell back on the bed
laughing, teasing him, pestering him, refusing to help with
her clothes.

"Oh, Beth," he said, and his voice was rough. "Beth,
God, I need you. God, I wish I understood you! Oh,
darling . . ." His groan thrilled her. She surrendered passionately to him and for a while she forgot her pain. For a
while there wasn't any pain, there was only a heady purify-
ing madness. She let her mind empty as her body was
fulfilled.

For a long time they lay in each other's arms, half asleep,
murmuring to each other, absorbed with each other.

"Feel better, darling?" he said. "Or do you want to go
out and get drunk again?" He laughed against her
shoulder.

"No. Don't have to . . . This'll last forever. Oh, Charlie,
I don't know what I'd do without you. I just don't know."

"I thought I caused all your troubles."

"Oh, let's not talk about troubles. Please . . ."

"Can't you tell me about it, honey?"

"Not now. Later. Please, later."

He lay still for a minute and then he said, with his lips
moving softly against her skin, "What am I going to do
with you, Beth? You worry me, darling. I don't know how
I'm going to leave you. I guess this is the first vacation I
haven't looked forward to since I started college. I'm—
almost afraid to leave you, Beth. I wish to hell I knew what
was the matter."

"Nothing's the matter. Nothing. Not now." She cuddled
against him.

He stroked her hair. "I wish I could believe that, honey."

After a while they got up. It was almost nine o'clock.
They were slow and sleepy getting into their clothes and
often they had to stop and hold each other. Every time they
separated, Beth felt the pain a little more. It was coming
back, little by ominous little.

"We'll stop on the way back and get something to eat,"
he said. "You must be starving."

Beth felt herself, as if that might clarify the matter, and said, "I don't know."

They stopped at a drive-in on the outskirts of town and got a couple of hamburgers and some coffee.

"Well," he said, "did you get Laura straightened out?"

"Straightened out?"

"Wasn't she giving you a hard time? Emmy said something—I don't know."

"Oh, she's just temperamental. She's just—I don't know. Let's not talk about Laura."

He was silent for a minute, eating his sandwich, and then he said, "Why didn't she want you to go out with me?"

"Oh—she had a crush on you. That's all." The bread and meat stuck suddenly as her throat went dry with alarm.

"No, she didn't."

"She did, darling. Anyway, how do you know she didn't?"

"Oh, hell, I don't know. I can tell. Can't you tell when someone has a crush on you?"

"Not always."

"Well, I can. And Laura didn't."

"Well, she did, Charlie. I talked to her. We—sort of had it all out."

"Why was this so hard to tell me?"

"It wasn't. It's not hard. I'm telling you."

"The last time I saw you you couldn't. It was so damn difficult you couldn't even think about it."

Beth forced herself to swallow; she was beginning to feel edgy with anxiety. "Oh, well—I hadn't talked to Laura, then. I didn't have a chance. I didn't want to say anything until I talked to her."

He raised an eyebrow at her. "Well? What did you say when you talked to her?"

"Oh, I told her she was behaving like a child. I was kind of nasty, I guess. I said she was acting like a spoiled brat and spoiled brats belong at home with their doting parents."

"My God, you *were* nasty. Jesus, honey, that was pretty low, wasn't it?"

She frowned at him. "What do you mean? It wasn't so bad. She *was* acting like a child. I just told her if she couldn't act grown up she'd better go back to her family where she belongs. Where somebody'll take care of her."

"She can't, Beth."

"She can't?"

"Didn't she tell you? I mean, didn't you know?"

"Know what?" Beth put her hamburger down, feeling suddenly sick. The incipient hangover, the passion, the overcooked beef, combined to aggravate her misery.

"They're divorced. Happened just before she came down to school. I guess it was pretty bad. Anyway, Laura was all upset about it." He paused. "You didn't know this?"

Beth shook her head.

"That's why I kept taking her out. She needed a shoulder to cry on. Poor kid. She really needed somebody. She was terribly alone. Still is, I guess. I felt sorry for her. My God, didn't she tell you all this?"

"She didn't tell anybody."

"You'd think she'd've told you. I mean, roommates . . . you know."

Beth held her head. "Oh, Charlie, I feel awful. Oh, I feel awful."

"Honey, are you going to be sick?"

"I guess so," she whispered.

"Yes, you are," he said with a swift critical glance. "Come on, here we go. Can you make it to the ladies' room?"

"I don't know."

He led her as fast as he could to the john. She made it just inside the door, fell to her knees and let the sickness flow out of her. Ten minutes later she came out, very pale.

"Charlie, I want to go home," she said. "I want to go home."

"I know. I'll take you home. You're going to be all right, darling, don't worry." He took her out to the car and drove her back to the house. She said nothing, leaning heavily against him and moaning a little now and then.

At the house he stopped and took her in his arms. "Poor little girl," he said. "Feel any better?"

"A little."

"Darling, that was my last exam today. How long will you be down here?"

"Day after tomorrow. Leave at noon."

"Will I see you?"

"Charlie— Oh, darling, I—"

"Okay," he said. "When will you be back?"

"February sixth."

"I'll be here the fifth. In case you come early."

"Charlie." She sat up a little and looked at him. "Darling, oh, I've been a bitch. Oh, Charlie, I'm a mess. Darling, I—"

"I love you, Beth," he said. And he kissed her.

She clung to him for a minute and then she said, "I love you, Charlie." It was plain and awesome honesty and it felt deliriously good.

He took her face in his hands. "Beth, take good care of yourself. Take good care of yourself, darling."

FIFTEEN

Eᴍɪʟʏ and Laura had a brief, bitter exchange of words. Laura precipitated it. She simply looked up from her studies and said, with no introduction, "Emmy, why did you call Charlie?" She was immediately sorry she had said it, but she was frantically worried about Beth and desperately unhappy.

Emily was startled. "Well—" she said. "She wanted to see him, Laur. It seemed as if it was the only way. I didn't mean to hurt your feelings about it."

"How did you know she wanted to see him?"

"I could just tell, Laur."

"Did it ever occur to you that Beth might not want to go out with him?"

"No, it never did," said Emmy. This wasn't the Laura Landon of last fall: passive, pleasant, unemotional.

"I don't understand why you don't know Beth any better than you do, Emmy. Sometimes I think you don't know her at all," Laura snapped.

"Laura, Beth wanted to go out with him. She didn't have to go, you know, even after I called him."

"Well, of course she had to go out with him, after she talked to him. What could she say?"

"I don't know, Laur. What could she say?"

Laura went suddenly cold. Her eyes dropped and she fumbled with her book. "I don't know," she said in a small voice.

"Why don't you want Beth and Charlie to go out together, Laur?" Emmy's voice was soft. If what she suspected were true, why hadn't Beth been honest with her about it? Beth had never deliberately lied to her before about anything.

"They just—aren't right for each other, that's all."

"How do you know?"

"Because I know Beth!" Laura flared.

"But you don't know Charlie very well."

Laura turned on her. "Emmy, what are you trying to say?"

136

Emmy, confronted with an angry challenge, was silent.

Laura rose slowly to her feet. "I'm going to bed," she said icily and walked stiffly to the door.

Emmy sat on the couch uncomfortably. She had no desire to stay in the room, either. It had suddenly become a sinister, unfamiliar place to her. She gathered some books together, scribbled a note to Beth and ran down the hall.

At ten thirty-five, Beth found the note on her dresser: "Laur's in bed. I'm in Bobbie's room. Come get me if you want me. I'll be up late. Love, Em."

Beth crumpled the note and tossed it into the wastebasket, and undressed. She looked at her blouse with the little rips now in place of buttons, and thought of Charlie. But all the cutting words she directed at Laura that afternoon came back to torment her.

She went to the washroom to clean up, and when she got back to the room, Laura was in it. She was standing looking out the window toward the street with her back to Beth. Beth said nothing. She put her things away and stood at her dresser for a minute, silent.

"Beth," said Laura softly. "I was wrong." She had learned her lesson. The only way to bring Beth back was to be gentle and yielding with her. It worked before where even the most righteous temper failed. Beth scolded her for being a child, but Laura knew she liked her best that way. Laura was willing to play the game—any game—if it meant keeping Beth.

"If you need Charlie, I guess you should have him," Laura said. She didn't turn around; she spoke to the windowpanes.

Beth regarded her back. "Laura, I was hateful to you. I was unforgivable."

"Let's not talk about it. I don't want to talk about it. You're forgiven, Beth."

Beth put her arms around her and her head down against Laura's. "Laura," she whispered.

"I understand. At least, I'll try to understand."

"Laura . . . I need you, honey." I can't just drop you, so hard, so suddenly. And besides, you're so sweet . . . so sweet to hold. Not good like Charlie, but . . . I wonder, if I could have you both.

Laura turned around and put her arms around Beth and looked up at her. "Beth," she said humbly. "Will we be together—just once in a while?"

"Yes, honey." Beth kissed her forehead. "Yes, we will."
Behind them Emmy pushed the door open. Beth had
forgotten to close it all the way and it didn't make a sound.
Emmy stood staring.

"Oh, I'm so glad," Laura whispered. "It's all right, then.
I'll be all right, if I can have that."

"Of course you can, baby. Oh Laur, I hurt you so."

"You could never hurt me too much, Beth. You can
never teach me by hurting me. I just come back for more.
I guess I'll never learn. I love you too much. I love you
so much."

They kissed each other's lips and Beth liked the velvety
softness of Laura's mouth. She could command Laura the
way Charlie commanded her. But the authority fulfilled
and invigorated Charlie; it only amused Beth and left her
empty.

Emmy stood watching them, transfixed and soundless,
while Beth rocked Laura gently in her arms and whispered,
"We'll work it out, honey. Don't worry." And then Emmy
pulled the door to very quietly, and without letting it catch,
and left. She walked down the hall shivering nervously,
wondering what to do. She stared unseeing at the bulletin
board in the hall with her head full of the strange scene
she had just witnessed and the details of it so vivid that she
could think of nothing else.

After a little while she heard soft voices down the hall.
She turned around and saw Beth and Laura coming toward
her.

"Beth?" she said, with a humane impulse to warn them
of her presence.

Beth looked up. "Oh, Emmy," she said. "I thought you
were in Bobbie's room."

Emmy hesitated, feeling strangely uncomfortable, and
Laura started up the stairs to bed.

"What, Em?" said Beth. She glanced quickly at Laura.
"Go on up, Laur," she whispered. "See you in the morning." She looked back at Emmy and Emmy found she
couldn't say it; she couldn't ask.

"How's Charlie?" she said.

Beth relaxed then and gave her a radiant smile. "Wonderful," she said. "I'm in love." And she went upstairs to
bed, leaving Emmy confounded. She knew she would
have to talk to Beth about Laura, she couldn't keep the
things she had seen and heard locked inside of her. But

she would wait, she decided, until the next night. Then Beth and she would be alone for the first time in months— Laura would have left for her semester vacation. So Emmy kept her peace for almost twenty-four hours and then discovered, when the time came for her to speak, that she didn't know how to broach the subject.

She looked at Beth with a sort of new timidity and said, dismayed to find her voice raspy, "Beth?"

"Hm?"

"Beth—"

Beth looked at her. "Why, Emmy, whatever is the matter? You look as if you—" She stopped, wondering. "Emmy, what's the matter?"

"Well—well, I— Beth?" She walked over to her, as if it were too difficult to send her words across the room, and took a deep breath. "Is Laura in love with you?" she asked finally.

"Oh," said Beth, and her face went very pale. She put her head down for a moment and said, "Oh, Emmy . . ."

"I know she is. I heard her say it last night. I had to tell you."

"Oh, Em."

"Beth, I won't tell. I won't ever ever tell. I promise." Emmy held her shoulders and watched her anxiously. Beth couldn't talk. "Do you love her, too?"

Beth lifted her head. "Emmy—come sit on the couch. Listen to me."

They sat down together and Beth tried to explain what had happened to her, and she tried to be honest. Emmy listened without saying a word, watching Beth's face intently. Finally Beth looked up at her and said, "You see, Emmy? Why it's been so hard? Now I'm in love with Charlie. Really in love. But I can't hurt Laura any more. I just can't. I can only wait till it wears off. Till she grows out of it and forgets about me, without my having to hurt her."

"Wouldn't it hurt her less just to tell her you don't want to do it any more?"

Beth played nervously with a cigarette. "Yes, I guess it would. But—you see—that's not it, exactly. I'm not in love with her. *That's* what I ought to tell her. But—"

"You mean you—still want her?" It was as weird and wonderous to Emmy as sorcery would have been.

"Yes," said Beth. She looked at Emmy with a worried frown. "Em, you must think I'm terrible."

"Oh, Beth, I don't think you're terrible at all." She leaned toward her sympathetically. "I couldn't think you were terrible—we're friends, Beth. I just—I just don't get it, that's all. Why do you want a girl when you could have a man? I mean, why does a girl want a girl? Ever? I mean —well—" She laughed a little. "What is there to want?"

"Oh, Emmy, I don't know how to tell you. I was just— we were both lonely. We just happened to be lonely at the same time in the same place, that's all. It was too easy. It was so good to have somebody to—hold, to talk to . . . sort of play with and play at making love."

"But Laura isn't playing. She is in love. I heard her say so."

"Oh, she thinks she is. She's just so young, she doesn't know. These things never last."

"How do you know?"

"Oh, Em, when you go to a girl's boarding school, you just know. It happens all the time. You grow out of it. It doesn't last. It's just part of growing up. Didn't you ever have a crush on a girl?"

Emmy searched her memory. "No," she said doubtfully. "I don't think so. Oh, once when I was about twelve, I guess . . . No, I don't think that was really a crush . . ." She looked at Beth.

"Well, maybe not."

"Anyway, there were always so many boys around and they were so much more fun. Well, I mean—" She hunched her shoulders.

"I know, I know. It never happens to some people. And it does to others. That's all."

"Beth, how do you know it won't last with Laura? I mean, some people never grow out of childish things, if this is a childish thing. How do you know?"

"Oh, because Laur's a sensible girl. She's sentimental, but she's—well, she's just timid. She hasn't known enough men. She's afraid of them. When she gets over that she'll be all right." She had to be all right.

"Well, I guess you ought to know. But some people go through all their lives queer. Oh, I don't mean you, Beth! I guess that's not a very nice word."

"Oh, it's just a word. What's in a word?"

"Besides, you're in love with a man."

"Yes, I am. Oh, I am, Emmy, I am!"

"Well, how can you love two people at once, Beth?"

"I can't. That's the whole trouble. I'm in love only with Charlie. But don't you see, Em—Laura can't be in love with me forever. I mean, a schoolgirl crush just doesn't last that long. I know, I've had them. You get over them. She'll get used to the idea of dating—of having me date, too—and pretty soon she'll begin to forget about it. And nobody gets hurt. Do you see?"

"Yeah. If it works."

"Emmy, you mustn't worry. Now that she understands about Charlie, there won't be any more trouble. That was the whole trouble before."

"Does she understand about him?"

"Oh, yes." Beth crushed the cigarette out in a bean-bottomed ashtray.

"Does she know you love him?"

"She knows I need him, Em." Emmy frowned at her. "Oh, Em, believe me, I know what I'm doing." She spoke heartily, in order to convince herself. "There won't be any more trouble now. We all understand each other. Everything's going to be all right. Really."

"Does Charlie understand about Laura?"

"Oh, no!" said Beth, and the idea shocked her. "He'll never know."

"I hope not," Emmy said. "Well, okay, Beth, I trust you." She had never seen Beth in a situation she couldn't handle.

Beth was right, for a while. She and Charlie were happy, Laura seemed to be happy, and even Mitch seemed to have deserted his books for a gay social life. He'd called Mary Lou and they were seeing a great deal of each other. Even Bud had settled down to a steady routine. He'd given Emmy his fraternity pin, which was in the nature of a minor miracle. Bud had managed to elude every other girl he'd known and leave them unscathed, his pin still firmly attached to his old tennis sweater. But Emmy had won and she was triumphant. She was teased, however.

As Beth put it to Laura, "That's just the first plateau. She's trying for the sixty-four-thousand-dollar ring." Laura laughed and Beth went on. "She'll never make it. Not with that guy. She'd better switch categories pronto."

Mary Lou said hopefully, "Maybe she'll calm down now and stop panting over him in public."

And so the month went by, peaceful on the surface, but boiling dangerously just below the surface.

The first week in March brought sorority initiation. Laura became a full-fledged Alpha Beta with a pin like Beth's. And she and Beth shared a sentimental bond that Charlie couldn't break.

It eased Laura to think about it on dreary weekends when Beth and Emmy were out with Charlie and Bud and she sat at home alone and studied, for she wasn't going out very much any more. She wouldn't have at all, except when Beth insisted on it, and then she accepted a blind date only to keep peace.

"You've got to go out once in a while, Laur. My God, you dated every week last fall. It'd look just too damn strange if you suddenly quit for no reason."

So she sighed and did as Beth told her. The nicest part of the weekend was at closing hours when Beth came in and Emmy went to bed. Emmy usually went off discreetly and it struck Laura as simple good luck. Beth never told her that Emmy knew.

Once, Laura asked, "Emmy doesn't suspect anything, does she? I mean, I was pretty temperamental a couple of times. Do you think she suspected?"

And Beth laughed and mussed up her hair and said, "Laur, honey, you worry about all the wrong things." And Laura, as always, took her cue from Beth. Beth wasn't worried, so there was nothing to worry about. Beth didn't think they were doing anything wrong, so they weren't.

Usually when Beth came in she was in a good humor. She wanted to tease and play and cuddle Laura and she was easily roused. It seemed to Laura then that Beth would always come back to her, however far she wandered; that she alone could satisfy her, make her happy. But now and then Beth came in quiet and uncommunicative, simply too satisfied for more passion. And then Laura wondered.

Sometimes Beth was a little drunk and then Laura sulked at her. Beth would tickle her to make her giggle and then laugh at her pout.

"Beth, you've been drinking," she would say.

"Not against the law, honey. I'm of age."

"That's not the point. I think it's disgusting." And she would turn her back on Beth's amusement.

"Laura, forgive me," Beth would plead and laugh at her.

"You smell of gin."

Beth squeezed her and said, "You don't even know what gin smells like."

"I do too!"

"Okay, I smell of gin. I guess you don't want me around. I guess I'd better just go off and leave you alone."

"No, Beth!" And she turned around and caught her arm as Beth started to rise.

Beth pushed her away. "Oh, but I smell of gin, remember? Laur, I don't know how you put up with me. I swear I don't know."

And then Laura would have to beg her to stay and protest that she didn't care what her breath smelled like. But she did.

SIXTEEN

In the middle of March Bud's fraternity gave a costume dance, an annual affair for which the girls were required to make their own costumes. They were given one square yard of bright colored cotton for that purpose and the one who returned the largest piece of unused cloth won first prize. Some used the whole cloth out of necessity, some out of modesty, and some used as little as they dared.

Emmy used as little as she dared. She achieved a sort of bikini effect much admired by the men and frowned upon by the conservative element in Alpha Beta, headed by Mary Lou. Before she went out Emmy modeled her creation in the upstairs hall.

"Emmy, I think that's a little—bare," said Mary Lou.

"Oh, heck, Mary Lou, there'll be a dozen others just like it."

"Well, I know, but it's awfully revealing."

The girls laughed at her and said, "Oh, they all wear 'em now, Mary Lou."

"I think she looks great."

"Emmy, if you don't win first prize, nobody can."

"Just don't sneeze," said Beth.

The buzzer sounded and Emmy said, "Oh, there's Bud!" and scampered down the stairs.

Laura watched her go a little spitefully. The thought that Emmy had brought Charlie and Beth together again still rankled inside her. Her sense told her it would have happened anyway; her heart told her it was Emmy's fault. She said to Beth, "Emmy has a pretty figure, doesn't she?"

"Oh, Emmy has a beautiful figure."

That was enough to make Laura hate it. She was even jealous of Emmy. Emmy and Beth were such good friends, Emmy was so pretty, Laura so plain. When Beth and Emmy laughed or talked to each other she found it irritating in the extreme. And yet she knew nothing could be less likely than erotic intimacies between them, and during the span of quiet rational daytime hours she calmed herself, combed out her snarled affections and sprayed them with logic so they might last smoothly through the evening.

After Emmy went out Mary Lou came in to talk to Beth.

"Hi, Mrs. Mitchell Grogan," said Beth with a grin. "When are you going out?"

Laura looked up from the couch, and Mary Lou laughed and said, "Oh, Mitch is coming over around eight. Say, Beth—" She grew suddenly serious. "Did you talk to Emmy?"

Beth felt a guilty pang shoot through her. "Why? Is something wrong?"

"Well—no, not really. But I just don't like it when she wears such a revealing costume to a big dance. I didn't know it was going to be that bare or I would have told her myself."

"None of us saw it before tonight, Mary Lou. In fact she finished it only this afternoon."

"Well, I didn't see it till just now or I'd've stopped her. But—what can you do?" She wrinkled her brow and sighed. "Bud came, and she was all ready to go out. Everybody stands around approving and it's the night of the party. I can't order her not to wear the thing. But I wish she'd use her head. I've been worried about her for months."

It made Beth feel rather nervously defensive. "She's been behaving herself," she said. "She doesn't act up in public."

"Oh, Beth, I've seen her so full of beer at parties—"

"That's just a big act, Mary Lou. Most of it."

"Well, not all of it. I've seen her drink the beer."

"She doesn't drink too much—just likes a good time."

"I'll say she likes a good time. Remember that afternoon at Maxie's when she was kissing Bud?"

"Oh, hell. Everybody kisses everybody at Maxie's."

"Yes, but not up on the bandstand. And not like Bud was kissing Emmy."

"Oh, Mary Lou, don't worry about her. You'd be surprised how sensible she can be."

"I certainly would."

Beth laughed and said, "Oh, come on. Don't worry. I'll answer for her."

"Okay, if you'll talk to her again. If you don't, I will."

"I will, Mary Lou." Bud was a party boy, and Beth knew it. He liked to whoop it up and he expected Emmy to keep up with him. He expected, in fact, quite a lot of Emmy, and Emmy wouldn't disappoint him. But she tried to make him play the game her way; he had to stay within certain bounds, and the bounds were simply discretion, meaning privacy. Unfortunately, the bounds became hazy and Bud began to step over them now and again.

Bud and Emmy hadn't gone to the dance directly, it turned out. They went to a party where beer flowed, spirits rose, and time wandered by unmarked. At a quarter of midnight someone shouted, "My God! The dance!"

They scrambled out and into their cars and made it over to the house five minutes before the orchestra packed up to leave. They were welcomed with a cheer and the girls surrendered their left-over costume material to a committee of judges, which, after a thirty-second squabble, gallantly pronounced Emily the winner.

Amidst the uproar following, Bud picked Emmy up by the waist and lifted her over his head. Flashbulbs flowered around them. He let her down again and she was giggling helplessly, clinging to him for support.

"Hey, pick her up again!" someone shouted. "Nielsen! Hey, boy, ya hear me? Pick her up again!"

"No!" said Emily, clutching Bud.

"Hey, we want another picture. Once more. Come on, Emmy!"

"No!"

"Emmy, you're chicken!"

"Hey, come on, Em," Bud said. "It won't hurt you."

"No, I won't do it. I don't want them to take pictures."

Bud dug his fingers into her ribs and she screamed and laughed, wriggling to be free. With a wretched disregard for discretion the top of her costume suddenly split open, and the evening took an unexpected saturnalian turn. Emmy gasped and covered her dazzling front with her arms and whirled to face Bud, who was laughing as he had never laughed before. He took her in his arms and the general hilarity got them both. Everyone shouted at Emmy to turn around again and somebody finally rescued her with a leather jacket, tossed over the heads of the crowd. The others booed the rescuer.

Bud reached out and caught the sailing jacket and Emily cried, "Oh, Bud, don't let me go!" and everybody cheered. When she had the thing safely on she went to the powder room and got her coat and wrapped herself securely in thick gray wool. She was indisputably the queen of the evening, and in spite of her embarrassment she was so roundly and good-naturedly flattered that the accident didn't seem like quite such a calamity.

Several of the girls who convoyed her to and from the powder room were Alpha Betas. They were laughing because the atmosphere of laughter was irresistible, but they knew, and Emmy knew, that there would be trouble.

"Well," said Emmy, "I certainly didn't do it on purpose. Nobody could say that."

"I hate to think what Mary Lou's going to say," said one of the Alpha Betas. "We can't possibly keep it a secret. Everybody'll be talking about it."

Emmy said in alarm, "Do you think they got any pictures of it?"

"Oh, my God! I hope not!"

"I don't think so," said another girl. "You turned around so fast. I don't think anybody had time."

"Well, pictures or no, Em, you're going to have to explain it somehow."

Emmy shrugged. "My costume broke, that's all. Heavens, it was double stitched. I don't know how it could have happened."

"Maybe you were sabotaged."

"What?"

"Maybe somebody cut the threads."

Emmy laughed, but she disallowed the suggestion.

She got home at closing hours, and ran breathless up to the room. Beth was just undressing and Laura was still up. Emmy came in laughing and threw herself down on the couch. Beth shut the door hastily and ran to her.

"Emmy!" she said, and Emmy laughed even harder. Beth had to laugh with her, while Laura remained disdainfully aloof. "Emmy, what happened? Tell me."

Emmy sat up slowly and said theatrically, "Look," and unbuttoned her coat. Laura gasped, and Beth stared wide-eyed at her for a minute and then she began to laugh.

"Oh, Emmy," she exclaimed when she could catch her breath. "My God, it broke!"

Laura watched their laughter, properly disapproving. Finally Beth began to get serious.

"Emmy, what happened?" she said. "Was it bad?"

"Oh—" Emmy slowed down a little. "It was just one of those things." She giggled again. "Bud was tickling me— Oh, guess what? I won first prize!"

Beth had to chuckle at her again. She threw her hands up and slapped her knees. "Emmy, you're impossible!" she said. "Okay, now be serious. What happened?"

"Well, it just ripped, that's all."

"With how many people gaping at you?"

"I don't know. Oh, I grabbed it, of course. I turned right around and Bud held me so nobody could see."

"After everybody saw."

"Well, Beth, I couldn't help it," Emmy protested, laughing again. "Oh, I was horribly embarrassed. But it was so funny!"

The door snapped open and Mary Lou bristled in. She shut the door after her and leaned on it.

"Emmy . . ." she said and paused, her face solemn. "What happened?"

Emmy stood up, still smiling. "Oh, it wasn't so awful, Mary Lou. It was just an accident."

"Well, I want to know just exactly what happened. Everybody's talking about it, Emmy. It'll be all over the campus by tomorrow. Now tell me." Her voice trembled with indignation and she was pale and earnest. She found no humor in the situation at all. It was a social fiasco that reflected directly on the good name of Alpha Beta.

"Well, I won first prize for my costume and everybody was sort of cheering and teasing me while they took pictures, and Bud tickled me and I sort of—jerked away from him, and the bra broke. That's all. I couldn't help it, Mary Lou. I didn't do it on purpose."

"They took pictures?" Mary Lou looked stricken, and Beth watched her with a worried frown. Anybody could have pleaded Emmy's case better than Emmy pleaded it herself.

"Oh, they didn't take pictures of that. I mean, I'm sure they didn't. Oh, Mary Lou, don't look so grim! You frighten me." She laughed, but Mary Lou didn't even smile.

"Emmy, we're going to have a talk about this. You and me and Sarah and Bobbie." They were the ranking house officers; Bobbie was one of Emmy's good friends.

"Mary Lou, you act as if you thought I did this on purpose. I'd never do such a thing."

"The house is in for a lot of bad publicity about this, Emmy. We have to agree on something to say. The dean is going to want to see you, and so are the alumnae."

Emmy sobered up suddenly. "Oh, no," she said. "Do you really think so? But it was just an accident."

"Be in my room tomorrow morning at nine," said Mary Lou. "And don't talk to anybody about it before then."

"Okay," said Emmy, and Mary Lou went out, leaving her honestly worried.

"Gee, Beth," Emmy said, turning anxious eyes on her. "What'll they do to me?"

"I don't know, Em. Depends on how it goes over on campus, I guess. Don't worry, Emmy, it wasn't your fault." Beth felt the weight of a new blame on her shoulders. She had failed both Emmy and Mary Lou. She could have warned Emmy to slow down, if she'd only had the eyes to see how fast she was going, if she'd only remembered Mary Lou's warning. But she had been too engrossed in her strange little triangle. Emmy was outside that triangle, so Emmy's troubles didn't count. Nobody had troubles but Beth Cullison, and now Beth was ashamed of her selfishness.

Beth wanted to go with Emmy to the meeting the next morning, but Mary Lou said no. So it was Mary Lou, Sarah, who was vice president, and Bobbie, who was secretary, who faced Emmy that morning.

Mary Lou, with her customary unbudging justice, and Sarah, who usually agreed with her, thought Emily and Bud should shake hands and call it quits. The dean had called and arranged a conference with Emily. The incident was in the town papers and the campus was having a good laugh. The faculty and the alumnae of Alpha Beta were furious. Emmy began to feel a little desperate.

"Can anyone possibly think I did it on purpose?" she said.

"Look, Emmy," said Mary Lou. "We know you didn't do it on purpose. That isn't the point. The point is that it happened and it happened to you. And you were very drunk and very bare and in mixed company at the time. Nobody's saying you deliberately undressed in public, but if you'd been willing to wear a little more costume in the first place this wouldn't have happened at all. And this came on top of four months of a pretty hot romance that everybody's been talking about. You just haven't been too careful, Emily. You just haven't cared very much about anything but yourself and Bud."

"But I have, Mary Lou."

"You've completely ignored your obligations to the university and the sorority. You've disgraced us all and it could have been prevented."

"I don't see—" Emmy was near tears.

"It could have, Emmy, if you hadn't insisted on being the barest girl at the party. If you hadn't gone out and gotten drunk."

"I wasn't the only one—"

"If you hadn't led Bud to expect that he could treat you—" she cast about for a word— "promiscuously in public and get away with it."

"It wasn't promiscuous. He was just tickling me. I mean —heavens, it was just—" She stopped, sensing that her own words did her a disservice.

"Well, just what kind of behavior do you think that is, Emmy—proper? What do you think a man thinks of when he sees a girl squirming and wriggling in practically no clothes at all?"

"I didn't ask him to tickle me, Mary Lou."

"Yes you did, Emmy. Don't you see? For the past four months you've been letting him tickle you; you just never told him not to. You let him do it and you let him know you like it. What more do you have to do for a man? Spell it for him?"

Emmy hung her head.

"Emily," said Mary Lou and her voice grew kind again. "I'm not trying to hurt you. Believe me, I'm not. I'm trying to do what I can for the sorority. And it, as a whole, is more important right now than the individual, because it's within the power of an individual to do the whole group a harm, to punish everybody for her one mistake. Well, we have to correct that mistake. We can't let everyone point at Alpha Beta and laugh because one Alpha Bete did something wrong. That one Alpha Bete has to correct the error. It's simple logic, and it's only fair."

Emmy rubbed her head. Simple logic was the hardest kind for her. It always struck her as being inarguable and senseless at the same time. She was awed by it.

Mary Lou sighed and ditched her cigarette. "Emmy, it's up to you," she said. "I don't want to impose any silly useless detention on you. I don't even want to campus you. You'll see the dean; you'll talk it over. I know you'll be sensible about it."

"What can I do?" said Emmy.

"Well . . ." Mary Lou looked around at the others and then sighed and looked back at Emily. "Em, I know you're terribly fond of Bud. I guess that's been the cause of the difficulty, really."

Emmy nodded. It seemed as if Mary Lou was beginning to understand her now and wanted to help her; it gave her a false sense of security.

"And I know too, how much affection you have for the sorority, for the university . . ."

Emmy nodded fervently again.

"Well, somehow the two just don't seem compatible. I know it's hard, Emmy . . ."

Emmy didn't get it at all for a minute.

"But—I think we have to take a positive step right now. Undo the wrong, sort of . . ."

"Oh, yes, I do too," said Emily, walking innocently, willingly, into the trap.

"And I think you just have to make a choice."

"A choice?"

"Yes. Because if you keep on like this, Em, the university and the sorority are going to suffer. That's all there is to it."

"Oh, but Mary Lou, I won't keep on. I mean, the party's over." She couldn't believe they would be so harsh. She laughed a little apprehensively as the light began to dawn.

"Is it, Emmy?" Mary Lou's bright, steady eyes hurt her.

"Well, of course."

"Emmy, I think it might be a good idea—for all of us, and especially for you—if you didn't see Bud for a while."

Emmy stared at her, speechless and appalled. "But I love him," she whispered finally.

"I think that's exactly the trouble, Emmy. I think you either ought to leave school and marry the guy, or not see him for a while. I think the temptation is just too great." She said it very kindly.

"But my parents would never let me leave school. My father has his heart set on my getting my degree." *And Bud might not marry me.* Brought face to face with the problem she admitted it to herself for the first time.

"Then I think you ought not to see Bud for a while."

Emmy was thunderstruck, trapped. "For a while?" she murmured in a hardly audible voice.

Bobbie put an arm around her and said, "Don't cry."

"For a while," Mary Lou repeated. "It's the only way, Emmy. I think you're headed straight for real trouble, otherwise. And you're pulling all of us after you. Don't you see, Emmy? It's for everybody's good, really. It won't be forever."

Emmy saw; she saw very clearly now. She tried to steady her breath. "What if I do see him?" She couldn't help asking; it was a last feeble gesture of independence. "What if I keep on seeing him?"

"It's your duty not to, Em."

"But what would happen if I did?" It had the fascination of calamity for her.

"Well—" Mary Lou looked down at her lap and found it hard to talk, hard to do what she cherished as her duty, to hit just the right tone—firm but compassionate. "Then I think—I think you would be happier outside the sorority."

It took Emmy's breath away from her for a minute. "You mean you'd jerk my pin?" It was preposterous. "You'd blackball me?"

"Oh, Emmy," said Mary Lou, and she patted her arm sympathetically. It was hard to do the right thing, but this was indubitably the right thing. "Emmy, don't say it that way. We wouldn't blackball you. I think we should just have a sort of agreement. If everything works out, you'll see Bud again. It just means time to think it over, time to get to know yourself."

"But you don't know Bud." Emmy put her head down in her hands. It might be love, all right, but with Bud she had to keep feeding the flame. She had to be with him every day, reminding him how pretty, how bright and sweet she was, or he would find someone else. It was that simple. *That* was logic.

She looked up. The three girls were watching her, a jury of friendly executioners, waiting for her answer. She knew they were all of the same mind—Mary Lou's mind. Even Bobbie, who gave her a squeeze and said, "Emmy, I think it might be a good idea."

Emily leaned against her and wept for a few minutes. The sorority had her in a corner; there was no help for her. At last she whispered, "All right," and got up and hurried from the room.

SEVENTEEN

Beth was warmly sympathetic in spite of her misgivings about Bud; she was needled by a sense of guilt and the thought of her own adventures with Charlie. She said over and over, "Emmy, I should have warned you, I should have seen it coming. It's my fault, Em."

But Emmy wouldn't have it that way.

"They're such damn hypocrites," Beth fumed. "They know you aren't the only one who's made a few concessions. My God, they do it themselves, a lot of them. It's just that the one who gets caught gets punished. You were just too much in love to be very cautious, I guess. I guess you really are in love, Emmy, aren't you?"

Emmy's tears answered her.

"Damn," Beth muttered. "They really cash in on that prestige of theirs, don't they? They know there's no disgrace quite so humiliating as getting blackballed out of the sorority. The whole campus talks about you for months. Suddenly you haven't any friends. Why? Because you left them all back in the sorority. And you've left the sorority for good. And then what happens? You can't stand it after a while. You're an outcast, a failure. You're nowhere socially. You're ashamed and lonesome. And pretty soon you call it quits and leave school. Maybe you go somewhere else, maybe you don't. But all over the country, on any campus, that sorority blackball will haunt you every time you try to join a club. They'll find out about it, and there you'll be, right back where you started. God, it makes me sick."

Bud exploded when he found out what had happened. He was furious, frustrated, bitter against the powers that be in universities and sororities. He cut his classes for a week and spent all his time, filled to his ears with beer, in Maxie's basement. He played till his lip gave out and he complained to anyone who would listen to him. It was his way of handling a problem. Bud could make sweet music and sweet girls; he could be supremely pleasant with anybody, anywhere; but he couldn't make or follow a plan, and order and progress were hostile to his happiness.

He was artist enough to admire ideals, but he never pursued them. However, they took Emily away from him at just the time when he had decided that she was one of his ideals, and the sudden loss made her more desirable—not less, as Emily had feared.

"I love that girl," he muttered moodily. "The only girl I ever loved. And what do they do? They take her away from me."

Charlie swatted him on the back. "Cheer up, boy," he said. "This won't last forever. You'll be seeing her. Beth says they'll parole her for good behavior." Charlie had heard the story a dozen times.

"Yeah, sure. When? What the hell am I supposed to do in the meantime? I tell ya, Ayers, I'm going nuts. I can't stand it. Who the hell do they think they are? Who the hell—"

"Okay, boy, take it easy."

"Yeah, take it easy. You gotta help me out. What am I gonna do? Help me out, boy."

Charlie gave him a lot of free advice. . . .

Beth complained to Charlie, too. "It's a damn dirty trick," she said. "God, it makes me mad! There's only one aspect of the whole thing that might do any good, and that's that Bud was never meant for Emmy—or any girl, for that matter. He couldn't support a wife or kids. My God, can you imagine Bud Nielsen with *kids* on his hands? He'd give 'em all slide whistles before they could walk and send 'em out to make their own living."

Charlie laughed at her.

"No one's fonder of Emmy than I am," she added, "but she'll do anything for a man she thinks she's in love with. She hasn't the sense she was born with. She'd never get caught if she'd use her head, but she wants to please Bud. Will she say no to Bud? No, she will not. And do they catch her in bed with him? No, they do not. That's too easy. Her damn silly costume breaks and all of a sudden she's a scarlet woman. An accident. God, it's ironic, isn't it?"

Charlie nodded.

"Well, maybe she'll cool off, now. See Bud for what he is."

"What is he, honey? You're pretty damn hard on him."

"Oh, Bud Nielsen is a bum. A born bum. Let's face it."

"A bum? I don't know, Beth. He's a nice guy."

"Sure, he's a nice guy. He's a great guy. Everybody likes him. And he'll never amount to a row of beans."

"Well, I don't know." Bud was a good friend of Charlie's.

"Oh, Charlie, he's been an undergraduate for six years. The guy hasn't even enough ambition to leave school, for God's sake. Emmy's as much in love with that trombone as she is with Bud. He's a big wheel on campus—talented, everybody knows him. I'd never tell her, but I'm kind of glad they'll be separated for a while. I think they'll both come to their senses. I hope they will."

Charlie disagreed. "Hell, if they took you away from me for a while would you come to your senses? Would I?"

"No, but—we're in love."

"Well, so are they."

"They just think they are."

"You just can't resist analyzing everybody you know, can you? No matter how little you really know about them. You figure them all out and slap a label on them and that's the end of them as far as you're concerned. You never consider that you might be wrong, or they might be different. Try analyzing yourself some time. It's no cinch."

Beth was temporarily confused. "Well—I know Emmy pretty well," she said.

"Yeah. And I know Bud. He may be a worthless character, but tearing him away from Emmy isn't going to cool either of them off. That's the best way I can think of to get them both hot. Right now Bud's in love with Emmy and he's damned unhappy. I feel sorry for the guy."

"Oh, so do I. It's not that I don't, it's just that all men are such—most men are such—oh, never mind."

He grinned at her. "What are most women?"

"You'd never understand."

"What's Beth Cullison?" His eyes were curiously bright and narrow and Beth felt suddenly uncomfortable.

"You tell me," she challenged him.

"I can't," he said. "I don't know. I thought you did."

She couldn't look at his eyes and she despised her sudden shyness.

"Maybe we'll find out together," he said with a light smile. . . .

And so the days went slowly by, with everybody bringing news to Emmy about Bud, with everybody discussing the situation over and over again.

Emily chafed and wept and wondered and beseeched her friends for more news. Bud griped and argued with anyone who would listen, and consoled himself with beer and music.

It got pretty bad. He liked to talk to Charlie because Charlie was a fraternity brother and Charlie saw Beth, Emmy's roommate. Charlie was a friend; he listened.

"I tell ya, dad, it's intolerable," Bud protested. "If I could just see her. Just once. The thing is, nobody'd have to know. If I could just talk to her, work it out somehow."

"They won't let you talk to her."

"If I could meet her someplace . . ."

"Hang on, boy. That's not going to kill you. They'll relent one of these days."

"Yeah, sure, I can hang on. But what I mean is, why hang on if you don't have to? Hell, this is a big campus. Nineteen thousand students. Who's going to check on each one? If I saw her some afternoon where nobody'd suspect anything . . ."

"Yeah, but you have to worry about where. Why don't you just forget it and let the thing ride for a few weeks? They'll give in. Emmy's acting like a damn puritan. They'll have to let her out."

Bud was quiet for a minute, and then he looked at Charlie with an intently confidential frown. "Charlie," he said, "listen. Is there any time during the day when your apartment is empty?"

"No," said Charlie firmly.

"Listen, boy—"

"No! It's never empty. We have a resident truant officer."

"Charlie, listen, it'd be so easy. Nobody'd ever know, believe me."

"No."

"Now listen to me, will ya, God damn it? Now listen. Look, Emmy has a two o'clock Tuesdays and Thursdays. She's out at three, walks south on Wright Street—"

"Listen, Bud—"

"Charlie, you've even got a car. My God, this is perfect. You could pick her up, tell her about it in the car on the way over."

"Way over where?"

"To the apartment, boy." Bud flung his hands out earnestly. "Use your head. Jesus. Now listen, when's your roommate in class? What's-his-name?"

"Mitch."

"Mitch. He there on Thursday afternoon?"

"Look Bud, that's beside the—"

"That's great. That makes it just about perfect. He wouldn't have to know a thing. Nobody'd know but you and me and Emmy. The fewer the better. Charlie my boy, listen to me—we'd be there only a couple of hours." He watched Charlie's face anxiously. "All right, an hour." Charlie was silent, sympathetic but dubious. "Charlie, you hear me?"

"Yeah . . . I don't know, Bud."

"Man, what's the matter with you? You so pure you never had a girl in your apartment?"

"No, but I was never under orders *not* to have her, boy. I was never shadowed by the university. If you get caught, we all get canned. The university doesn't sponsor extra-curricular love-making, in case you didn't know."

"Look, Charlie, if we get caught, which we won't, nobody gets canned but us. Emmy and me."

"Are you ready to do that to Emmy?"

"It won't happen. Believe me. Besides, if it did we'd go on pro, we wouldn't be expelled."

"Who wants to be on probation?"

"Charlie, we're just wasting time talking about it. It won't happen, man."

"It's my apartment, my car—my *bed*, for God's sake."

"Okay. And I'm your friend. A brother. I could've asked to use the apartment without telling you why. You can make like you're shocked as all hell if we get caught. Oh, hell, this is a lot of crap—we're not going to get caught. Who's gonna catch us? When does Mitch get in?"

"Oh—about five-thirty."

"Any sooner? Ever get in sooner?"

"No." Charlie shook his head.

"Okay, we're out at five. Emmy walks one block to the bus, I go the other way, toward campus."

Charlie shook his head doubtfully. "Bud, I hate to risk it, boy. Not because I'm afraid for my own sake, but—God, it would be the end for Emmy if she got caught."

"Charlie," said Bud, as if he were talking to an unco-operative first-grader, "we won't get caught. Who the hell's gonna catch us? As long as I don't have to call her, as long as you pick her up and everything, what's to go wrong? Oh, Charlie, be a friend. I need help, believe me. How would you like it if they cut you off for months? And don't tell me there's other girls. I know that, I know. I want Emmy. Like you want Beth, I want Emmy . . . Charlie, I'd do it for you. I swear I would, boy."

Charlie drained his beer and stabbed his cigarette into an ashtray. "You really want to see her that bad?" he said.

Bud looked up at the ceiling as if searching it for his self-control. "Yeah. I want to," he said. "That bad."

"Okay. I'll pick her up. Thursday at three."

"Charlie—" Bud grinned at him and gripped his hand.

"Be at the apartment. And by God, be out at five."

"I will. Jesus, Charlie, I can't tell you—"

"Never mind, boy. Save it. Just keep it quiet."

"My God, you're telling me!"

At three o'clock on Thursday afternoon Emily stood on the steps of Bevier Hall on Wright Street, chattering with some classmates. Charlie didn't see her until she came down the walk with a friend, and then he pulled the car toward her and called to her.

"Emmy!" he said. "Hey, Em! How about a ride?"

She looked up, surprised, and broke into a sudden smile.

"Thanks!" she exclaimed, running over. "Can you take Jane too?"

Charlie was alarmed. "Where's she going?"

"Gamma Delt house." The girl thrust a pleasant young face over Emmy's shoulder.

"Okay, hop in," said Charlie.

"It's right on the way. I hope you don't mind," Emmy said, sensing his reserve.

"Not at all." He had little to say until Jane was delivered and they were a mile off course from the apartment. He turned the car around while Emily watched him with big questioning eyes.

"Where're we going?" she asked.

"We're going to my apartment, Emily," he said.

"Your apartment?"

"Yeah." He looked at her and said with a smile, "Bud's there."

Emily gasped. And then she cried.

"Emily!" he said. "My God, don't tell me you don't want to go!"

"Yes, I do," she said. "I do. You scared me, Charlie. Oh, is he really there?" She put a hand on his arm.

"Yeah, he's there all right."

"Charlie—it's safe, isn't it? I mean, we won't get caught?"

"No, Em, don't worry. Mitch is out for the afternoon. I won't be there. You'll have till five o'clock."

"Ohhh," said Emily with an uncertain smile. "Charlie, thanks."

"Don't thank me, honey. I wasn't very nice about it. I don't want you to get into trouble. But I guess there's not much chance of that. But Emmy—"

"Yes?" Her heart gave a thump.

"Don't tell anyone about it. Not anyone. Not even Beth. Understand?"

"Yes. Not even Beth?"

"Not even Beth. Promise?"

"Yes," she whispered.

Charlie dropped her off. She walked up to the door with her knees shaking a little, opened it, and went in. For a moment her sun-dazzled eyes saw nothing and then she heard Bud jump to his feet. "Emmy!" he said. He pushed the door shut behind her, and held her against it, leaning on her and kissing her almost savagely.

He pulled her against him and said, "Oh, Emmy. Oh, God, God, God, Emmy! Darling . . ." He could not have said more or said it better. He looked at her as if she were all miraculously new to him. He pulled her down and took her like a man who had never had a woman before and thought never to have another. He took her over and over and over and yet again in a fight with time that raised his passion to a frenetic pitch and made a wild, tireless thing of Emily. And then they lay beside each other, whispered to each other of love and loneliness and relentless longing. Bud wrapped her in his arms, still lightheaded with emotion, and said, "Emmy, darling, I love you."

"Oh, Bud," she half sobbed. "They'll never do this to us again."

"Never," he echoed. "Oh, Em—I'd do anything for you. I love you, chicken."

She clung to him hopefully. "Anything, Bud?"

"Anything," he murmured, kissing her. "They'll never take you away from me again."

"Bud—" Her voice was light and supplicating. "Marry me?"

"What?" He stopped kissing her just long enough to raise himself on one elbow and gaze at her. "Marry you?"

She held her breath, not daring to answer nor yet to keep still, and her perishable perfection ensnared him, enflamed him, wrenched his heart like a lovely tune.

"Yes, Em. I guess I would. I never thought of it, but I guess I would. I will if you want it, Emmy. I'd be one hell of a lousy husband, but I love you. Maybe that'll make up for it."

"Oh, Bud," she cried softly. They leaned toward each other until their lips were together again, and far away, as in the gentlest of reveries, the latch clicked and the door opened. They lay, quiet and complete, whole and serene in each other's need, fulfilled and reassured, lovely and beautifully human.

"Emily!" A poison-tipped voice split them asunder; a girl's voice, high and hard with indignation.

"Oh, my God!" cried a boy at almost the same time. "Oh, my God!" he said again, helplessly.

Bud and Emmy sat up suddenly in a fit of alarm, gazing at the silhouettes, straining against the head-on sun streaming at them from the window to see their faces.

"I'm terribly sorry," said the boy. "I didn't know. I mean—God. We'd better go, Mary Lou."

"We'd better go, Emily," said Mary Lou. "You and I."

Bud looked at his watch. "But it's only four-thirty," he said.

Beth found Emmy just before dinner, face down on the couch and sobbing. The shades were all pulled down and the room was dark and sad and overheated. Laura followed Beth into the room and stood soundless and motionless while Beth dropped her books and shut the door.

"Emmy!" Beth said. "What's the matter?" She threw her coat off and sank to the floor on her knees by Emily's head. Emily turned away. "Emmy, honey," she said, and stroked her hair. Laura watched her without expression. "Tell me what's the matter."

Emily tried to repress her tears. She turned to Beth and whispered sporadically, "They found us. Mary Lou and Mitch. We couldn't stand it any longer. We had to see each other. They found us."

Beth was astounded. "You saw Bud?" she said, squinting incredulously.

"Yes," said Emmy in a tiny voice.

"Emmy! Where? How?" Beth felt the impending catastrophe.

"The apartment. I didn't know. Charlie picked me up. I never thought we'd get caught."

"Charlie? Charlie's apartment?"

"Yes. He told Bud he could use it. Nobody was going to be there. It was just a mistake—"

"You met Bud in Charlie's apartment?"

"Yes." Her voice tricked and trapped and deserted her; her breath came hard and then not at all.

"Oh, Em . . ." Beth put her arms around her and comforted her. Laura watched them, cold and remote as a winter sky, silent as the snow. "Tell me about it."

Emmy pulled herself up and sat gazing at the dead face of the window shade behind the desk. "Mitch wasn't supposed to get in till five-thirty. He cut class. He had coffee with Mary Lou. They came back to the apartment to get some books. We would have left in another fifteen minutes. But they caught us. I'll be blackballed, Beth." She looked desperately at her.

The dinner chime sounded and Beth remembered Laura. "Run along and eat, honey," she said.

Laura stood stolidly in place. There were times when she actively resented the childish role Beth forced on her.

"Go on," Beth said. "I'll be along in a minute."

Laura stayed where she was and Beth turned to Emily again. "Can I bring you a tray, Em?"

Emmy shook her head. "I can't eat," she said, leaning limply on Beth's shoulder. "They're going to kick me out, Beth."

"How bad—I mean—what were you doing when they came in?"

"We were in bed. We were in Charlie's bed."

Laura shuddered with a sharp involuntary disgust.

"We were making love. Oh, Beth!" Emmy wept. "I love him so much. Is it such a terrible crime to love somebody?"

"No," said Beth with a sting in her voice, "but it's a terrible thing to get caught. It's good to love, Emmy, but it's hell to get caught. I'd just love to know," she went on, with her voice getting surer and harder, "just what the hell Mary Lou and Mitch were doing going to the apartment this afternoon? Going to do a little intimate homework, maybe? A little research . . . anatomical variety? We'll never know." She rocked Emily in her arms and Laura, seeing their bodies move together, could feel nothing but spite for Emily. . . .

Laura held her tongue until late that night, after Emmy had gone to bed. "What will they do to her?" she asked.

"Kick her out. Jerk her pin. Disgrace her." She spat the words out.

"Well . . ." Laura studied her nails. "I guess she disgraced them."

Beth looked at her narrowly. "She fell in love, Laura. Is that so disgraceful to you?"

"I didn't mean it that way, Beth," Laura said softly. "I only meant she didn't have to be so obvious about it. Everybody knew—"

"Yeah, everybody knew she loved him. That's good enough reason to expel her, isn't it?"

Laura sighed ill-naturedly. "She got what she deserved," she said. "She broke every rule. She defied authority."

"Laura," said Beth with pointed irritation, "what do you think would happen to you if everybody knew you were in love with me? You'd get the same treatment, honey, and don't forget it. You'd get worse."

Laura stared at her, startled and scared.

"What's so wonderful about rules?" Beth snapped. "Is it obeying the rules for two girls to make love to each other? Don't you think we're defying authority ourselves?"

"I—never thought of it that way," Laura faltered.

"No, of course not. Maybe you never thought of it at all."

"Beth, for heaven's sake! Emily was caught in bed with a man with no clothes on when she wasn't supposed to see him at all. She was—she was—making love to him—"

Beth came over to the couch and sat down beside

Laura, leaning forward with her elbows on her knees, a cigarette in one hand. She pulled on her cigarette and brought two jets of smoke through her nose. "We've made love, Laura."

"But that's different, Beth. That's clean. It's beautiful." She grasped Beth's arm and leaned anxiously toward her. Beth studied the tip of her cigarette.

"A man and a woman are beautfiul, too. And we've been caught making love, Laura . . . you and I. Just like Bud and Emmy."

Laura snatched her hand away as if from a flame and sat for a wounded moment, terrified. "Beth, what do you mean?" she said in a strained whisper.

Beth flicked her ashes thoughtlessly toward a tray. "Just that. We aren't any cleaner or any more beautiful than Emily and Bud, just because we're both women. And we were caught, too."

"Beth!" Laura stared at her with horrified eyes. "We were never caught."

"Yes we were, Laur. We were seen in here one night— right here in this room—kissing each other and talking about it."

"Why didn't you tell me? Why didn't they ever say anything?"

" 'They' don't know. We had the good luck to get caught by Emmy."

"Emmy!"

"Yes. Emmy. Emmy found us in here one night. Just before semester vacation. She heard enough to guess the story. She never told a soul except me. She never will." Beth's quiet, angry voice contrasted vividly with Laura's high anxiety.

To Laura, her love had seemed as secret as it was sacred. That someone else should know; that someone else had known for months; that the someone else was Emily, and Emily would never tell, would spare them what had been inflicted on her—all these thoughts struck Laura at once and she felt a sudden twist of guilt in her heart.

"Oh, Beth . . . if I'd only known," she said, and her voice broke.

"Oh, it would only have worried you, Laur. I hoped you could see some good in Emmy. I hoped you'd learn to like her." She looked up at Laura's face. "I guess you were jealous of her."

"Beth . . ." Laura rested her forehead against Beth's shoulder. "Beth, I'm so sorry. I thought she was—oh, I don't know why she didn't just tell them about me. I was so nasty to her. I couldn't have blamed her if she did."

"She's not that way, Laur. Besides, if she told them about you she'd've had to tell them about me." She fingered her cigarette, musing. "But she wouldn't have said anything anyway. She likes you, Laur . . . or at least, she wants to. I don't know why."

"Oh, Beth, I'm so sorry—"

"Don't tell me, Laur, tell Emmy." Beth wasn't cross with her any more. She was too worried about Emily to think about other feelings.

"Don't cry, Laur." She turned and held her then and chided her gently. "I've had all I can stand of crying today."

Laura stopped slowly, in jerks. "Will they really blackball her, Beth?" she whispered.

"They have to. You can break the rules, but you can't get caught."

"Isn't there anything we can do?"

"All we can do is remind them of what they're going to do to Emmy: her family, her education, her friends . . . all the heartbreak, and things never patch up to be quite the same as they were before."

"Never?"

"Oh, those things get all over your home town. There's always somebody around to let them out. And once it's out they never let you forget it."

"Will they kick her out of school, too?"

"They'll probably just put her on social probation. But she won't want to stay in school. My God, when the whole damn campus knows what happened?"

Beth knew what she was talking about. In no time at all there was the secret chapter meeting of the sorority, with one of the national officers in attendance. Representatives of the alumnae were there, too.

Mary Lou was pale and distressed and she let the alumnae carry the burden of the meeting. They were impressive women, businesslike and efficient, real club women. They enjoyed tackling problems; Emmy's was one of the juiciest in years. They spent a good bit of time congratulating the girls present on their presumed virginity and their unblemished reputations; and a good bit demolishing what was left of Emmy's. They did it with masterful tact.

"Emmy is a good girl at heart, but . . ."

"Of course, you all feel terrible about this. I know she had many friends in the house . . ."

But an hour and a half later, Emily was an ex-Alpha Beta. Her career at the university was ruined.

Emmy was spared the meeting. She sat alone in her room while it was going on with a number of open suitcases around her and tried to find the courage to start packing.

Beth had stood up at the meeting and made an eloquent plea for her. And when that failed she got sharp and sarcastic, and still it didn't change the vote. The sisters were sympathetic but restrained from mercy by the stifling good sense of their elders.

Laura sat in wretched silence, helpless. She couldn't speak as well as Beth, she hadn't nearly the influence, and yet she wanted to stand up and say something, but after Beth sat down there was nothing more to be said.

Beth and Laura went up to the room together. Emmy had one bag packed when they came in. She sat on the floor staring listlessly at her belongings, and she looked up at them when they came in. Their faces were painful to see.

"I know," she said. "I've called home. Dad's going to pick me up tomorrow."

Beth went to her and said, "We did everything we could, Em."

"I know. I knew it would happen. It had to happen, that's all. It couldn't be any other way. I was a fool."

"Did you talk to Bud? They said you could call him."

Emmy gave a bitter little smile. "Now that the damage is done, I can call him. If they'd let me talk to him before, maybe it wouldn't have happened."

"Did you talk to him?"

"Yes. I called while you were all downstairs."

"What'd he say?"

"Oh, you know Bud. He feels terrible. He was furious. But he doesn't know what to do; he never could handle a problem." Her smile became reluctantly tender. "He just rants and raves and says he'll quit school too, as if that would do any good, and they can't do this to me, and . . . Oh, I don't know." She looked at Beth sadly.

"Come on, Emmy," Beth said gently. "I'll help you get your things together. You don't have to go right away. You can take a few days to pack and—" She stopped.

"I want to get out of here as fast as I can," Emmy said harshly. "Oh, Beth, he—he cried!" she said with a sudden hard sob. "My dad cried!" And the stress of that sorrow nearly tore her apart.

Beth got Emily packed by three in the morning. Laura had tried to help but soon realized that she was neither needed nor wanted and left for the dormitory. Emily was afraid to face anybody and Beth sat up with her all night and helped her get ready to meet Bud for breakfast so they could say good-by. He promised to go to see her every weekend, he swore he loved her, he denounced the university, the sorority, the world for his mistake.

He said, "Emmy, darling, I did this to you and I'll make it up to you somehow, by God, I will. I don't know how, but—there must be a way. Oh, honey, I hate to see you so unhappy. And I did it, I did it." He was so miserable that Emily had to comfort him, and it seemed to give her strength. She listened to him, knowing that he sincerely meant what he said when he said it, wondering how long it would affect him so.

"Emmy," he said, "I love you. If only there were something I could do."

"There is," she said, nervously determined. "Don't you remember?"

He looked at her in puzzlement.

"Marry me, Bud," she said.

He dropped his glance and stared at the table for a minute and then he took her hands and nearly crushed them in his. "I will, Em," he said. "If that's what you want, I will." He looked up at her.

"Oh, Bud," she said, and began to smile a real smile for the first time since their disaster. "If I could know that —if I could look forward to that—"

He kissed her hands.

"When?" she urged him.

He shook his head. "I don't know." And seeing her face cloud over again he added, "June, maybe. Or Easter. I don't know."

"Oh, Bud, darling," she whispered, and the world steadied a little.

EIGHTEEN

Beth brooded for days. She didn't want to see Charlie, she didn't want to go out, she didn't want to do anything. Her every bitter thought had a wicked stinger in it: she and Charlie had done the same as Emily and Bud, and got away with it.

Beth felt a wave of irresistible disgust with herself, her little duplicities, her evasions. In a restless temper she got up and paced the room fretfully. Laura watched her anxiously, wanting to talk to her, to help, but afraid to. Beth pulled the window open and stood in the wash of early April air, chill and dark and soft, and thought of the sorrows that a man can heap on a woman. She thought of Charlie's complicity, she thought of Bud's worthless charm and useless contrition, and she hated them briefly, with violent energy.

The phone on the desk rang. Laura picked it up, watching Beth all the while.

"Hello?" she said, and she frowned. Beth shook her head without a word, and then shut her eyes tight as if that might eliminate the sound of Laura's voice.

"No, Charlie, she's not here. I'm sorry—please, Charlie —I don't know, but—" And she listened a moment longer and hung up. She looked at Beth apologetically. "I hung up on him," she said. "I didn't know what else to do. He sounded sort of—frantic. I didn't know what else to do." She watched Beth hopefully, tenderly, afraid to go near her. Beth leaned against her dresser and stared out the window again, silent.

"Beth?" Laura said softly. Beth turned toward her suddenly and pulled her hard and close against her and put her head down against Laura's. Her hot hands probed and pushed back and forth across Laura's shoulders, the small of her back, her hips, catching in her clothes, rumpling them, and finally her arms tightened around the younger girl and she whispered, "Laura. Look at me."

Laura looked up and Beth kissed her full on the lips, a yearning kiss, warm and deep and slow. She didn't stop

167

for a long while, not until Laura was shivering wildly in her embrace, answering Beth's passion with her own.

"Oh, Laur," Beth said into Laura's ear, "what a fool I am. What a simpleton."

"Beth, I love you," said Laura, clinging to her and letting the delicious tremors shake her body, wondering where this revival of desire came from, but not caring. It had happened; Beth wanted her again the way she had in the beginning.

"Laura," Beth said. "Oh, I hate them! God damn them all, I hate them!" Laura didn't have to be told that "they" were men; she knew it and her heart expanded joyously and floated in her chest.

"You can't trust them," Beth muttered. "You can't trust them. God, I don't know why I ever bothered with them. All they know how to do is hurt. They all want the same damn thing." She hugged Laura tighter and Laura's hope bloomed again like a forced flower. "I'm sick and tired of it," Beth went on. "I'm sick and tired of the whole thing. If you get caught they treat you like a slut, they kick you out. If you don't get caught your conscience gives you hell. I've had enough, Laura. It makes me sick the whole damn business—authority—stupid, stuffy, blind authority—men, deans, school, everything. I want to get out of here." They whipped Emmy in public, she thought; I'll whip myself in private. Exile myself. It was the only way to square with her conscience.

"What about Charlie?" Laura's voice was faint and frightened.

"Charlie can go to hell. Charlie's as guilty as Bud. You don't know how guilty Charlie is. You don't know." She put her head down again.

"Beth, would you really leave school?"

"Yes. Yes, I would, damn it. I would!"

"Will you let me come with you?"

Beth pulled away from her a little and started to shake her head.

"Beth!" Laura cried, "I want to go wherever you go. You said we weren't any better than Bud and Emily; you said we were doing the same thing. Well, we haven't any more right to stay here than she does, then."

"Your family?" Beth said.

"Oh, my family . . ." Laura said, making the word curdle with her contempt. "My family doesn't care what happens to me, just so they have something to tell their friends."

"They won't like it, Laur."

"I won't ask them to like it. There's nothing they can do about it, Beth. I'm of age, in this state anyway. Oh, Beth, you can't ask me to stay here without you—you can't!" She clung tightly to her. Laura was aware that Beth couldn't resist her at that moment, and she made the most of it.

Furious with men and intensely sympathetic for a girl, angry with herself, yet in need of reassurance, Beth turned to Laura again with all the unreasoning joy of their early romance. She said weakly, "I don't know . . ."

Laura said quickly, "Beth, darling, I wouldn't be afraid of anything as long as you were with me."

Beth laughed gently at her, flattered, seeing the exaggeration and yet enjoying it too much to deny it. "I can't do everything," she whispered.

"Yes you can," said Laura positively.

Beth looked down at her with a spellbound smile. "Laura," she said, with her lips against Laura's cheek, drifting over her face toward her lips. "I love you." Laura's arms tightened about her and brought her desire hot to the surface. Beth pulled her over to the couch and down beside her.

Suddenly, unexpectedly, completely, Laura had Beth again. Whatever the sorcery that won her, it was potent, and it lasted. A week passed and they made plans in secret to leave the house. Every night, in defiance of chance, they slept together in the room, and strangely enough, nobody noticed. Nobody barged in on them. Nobody suspected anything.

Beth laughed at their luck. "Wouldn't you know," she said. "We might as well be kicked out as leave by ourselves. Might even be more honorable. But as long as we don't give a damn we're perfectly safe. They'd never dream of anything amiss in this room. Lightning never strikes twice in the same place."

Laura laughed with her.

Charlie was getting desperate. He called, and almost never spoke to Beth. When he did, she was brusque with him. He saw her at the Union, where she couldn't escape him, and she gave him only a few cursory minutes in public. He tried to pick her up after classes and she ignored him or took refuge in the ladies' room.

He was aching to explain, to talk, to hold her and to restore the love and logic to his world. Every time he saw her he felt a frantic need to touch her, to force her to listen. Nothing was sensible any more. He stopped her in the hall at the Union one day and said, "Beth, this has gone far enough. For God's sake, talk to me."

She eyed him coolly. "I have nothing to say to you, Charlie."

"Well, I've got something to say to you."

She folded her arms patiently. "All right," she said.

"Here?" His voice was hard.

"This is as good as any place."

He studied her for a minute in silence. "Not quite, Beth," he said finally, and walked off and left her alone. It was the first time he had done it, and he caught Beth by surprise. She stared after him for a minute and then went down the hall in the opposite direction. Charlie went off tormented and angry, wild with impatience and doubt, afraid he might never reach her, never touch her again, and the idea made him half mad.

He went home to the empty apartment, poured himself a stiff drink, and threw himself into a chair. He fixed the wall with an angry stare while he finished the drink and poured another. And then he said to himself, Why? What the hell's wrong with the girl? And then he said it out loud, as if he expected an answer from the listening wall: "What the hell *is* wrong with her?"

He stood up, glass in hand, and began to walk slowly up and down the room. "I'll tell you what's wrong with her," he told himself aloud. "She doesn't want to see you." He turned sharply around and demanded sarcastically, "Does that mean there's something wrong with her?" He emptied his glass and then glared balefully at the wall, filling the glass again. "Be sensible, be sensible . . ." he admonished himself. "Okay, we'll be sensible," he said. "We'll be logical. We'll start with her family. Anything wrong there? No, she gets along fine with them."

He fortified himself with a swallow. "Now," he said. "Friends. First category: men. God, let's see. Men." He sat down suddenly. "Damn them," he murmured. "God damn them all." When she had told him about the others, he had taken it in stride. He had been full of her, warm and passionate and wildly in love. He had her in his arms, and she had made a brave and painful confession to him. It had stunned him, but he rallied. It was easy to forgive her; she loved him, she needed him, she hated the others as much as he did. But now, thinking of them, with Beth remote and icy, with the same room they had made love in cold and lonely and haunted with Bud and Emily's sorrows as well as his own—he broke down, enraged.

"Oh, God," he snarled through closed teeth, "send every one of those stinking bastards straight to hell." His voice subsided to a whisper. "And as for her—as for her—" He drank a little more, and then dropped his head in his hands. "Make her love me," he said in a broken voice. "Just make her love me."

After a few minutes he straightened up again and refilled his glass. "Men," he said softly. "I know she has no other men. I'd know that right away—Mary Lou would tell Mitch and he'd sure tell me."

He drank. It was becoming rather difficult to pursue the logical approach. He tried to retrace his steps. "Family," he muttered. "Friends. Men. Women." He laughed a little and lifted his glass and then put it down again on the table. He shook his head to clear it. "God, how drunk am I?" he said, looking at the glass and then at the bottle. After a long pause he said it again, aloud but very quietly, "Women?" And then he took a long swallow. He stood up again and walked uncertainly around the room, pulling at his chin, rubbing his head, squinting with concentration. Finally he walked up to the wall and stopped, leaning against it. From months past came a hazy argument with Beth. He remembered gazing at her over the top of a diner table. He was saying, "I can tell when a person has a crush on me. Can't you? Laura doesn't."

"Well, she does," Beth had said.

She had said it several times, insisted on it. Charlie raised his clenched fists over his head, his whole body relying on the wall. "Laura?" he whispered, and the strength seemed to go out of him. He sagged against the wall. "If I weren't so drunk," he told himself sternly. He slid slowly to the floor and fell asleep where he lay.

While Charlie got drunk that afternoon, Beth began, for the first time, to have doubts about leaving school with Laura. When she got back to the sorority house that evening she, quite unconsciously, gave herself away by saying to Laura, "I wonder if we're doing the right thing?"

"Beth!" Laura exclaimed. She grasped Beth's hands and held them tight. "Of course we are. What a thing to say!"

"I guess so, but—I don't know. As time goes by, I begin to wonder."

"Beth, don't you remember what you said? Don't you remember what they did to Emmy? What they'd do to us if we got caught? Beth, you promised me. Oh, darling— we were going to be so happy, all to ourselves with no house rules, no deans, no men to worry about. Beth . . ." She pulled her hands up and pressed them to her lips and Beth watched her with a warm feeling in her chest. Laura looked up. "Beth, you promised. You said whatever happens. I said it, too. It's like an oath. You can't break it. Oh, Beth, my love!" She threw her arms around her.

"Yes," Beth whispered. "Yes. Oh, Laur, I'm just—I don't know. I'm crazy. Don't listen to me, I don't know what I'm saying."

"Then we *will* go?"

"Yes. We'll go."

But if she could calm Laura she couldn't do as well by herself. Laura could believe in Beth and lean on her, depend on her for everything. But Beth had no one to look to and she was suddenly responsible not just for herself but for Laura as well. It was unnerving. She hadn't expected Laura to take to her idea with such enthusiasm; to take so seriously and so finally what began in Beth's mind as a private emotional revolt. The thing seemed somehow foolhardy and stupid. And yet, when she looked into Laura's face and saw the endless warm love in it, all hers, her reservations faded away.

Laura said, "Beth, when will we go? Let's go soon." She knew if they postponed the thing much longer, Beth wouldn't go at all. The main thing was to get Beth out of Champlain before she changed her mind. And Laura had a sure idea that Charlie was behind Beth's doubt.

"Did you see Charlie today?" she asked.

Beth looked surprised. "Yes," she said.

Laura stroked Beth's cheek with her finger. "He always upsets you, Beth," she said.

Beth kissed the finger. "He reminds me of things I'd rather forget. Laura, you're adorable."

Laura smiled gratefully at her. "When shall we go?" she said, capitalizing on Beth's mood.

"Oh . . ."

"Beth, tell me."

"Oh, I don't know. When do you want to go? Your eyes are such a pretty blue. Where'd you get such blue eyes, Laur?"

"Let's go Friday."

"This Friday?"

"Yes." She watched her hopefully, with parted lips. Beth kissed them.

"Isn't that kind of soon?"

"We have to, Beth. It's now or never," she added truthfully.

Beth kissed the corner of Laura's mouth. "Is it?" she murmured.

"Yes. Beth, answer me."

"Kiss me." Beth's eyes were bright, teasing.

Laura obeyed her. "Now, answer me," she demanded.

"Answer you what?"

Laura smiled. "Say yes, Beth. Say yes, darling."

"Yes, what?"

"Just yes. Never mind what. Say it." She kissed her hard.

"Yes," Beth whispered, smiling. "Yes, yes, yes . . ."

That was Monday night. Laura spent the next few days worrying about Charlie. She was afraid of any further contact between Charlie and Beth, though it seemed inevitable, the way Charlie was trying to see her. She wanted to prevent him from talking to Beth before he could do any real damage, before Friday came and Beth was safely on the train. But she didn't know what to do about it, how to go about it. Unexpectedly, Charlie solved her problem before the week was out.

NINETEEN

BETH and Laura told their friends simply that they were going home for the weekend, a normal thing, especially in spring, for most of the girls to do.

By Thursday afternoon Laura was irrepressibly happy. Her only difficulty lay in trying to keep her excitement from showing. It was wonderful to escape from classes and campus and meetings and people, into her room and Beth's arms; wonderful to free her feelings and see how strong and deep and solid they were; best of all to know that after tomorrow Beth would be hers, irrevocably committed.

Beth, as the time grew closer, began to worry in earnest, but Laura's drive and devotion seemed to pull her inexorably toward the train on Friday. She was sure she loved Laura, but not so sure she didn't love Charlie. She wavered, she wondered, she weighed a thousand things in her mind: freedom against her college degree, a tormented conscience against the sweet warmth of Laura, and all the countless little details that trailed in the wake of either decision.

She tried to keep her mental seesawing from Laura; it would only hurt and confuse her. She felt that Laura had to be protected like a child. She had failed to see that every time she treated Laura to a little adult honesty, Laura responded like an adult. She didn't want to see. Laura was her baby.

By Thursday, Beth had an almost oriental fatalism about leaving for New York. There was nothing she could do to stem the tide of Laura's enthusiasm, no way she had any control over the situation any more.

That afternoon, Laura went over to Campus Town after class to get some last-minute supplies. She walked into the university drugstore and got some toothpaste—one for Beth, she was always running out—and some emery boards. She was standing at the counter waiting for her change when she heard Charlie next to her say, "Hello, Laura."

She looked up with a start. "Hi, Charlie," she said. He smiled down at her while she faltered, a little confused. She had the distinct feeling that he had followed her.

"Your change, miss," said the clerk, dangling a bored hand over the counter.

"Oh, thank you." Laura took it and Charlie simultaneously pulled her books out of her arms and held them while she put the money in her wallet. She stuffed the money away and reached quickly for her books, but he held them out of reach.

"Let me take you home, Laura," he said, steering her toward the door. She didn't like the tone of his voice. "My car's just a block away."

Laura protested; she didn't want anything from Charlie Ayers, not even a ride home. "Oh, please don't bother," she said.

"No bother." She understood then that he intended to take her home, no matter what she said. He had made up his mind and she resented his easy authority. It made her apprehensive.

She walked along beside him in nettled silence, dragging and wishing she could give a hard shake to get his hand off her arm. They reached the car and he held the door for her while she hesitated.

"Get in," he said pleasantly, and when still she hung back he smiled and said, "I'm not going to attack you, Laura."

Laura blushed angrily and got into the front seat.

He watched her with a curious smile and then came around and got in and started the car. "I thought maybe you'd answer a couple of questions for me," he said.

"In return for the ride?" she said. He must have been following me, she told herself.

He laughed. "No," he said. "In return for the sympathy. You cried on my shoulder last fall, Laura. Now I'm going to cry on yours—figuratively," he added when she gave him a cold stare. They pulled away from the curb.

"Well," she said, "I don't know if I can answer any questions, Charlie."

"I think you can," he said. "I hope you will." He paused and then looked at her out of the corner of his eye, amused to see that she was staring spitefully at his long legs. She looked up hastily, sensing his gaze. "Of course you're under no obligation," he said.

"Oh, no." She looked down at her hands, knowing it would be about Beth and tempted to fear Charlie again. He was impressive competition; she had almost forgotten the lines of him. But tomorrow, she told herself. Tomorrow! And thinking of Beth and of the things she did and said and the way she looked, Laura felt a flush of strength and certainty. Beth loved her. You can't be in love with two people at once, and Beth loved Laura. She said so and she meant it. Laura was sure. She looked up at Charlie again. He was lighting a cigarette.

"I want to know," he said, taking it out of his mouth and spewing smoke over the dashboard, "why Beth won't see me."

"Well," Laura shrugged. "She's been terribly upset."

"So have I."

"Well, Charlie, I don't know. Emily was her best friend."

"Does her best friend mean more to her than the man she's in love with?"

Laura turned surprised eyes on him and then she laughed, in spite of herself. He gave her a quick inquisitive glance. "What's so funny?" he said.

"She's not in love with you, Charlie. Oh, I'm sorry, I didn't mean to laugh. You just—surprised me." It was glorious to talk to him like this.

"The hell she isn't," he said. "She's mad, she's insulted, yes. Maybe she hates me, I don't know. But I do know she's in love with me."

Laura smiled at his certainty, suddenly enjoying her ride.

"What's so damn funny, Laura?" he said.

"Nothing," she said, but it was too tempting. "Your egoism, Charlie."

"My egoism?" He smiled a little, suddenly cautious, wondering at Laura's change of mood.

"Charlie," she said solicitously, with the thought of Beth in bed the night before, of Beth's kiss in the morning, of Beth's arms around her that afternoon, "Charlie, I didn't mean to be rude, really. I'm sorry. I know you think a lot of Beth."

"I love Beth, Laura."

Laura smiled into her lap again. Charlie watched her and then pulled the car up. He had been taking the long way back to Alpha Beta. They were at the edge of the university's experimental farm on the south campus. Charlie switched the ignition off and turned in his seat to study Laura. She glanced out the window and then questioningly at Charlie.

"I want to know what's so damn funny about my being in love with Beth. Or Beth with me." He looked straight at her.

Laura fought her smile down. "Nothing, Charlie. It isn't funny. It was wrong of me. I'm sorry." He said nothing. "I think we'd better get back to the house," she said.

"We will. When you explain the joke."

She couldn't feel any alarm, somehow. She just felt delightfully secure, smug as only a successful rival can feel in the presence of the loser. She looked out the window again at the adventuring green of mid-April. "There's no joke, Charlie," she said.

"Then what are you laughing at?"

"I'm not. I just—I don't know." She ached to tell him. Half the joy of a victory is the look on the face of defeat.

"Look, Laura," he said, leaning toward her. "I thought we were friends, you and I. Maybe I was wrong." He watched her narrowly.

"No." She shook her head slowly, letting him work for every word from her.

"Well, then will you clear up the mystery for me? What's the matter with Beth? Or me, for that matter?"

"Nothing's the matter with you. Or her."

Charlie lighted another cigarette from the last leg of the old one. "What's the matter, Laura? Why don't you want to tell me?" She frustrated him, made him feel hoodwinked; he had never thought a transparent girl like Laura could be so enigmatic. "What's all this about my being egotistical?" He watched her. No response, except a little maddening smile. He put his arm over the back of the seat and leaned toward her. "Come on, Laura, deflate my ego," he said cannily. "It seems to be the only way I'll learn anything."

Laura laughed again. "I don't want to deflate your ego, Charlie."

"Come on, Laura," he insisted. "Don't I have a right to know?"

"Well," said Laura, savoring each word, "it's just that

Beth isn't in love with you, Charlie. She was never in love with you." She gave him a sympathetic look. "That's all. I'm sorry."

He knew better. "Yes, she is," he said. Laura shook her head with a smile. "How do you know she isn't?" he said.

She looked at her lap and finally Charlie sat forward and knocked some ashes out the window and said some words he had only thought of once before, vaguely, when he was very drunk. "She's in love with you, I suppose," he said with a taste of sarcasm in his voice.

Laura looked up at him and smiled. It was intoxicating. Charlie gazed thoughtfully out the windshield, waiting for her denial, not taking his own words seriously until the silence forced him to review them. And suddenly, with painful lucidity, the light came; the sense and the reasons fell deafeningly into place.

Laura watched him minutely; saw the tiniest line between his eyes grow and deepen; saw the hand with the cigarette start for his lips and drop slowly back to the steering wheel; saw his lips part a little and his eyes widen. And then he turned and stared at her and she looked full into his face and smiled. He stared, and all Beth's little mysteries and refusals and anxieties and half-finished sentences smiled back at him. Laura never said a word; she just smiled serenely at him.

Charlie shut his eyes for a moment, wishing he were stone drunk, and then looked unwillingly at her again, and then at the floor. Laura watched him hungrily, remembering every second, every detail of him, every sound.

Finally he said in a husky voice, "Laura—is it true? Is it possible?" He looked at her. "Beth?"

Laura didn't answer him. Her lips parted a little as if she meant to, but she didn't. Then she succumbed to temptation. "Is what true?" she said softly.

"Is Beth—is she—" It was hard for him to say, and Laura enjoyed his difficulty. She felt like patting his arm and saying the question for him and then answering it lightly as if it were the easiest thing in the world. Charlie breathed deep. "Is Beth—in love with you, Laura?"

Laura looked down for a moment and her smile widened. And then her eyes came up slowly to his face. Charlie took her shoulders and shook her.

"Answer me!" he commanded. "Answer me, Laura! Is she?"

Her shoulders hurt from the grip of his hard hands and she saw the ripple of movement in his cheeks as his jaw clenched. Laura let her head fall back a little and she smiled gently at him and said, very slowly and luxuriously, "Yes."

They gazed at each other for what seemed a very long time—a tortuous time for Charlie and an exultant one for Laura. And then he let her go suddenly and turned back to the wheel and put his arms across it with his head down on his arms. Laura hoped he would cry. For a few minutes they sat in utter silence, with only April noises to disturb them.

Laura put her head back on the seat and gloated over the handsome broad-shouldered boy beside her, thinking how charming he was, how pleasant, how cock-sure. She let herself feel sorry for him, and her pity threatened to exhilarate her uncontrollably. This was her irresistible rival, a desirable man. And Laura, a plain girl, had vanquished him. She smiled again.

At length, Charlie straightened up. "I could never have believed it," he said quietly. "I thought of everything, but some things you just don't believe."

He started the car without looking at her, without saying anything more. They pulled back onto the road and headed for the sorority house. Laura watched him, but his face was set and blank; not the least tremor, not the palest line betrayed the tumult inside him. She said nothing, respecting his unuttered wish for silence.

Five minutes later they pulled up in front of the house. Charlie stopped the car and turned to look at her. She gathered up her books and opened the door, and then she looked back at him; she couldn't help herself.

"Thanks for the ride," she said.

"You're welcome," he answered. His voice was deep and quiet. She admired his control.

She got out and went up the walk to the front door and opened it and went into the house, knowing that he was sitting in the car watching her, never moving. When she was inside she rushed up the stairs to the first landing and pushed the heavy drapes carefully aside to peek out and see him start the car up and move down the street. He was driving in the direction of Maxie's. He's going to get drunk, Laura thought jubilantly, he's going to get drunk because he can't take it!"

Charlie's first thought was go to Maxie's and drink himself insensible. But he dismissed the idea almost as soon as it came to him. This time he needed a clear mind, uncluttered with alcoholic confusion. He turned the car around and drove slowly in the opposite direction. He was thinking, concentrating intensely in an effort to keep his emotions at bay. "A clear mind," he thought over and over. It occurred to him to go to the library. He hadn't any specific idea why. The library was a temple of learning, of wisdom. He would go there and soak it up. He would find a good sensible book and discover what made Beth and Laura want each other. He would understand.

But he no sooner parked his car by the library and started walking toward the big building than he knew how futile it was. He would be unable to read a single line of print. He paused uncertainly on the steps, looking into the great dark hall beyond the doors, and then he turned around. He didn't know what to do.

He sat down finally in the shade of a statue and leaned against the base. Above him drooped a lush woman in rough stone, rich with female curves. Some feet away a sister statue straddled her pedestal with muscular thighs. Charlie glared at the two women of rock, so warmly shaped that he never passed them without wanting to reach out and touch them. He knew them today for their cold, hard, unknowable selves.

For a long time he sat on the library steps between the stone sisters, and after a while it became possible to think. Just a little at first. It was one thing to reconcile himself to Beth's mistakes of the past; mistakes that were over and done with, mistakes that were above all normal. But it was quite another to accept her strange transgression with Laura.

Charlie thought back over the year. He knew he had satisfied Beth, he knew she wanted him. He had not been putting up a front when he told Laura that Beth loved him. Beth did love him. That could only mean one thing: that her feelings for Laura were not true love, not the kind of love she had for him.

He began to breathe a little more freely. Beth was an iconoclast, he knew that. She was an experimenter. And her failures, her frigidity with men might have pushed her to make this most extraordinary experiment of all: to look for release with a woman. Coming at it from that angle it wasn't quite so shocking—and it gave him hope. If Laura were an experiment for Beth, she wasn't a permanent thing. She represented a phase Beth had to go through.

Charlie smacked his fist into his palm. He stood up and slapped the nearest stone woman on the rump. He had made up his mind. Beth needed someone to guide her, to talk to her and straighten her out. She needed someone to love, with real love. He would see to it that she got it.

TWENTY

BETH was pensive that evening, but Laura was so gay that she had trouble concentrating on her misgivings. Laura was learning from her how to tease, and she could rouse and delight Beth very skillfully now. She rarely missed an opportunity to do it. Beth sat on the couch with a book in her hands, and Laura came up to her and pulled it out.

"What's that?" she said, glancing at it as she sat beside Beth.

"James."

"What's it for?"

"Class tomorrow."

"Class doesn't matter any more," Laura said. "Nothing matters any more but you and me. You have to study me now, Beth."

Beth laughed and caressed her, but her doubts grew stronger, nevertheless. She might have revolted against the plan, begged Laura to wait till the school year was up, if a letter hadn't come the next day from Emmy.

There had been several; Beth answered them all and they had been brave and hopeful. But this one was forsaken and bitter for the first time. Emmy hadn't seen Bud for two weeks, her parents were needling her, she couldn't find a job. She said:

"Beth, whatever happens, don't ever let yourself get into a mess like this, ever. Everybody knows what happened—it's so hard to face them all.

"I'd always thought men would give you a fair shake if you were honest with them. But now I'm beginning to wonder. I haven't heard from Bud for two weeks—not a word. And I've written every day. I'd call, but I'm afraid I'd embarrass him—make him mad, or something."

Make Bud mad! What's Bud done to deserve any consideration?

"Besides, I have some unwelcome news for him. He may *have* to marry me, whether he wants to or not."

182

Beth crumpled the letter harshly in her hand, too angry and vengeful even for tears.

Laura came into the room, back from her last class. She was breathless and happy and she threw her arms around Beth and said, "Oh, Beth, I can't wait!"

Beth hugged her. She felt good, the weather was good, the idea was good, the time was right. Emmy was right, there was no good in men.

They planned to meet at the station at four-thirty. The train pulled out at five-fifteen; they'd have time for a sandwich, plenty of time to get good seats.

A lot of trunks went home in April full of winter clothes. Theirs had left with a bunch of others, unnoticed. Beth simply left most of the room furnishings. They were hers and she didn't care about them.

"I'm rich, Laura," she said gaily. "I'm twenty-one and I've got my own money now, and no one can take it away from me, not even Uncle John. I'm free." And it was wonderful.

Beth had an afternoon class, and as Laura didn't, they planned to go down to the station separately and meet there.

Beth got out of her last class at three and headed for the Union. Her conscience troubled her; she was leaving a big job in a big mess. She went up to her office and tried to straighten things out.

"Leaving us?" someone called out, eying her little traveling bag.

She was startled for a minute. "No," she said. "I mean —home for the weekend."

"Lucky girl. Wish I could take a weekend off."

She laughed nervously and went to work. It was after four when she stopped. She tidied up her desk with an unsettling sense of finality, pulled her jacket on, took her bag firmly by the handle, and walked out of her office, through the Student Activities room and into the spacious hall, heading for the elevator.

Charlie stood up from a bench by the stair well. "I've been waiting for you," he said.

She stood frozen for a minute, and then she started briskly for the elevator. "I haven't got time, Charlie."

"Well, make time," he said. He caught her arms and took her bag from her. "Going someplace?"

"Yes. Let me go."

"Not this time, Beth. Where're you going?"

"That's none of your business."

"All right," he said. An elevator stopped and the doors opened and people spilled out. "I'm going to talk to you, Beth, whether you like it or not," Charlie said. People looked at them curiously. "I'm going to talk to you right here and now, in front of anybody and everybody—unless you'd care to give me a little privacy."

"Charlie, don't be a fool," she said sharply. "Give me my bag."

"Beth, there's something I've been meaning to tell you for a long time."

People stopped and watched them.

"All right, Charlie," she said in a brittle voice. She went to the door of a conference room, looked in and found it empty. "We can use this," she said. "But make it snappy."

He followed her in, shutting the door behind him. "Beth, where are you going?" he said seriously, indicating the bag.

Beth sighed impatiently. "I'm going home for the weekend. With Laura. On the five-fifteen." She looked significantly at her watch.

Charlie looked at her in alarm, suddenly alerted. "With Laura?" he said.

Beth turned her back on him. "Yes, with Laura. Now, what is it you're so anxious to tell me?"

Charlie knew he might lose her, then; really lose her. The bag looked ominous, sitting quietly on the long polished conference table. He leaned against the wall, watching Beth pace up the other side of the table, wondering if he could flush the truth out of her with a scare. "Why don't you take her to New York?" he said.

Beth stood absolutely still. The click of her heels died abruptly and she was tense as a guy wire, motionless. He hit home—her back told him so. Finally she turned and looked at him.

"What do you mean?" she said, and her voice was very soft.

He straightened up. "If you're in love with her, go live with her." His eyes were relentless.

Beth gazed at him with a stricken frown on her face, and suddenly she hurried toward the door. Charlie stepped in front of it, and she stopped, unwilling to touch him. She turned her back to him again.

"Is that all you have to say to me, Charlie?"

"No," he said. "Do you love her, Beth?"

"What are you trying to prove, Charlie?"

"What are you trying to hide, Beth?"

"Nothing!" she flared.

"Then be honest with me. Do you love her?"

She paused, looking anxiously for an answer. "What makes you think I love her?"

"Answer me, damn it!" he said.

She said, in a haggard, scarcely audible voice, "I don't know . . . I don't know." And then she turned angry eyes on him. "How did you know?"

"I figured it out. Look, Beth—all I want is a chance to talk to you. I'm not going to strong-arm you into anything; I'm not going to beat you over the head. You ought to know that by this time. I didn't expect to find you running away, but—"

"I'm not running away. Damn it, Charlie, I'm running *into* more problems than I'm running away from. I'm not a coward."

"Listen to me, Beth," he said, and his eyes were intense and his voice was soft. "Just listen to me for a minute. And remember, no matter what I say, no matter what you feel, I love you."

That silenced her. For a minute he regarded her quietly and then he said, "Grow up, Beth. I don't know how much there is to this thing between you and Laura, honey, but it's all off balance, I'll tell you that. It's cockeyed because Laura's in love with you and you aren't in love with Laura."

"I am!"

"A minute ago you didn't know." Her eyes fell, and she rubbed them in confusion. "And what's more," he went on in his firm voice, "she doesn't know you're in love with me. She doesn't know you ever were."

"I'm not."

He ignored her. "This is child stuff, Beth, this thing between you and Laura. You're deceiving yourself, denying yourself. You're a woman, honey—a grown woman. An intelligent, beautiful girl with a good life ahead of you. And that life has a man in it and kids and a college degree. Maybe it can't be that way for Laura. But it's got to be that way for you."

"I want something more than that." Her voice was contemptuous.

"Then you'll find it. But not by running away. And certainly not by running away with a girl, and a girl you don't love, at that."

"Charlie, damn it—"

"You can't run away, Beth." His voice, his gestures, were urgent. "My God, you've read the books. What do they all say—every damn one? They say running away won't help, it won't solve the problem. You can't run away from the problem, you have to stand pat and face it. Look, darling," he said, "you aren't in love with Laura. Laura's in love with you, yes, but—my God, don't you see what you're doing? You're using her as an excuse. You're sorry for her, you want to take care of her as if she were a little girl, without thinking what harm that's doing her. You're sorry for Emmy, you're sorry for yourself. You're mad at the whole God-damned world and me in particular because there are rules that you don't like, and when somebody breaks the rules somebody gets hurt.

"Don't you see how young that is? It's kid stuff, honey. That's the kind of thing you did back in grade school when the world was a big mystery and rules didn't seem to make any sense. You couldn't fight them, you couldn't make sense of them, so you either kicked and screamed or you ran away."

"Charlie," she whispered, and he could hear the tears in her voice, "I can't hurt Laura. I can't hurt her. Not now. It's too late."

"Beth . . ." He came up behind her and took her shoulders in his hands, bending his head down close to hers. "Jesus, Beth, don't you see how much greater the harm would be if you let her go along thinking you love her—let her leave school and home and everything she knows for you—and then let her find out some day that you don't really love her? That you never loved her? That you've only been playing with her, using her for your own self-assurance, lying to her all along?"

"Oh, Charlie." Her shoulders trembled. "You make it sound so terrible."

"It is terrible, darling. But it hasn't happened yet." He felt the first twinge of hope. He was right; she was frightened. The premise he had gambled on was true. She loved him, not Laura; it remained only to convince her of this herself.

"It would hurt her so awfully if I—if I—"

"Not like it will a few months from now. Or a year. Then it could hurt so much that she'd never recover. Beth, my love . . ." He put his arms around her. "Running away now won't help Emmy either. It won't undo the wrong. It won't make Laura happy. And think what it's going to do to you. Face it, honey, look ahead. Think, not just of Laura or Emmy or me, but of yourself. What will this do to your life? Beth," he said, turning her around and lifting her chin.

She looked at him through welling tears.

"You don't need to be loved right now, my darling," he said, and she frowned in wonderment. "You are, but that's not the point. You don't need to be loved one half so much as you need to *love*, Beth. And you need to love a man . . . and you do."

They stared at each other for a long time while her tears slowed and stopped and his face came into focus and his strength held her fast and warmed and thrilled her.

"Charlie?" she said.

He kissed her wet cheeks and her lips for a long lovely while, cradling her body against his own, letting her forget a little, find her courage and will again, pressed hard against the clean friendly power of himself. And then he pushed her firmly away.

"Your train leaves in half an hour," he said. "I'll drop you off at the station."

He picked up her bag and led her out of the room. She followed him in confusion, her mind in an alarming uproar, her heart in knots. They left the Union and walked half a block to his car without saying anything. She got in and settled herself, trying at the same time to settle her frantic nerves.

They drove to the station. He stopped at the corner, some distance from the entrance, in case Laura should be there waiting. Beth hesitated, her hand on the door handle. Charlie watched her.

"It's your decision, Beth," he said.

She closed her eyes and clamped her teeth together, and pushed the handle down. The door gave a little, and still she waited, agonized.

"It's five o'clock. Better get going," he said. "Train leaves at five-fifteen."

"Charlie—" She turned her tortured face to him. "Charlie—"

"I'm going over to Walgreen's and get a cup of coffee," he said. "I'll be there until five-thirty."

Slowly she got out of the car, pulling her bag after her. She gave him a long supplicating look and then shut the car door and watched him drive off. He didn't look back. She turned and walked up the steps and along the station to the entrance and went in. Laura saw her instantly.

"Oh, Beth!" she said thankfully. "For a minute I—I— oh, never mind. You're here. Thank God, you're here."

Beth tried to smile at her. "Laura, I—" she began.

"I got your ticket, darling. It got so late, I— What happened, Beth? Why are you so late?"

"I—I got held up at the Union." Could she never tell the truth?

"Oh," Laura laughed. "I nearly had heart failure. It got later and later and— Well, anyway, you're here. We'd better go on up if we want seats. The train's loading." She gave a little tug at Beth's sleeve.

"Laura—wait. Wait. I—" She stopped, unable to talk, hardly able to face Laura.

With a forced, frightened calm, Laura took Beth's bag from her and led her to a wooden bench near the ticket windows. She made her sit down and then she took her hands and said, with inexplicable dread, "What is it, Beth?" Far away inside her it was turning cold.

"Laura—" Beth's cheeks were hot with a needling shame and uncertainty.

"Beth, you've been crying. What's the matter?"

"Oh, Laura . . ." Beth couldn't find her tongue. Her voice was rough with sorrow.

"Don't you want to go, darling?" Laura sounded unbelievably sad and soft and sweet.

"Laura, couldn't we—couldn't we wait till June? I—"

Laura shook her head gravely. "No, we can't wait, Beth. We have to go now, or we'll never go. You know that."

She did know it, but she couldn't come right out and admit it. "No, Laur, we could do it later. Couldn't we?" For the first time she was asking Laura instead of telling her.

Laura shook her head again and murmured, "No, Beth, tell me the truth. We haven't much time. What's the matter?"

"Laura—darling—I just can't do it. I just can't. Oh, Laura—hate me. Hate me!" And she put her head down against the bench and wept, unable to look at Laura, pulling her hand free to cover her face.

Laura held the other one hard. When Beth was quieter she raised her eyes and saw Laura's face, white and heartbreakingly gentle, and there was a curious new strength in it, an almost awesome dignity that Beth, in her distress, lacked completely.

"Laura, stay with me," she said a little wildly. "Stay here. We'll go back to the house. It's only another month or so. Please—"

"No," said Laura. "I have to go." She was cold all over now, but the frost brought clarity as well as suffering. She began to understand. She heard Beth start to implore her and she stopped her.

"Beth, I have only a few minutes. Listen to me. Tell me one thing—only one. Do you love Charlie? Is that what's the matter?" Beth started to shake her head, but Laura said, "Don't try to protect me any more, Beth. I want to know the whole truth. Do you love him?"

Beth was surprised and touched by her self-command, and she gazed at her a moment before answering, "Yes," in a whisper.

"Then I'll go. And you'll stay."

"No—"

"Listen to me!" Beth was startled into silence. Laura's voice dropped. "Beth, I love you. I'm not like other people—like most people. I can never love more or better than I love you—only more wisely maybe, some day, if I'm lucky. It can never be any other way for me. What I mean is—there can never be a man for me, Beth. I'll never love a man like I love you."

Her voice never lost its steady softness, her eyes never lost their deep hurt, her hand never relaxed its tight constriction over Beth's. She talked fast, racing the clock.

"It's different for you, Beth. I guess I've known all along, when you met Charlie and everything. I just wanted you so much, so terribly, so selfishly, that I couldn't admit it. I couldn't believe it. But you need a man, you always did. Emmy was right, she understood. If I'd only listened. I was the one who was wrong, about you and her. But I'm not wrong about myself, not any more. And not about you, either."

"Oh, Laura, my dear—"

"We haven't time for tears now, Beth. I've grown up

emotionally as far as I can. But you can go farther, you can be better than that. And you must, Beth, if you can. I've no right to hold you back." Her heart shrank inside her at her own words.

"Laura, I misjudged you so. I thought you were such a baby, such a—"

"We've both made mistakes, Beth."

"Can you forgive me? I've been so—"

"You taught me what I am, Beth. I know now, I didn't before. I understand what I am, finally. It's not a question of forgiving. I'm grateful. I can face life, my family, everything now, knowing. That's terribly important. I couldn't before. Don't you see?" She couldn't cry; there were no tears potent enough to relieve her grief. Her control was almost involuntary.

"But I—I've deceived you so. I—"

"It was just an accident, the whole thing, Beth." The train whistle blew. Laura drew nearer, her eyes profound and wise and wounded. Only five minutes left. "Don't you see what happened, Beth? We were in the same place at the same time and we both needed affection, darling. If it hadn't been that way, I wouldn't have known, I wouldn't have learned about myself, maybe not for a long time. And then it could have been a brutal, terrifying lesson. You made it beautiful, Beth.

"I guess that's all loving ever is—two people in the same place at the same time who need it. Only sometimes, for one, love has all the answers. For the other, it's just a game, a beautiful game. That's what happened to us, Beth. Neither of us willed it that way, it just happened. For you it was an accident, a sort of lovely surprise, and you took it that way. You took me for the little girl you thought I was. It was that little girl you wanted, not me. I had to be that little girl to keep you. I should have faced it then, but I couldn't. I couldn't even think about it.

"You see, for me it was love. A revelation, a forever sort of thing. Only nothing lasts forever. You told me that once."

The whistle called again. Laura got up from the bench and walked swiftly toward the exit. Beth ran after her.

"Oh, Laura, Laura, please don't go, not like this. Please."

"I have to, Beth."

"You're running away." She followed her outside as Laura hurried toward the stairs up to the train platform.

"No, I'm facing it," Laura said. "I know what I am, and I can be honest with myself now. I'll live my life as honestly as I can, without ruining it. I can't do that here and I can't do it with you. That's over now."

Beth listened to her words, feeling for the first time the maturity in them; knowing Laura was right and admiring her with a sudden force because Laura had the courage to say these things, these truths, and the strength to do what she knew was right. Beth rushed along beside her, holding her arm, knowing that when she released it, she would release Laura forever; she would never see her or touch her again—and yet knowing that it had to be that way. She would come to Charlie chastened with the knowledge Laura had given her; she would come to him wiser, older, and richer in love because of Laura.

"Laura," she said as they made their way down the platform, "I'm the one who's been acting like a baby, who's been childish about the whole thing. I never dreamed you were so—so brave." She couldn't think of a more fitting word. "Laura, I know I'm not making much sense, but I—you do mean so much to me, Laur. So very much. I want you to know. You're not the only one who's learned and who's grateful."

They reached the last car and Laura turned to her. There was the shade of a smile on her face. The pain was awful but the wound was clean. It would heal.

"Beth, I'm not angry. I thought I'd be bitter. I thought I'd hate Charlie if this ever happened. I thought I'd hate you more than anyone else on earth. But I've thought about it a lot, when you were seeing him so much and so happy with him, and I was spending those long nights at home alone. Even now, when you were late getting to the station, I kind of imagined what it would be like. I knew it would hurt, but—somehow I guess I always knew it would happen. It had to; you can't need men and spend the rest of your life with a girl. I knew you weren't— queer—like I am."

The word slapped Beth cruelly in the face. "Laura—" she protested.

"I knew as well as you did that it wouldn't last. Only I couldn't admit it, because I love you."

"Oh, Laura, darling—"

The conductor shouted, "All aboard!"

Laura put her bag on the steps and took Beth's hands

again. "Beth, you're meant for a man. Like Charlie. I'm
not. I'm not afraid to go, I'm not sorry. It hurts, and I
love you—" Her eyes dropped and she almost faltered. "I
love you—" she whispered, And Beth felt the pressure of
her hands as the train gave a preliminary jerk.

"Laura!" Beth cried, walking by the train, and Laura
looked up again.

"But I wouldn't have the strength to face it if I didn't."

Beth reached for her and pulled her head down and
kissed her, there on the train platform in the late afternoon sun with the train inching away from her and all
Champlain free to watch.

"Laura, I love you," she said, letting Laura slide from
her arms as the train pulled her away. And she meant it,
for the first time. She loved her; not as Laura would have
wanted her to, but sincerely, honestly, the best love she
could offer.

She leaned exhausted against a post and watched the
train pull out and her eyes never left Laura's. She stood
with quiet tears stinging her cheeks and watched till the
train wound its way out of sight.

Then she turned and walked slowly back down the
steps and over to the station. She picked up her bag where
Laura had left it and walked outside into the sunshine, set
it down, and looked at her watch. There was a sudden
flutter of new joy in her heart.

She had to hurry; it was almost five-thirty.

THE END
of a Gold Medal Original by
A. BANNON

Made in the USA
Coppell, TX
31 August 2021